He's Amish.

Rose held out her hand, and I grasped it. She avoided my gaze, leading me to her barn. I followed along, very nervous about what she had to say.

When I was seated on a hay bale in the loft, I watched her pace back and forth in uncomfortable silence for a minute or so before curiosity overcame the worry, and I blurted out, "Rose, come sit down and talk to me. Please."

She's not.

She stopped and looked at me with her own fear clearly showing. The loft felt very different in the brightness of late morning than it did in the dark of night when we'd met before. Somehow the light beams shining through the gaps in the wood made the moment feel more real…and frightening.

With reluctant steps, she approached, stopping in front of me. I spread my legs and pulled her forward into a hug. Breathing in the lovely lavender scent, I tried to relax. Rose needed my strength now.

She whispered against my cheek, "I'm pregnant."

But everything's about to change.

Books by Karen Ann Hopkins

The Temptation novels
in reading order

TEMPTATION
BELONGING
FOREVER

forever

Karen Ann Hopkins

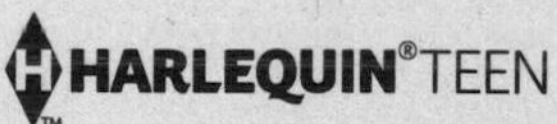

Recycling programs for this product may not exist in your area.

ISBN-13: 978-0-373-21106-7

FOREVER

This edition published by arrangement with Harlequin Books S.A.

For questions and comments about the quality of this book, please contact us at CustomerService@Harlequin.com.

Printed in U.S.A.

This book is dedicated to my close friend Opal Dickerson, who has been lucky enough to call both the Amish and English worlds her home.

Your strength and kindness inspire me.

Acknowledgments

As Rose and Noah's story comes to an end, I want to express much appreciation to my awesome agent, Christina Hogrebe of the Jane Rotrosen Agency, for being on this literary journey with me from day one; my exceptional editor, TS Ferguson, for his wisdom and patience in the process; to my fabulous publicist, Lisa Wray, for all the little things; to the cover art department for the dazzling cover on this book; and the rest of the Harlequin TEEN team for their professionalism, friendliness and guidance along the way.

I could never have succeeded in this crazy endeavor without the love and support of my family. Kisses and hugs to my five children, Luke, Cole, Lily, Owen and Cora. Many thanks go out to my mom, Marilyn; my dad, Anthony; my brother, Tony; and my nephew, Jamey, for everything. I love you all.

With gratitude to Jay, Carey, Devin, Marian, Kelsey, Kendra, Jackie, Eric and the Mast family. The last few years have had ups and downs, and each one of you has helped out in some special way. Thank you!

"There can be no assumption that today's majority is 'right' and the Amish and others like them are 'wrong.' A way of life that is odd or even erratic but interferes with no rights or interests of others is not to be condemned because it is different."
—Warren E. Burger, Supreme Court Justice

1

Noah

It was dark except for the light slicing through the gaps in the barn boards. The silence made my skin crawl, and I shook the feeling away. I took a deep breath. Leaning back against the stall, I closed my eyes, and a picture of Rose immediately appeared.

She sat alone on her bed. Her head was bowed and her shoulders jerked with rocking movements. When she lifted her face, her cheeks were wet. The same moon that sprayed soft light into her bedroom was the one that lit the barnyard beyond the door. I wanted to go to her, gather her up in my arms and tell her that everything was all right. The pain of knowing that I couldn't hold her stabbed my chest.

Was it just my imagination that she was crying this night? I had no way of knowing; we were still being kept apart. Would it ever end? Was a time of peace and acceptance in our lives possible? Rose needed me. I could feel it in my bones, but I couldn't be with her—at least not yet.

Elijah Schwartz's voice hissed into the quiet air, snapping my eyes wide open.

"This is unacceptable, Amos. I only allowed my eldest daughter, Constance, to become betrothed to your son, because of your promise that his association with the English girl was over. Now, you're telling me that he wants to break off the engagement, only weeks before the joining? You can't be serious."

To Father's credit, his voice came out restrained and sure. As my head turned to him, he said, "Things have changed. I feel terrible that Constance will be hurt by the breakup, but the consequences if Noah went through with the wedding would be a greater travesty. He is in love with another girl."

The three long strides that Elijah took toward me brought me off the hay bale and into a standing position right quick. The older man looked at me with a tight frown.

His gray eyes glittered dangerously when he raised his finger to my face and said, "You are making a mistake, boy. Not only will your life with an outsider be filled with pain, lies and deceit, you have created a rift with me and my kin. Mark my words there will be no peace in your life with this decision."

Elijah stormed to the doorway. His eldest sons, Paul and Micah, were fast on his heels. Paul made a huffing noise and ignored me as he followed his father, but Micah took the time to meet my gaze. He frowned and shook his head sadly, and I quickly searched my memories for the reason for his distress.

I suddenly understood. The numerous times that I'd spotted Sarah lingering in the kitchen or barnyard while Micah was a few feet away finally made sense. But confusion peppered the realization. I thought Sarah had been moving in the direction of courting Edwin. It showed how out of the loop I'd become that I had no idea what was going on with my own sister.

As Elijah was pushing the door open, Bishop Abram caught his arm in a loose grip.

"Those are harsh words, Elijah. It's not with malicious intent that Noah has done this. Rose's family manipulated the younger boy to write a letter convincing the Millers that she was leaving on her own accord, but that wasn't the truth of it."

"Do you think that matters to me? My daughter will be humiliated. Our family will be made a laughingstock before the community." Elijah stood up straighter before passing his gaze between Bishop Abram and Father. "The acts of this boy—" he paused and pointed at me "—will not be ignored by our people."

When Elijah disappeared into the night with his sons in tow, the barn became quiet once again. With a groan, I dropped to the hay bale and rubbed my face vigorously.

"What a mess of things I've made," I mumbled into my hands.

Bishop Abram sighed and sat down beside me in a smoother movement than my own. He placed his hand on my knee and said, "Yes, a storm is brewing on the horizon. Elijah won't let the matter rest. He is a prideful and stubborn man. Any difficulties we've had dealing with Mervin Weaver will be mild in comparison to what the Schwartzes will bring down upon us."

"Yet he's only lived within our community for a few months. Perhaps you're overestimating his influence," Father suggested, rubbing his beard thoughtfully.

Bishop Abram shook his head before raising his gaze. "Don't take that man lightly, Amos. He's already been talking with the other men in the church with the desire to take a place as their minister. He may be new to us, but he's strong-willed and intelligent. I have no doubt the matter will go before the church, regardless of my wishes."

A chill passed over me at his words.

Rose's reputation would forever be clouded within the community if she was with child. Elijah would use it against us…and my entire family. If Rose and I could hold on for a while longer, she'd be old enough to marry me without her father's approval. Then we could begin our lives unsullied.

With a sudden change of heart, darkness settled over my spirit. I said a silent prayer that Rose wasn't pregnant.

2

Rose

I was glad they couldn't see the fresh tears on my cheeks. They'd been so good putting up with me the past few days—I didn't want them to think I was turning into a sputtering fool again. I had to be strong.

"What are you thinking, Rose?" Summer's voice was soft and muffled. She must be leaning against Sam's chest, but the way I was resting on the bed in Aunt Debbie's guest room, I couldn't see them on the floor, and I didn't even have the energy to turn my head to look their way.

"Everything...and nothing at all." I sighed and dropped my head on the pillow.

"God, please tell me you've changed your mind," Sam said.

His rough words made me shiver. He was becoming irritated again. Things were always so cut-and-dry with him. Couldn't he understand where I was coming from?

"No, Sam, I've made up my mind."

"You just keep making dumb decisions—why won't you ever listen to the voice of reason and good sense?" Sam's voice rose with each word.

"Shhh, your aunt will hear, and that's the last thing we

need right now," Summer chastised. She pulled away from Sam and climbed on the bed beside me. "We've gone over it a million times. This is the best plan for now."

Even in the semidarkness I could see Sam's head jerking back and forth. "I don't agree. As much as I hate the guy, he should know what he did to Rose. She shouldn't have to deal with it by herself."

"I'm not alone. I have you guys," I piped up.

"And, Sam, it's only for a few weeks. Really, you're making more drama than necessary." Summer said it quietly and slowly enough that I was betting Sam wouldn't argue.

But I was wrong.

"Dad should at least know. This is serious business—" his hand waved into the air at me "—she needs to see a doctor."

"Women have been having babies forever, a few weeks won't make a difference," Summer said with a shrug.

"We aren't even certain she's pregnant, though."

"Don't be dumb. She took five prego tests. She is, and that's the end of it."

Sam muttered under his breath, "Damn, females are diabolical."

I heard him loud and clear, though...and I was suddenly afraid.

3

Sarah

Glancing sideways, I quickly looked back into the laundry basket and blushed. Micah had been watching me.

Oh, goodness, what should I do?

Trying to ignore what my eyes had just told me, I reached into the basket and pulled out a pair of pants still heavy with dampness. Snapping them on to the line, I nearly jumped out of my skin when Micah spoke close behind me.

"Would you like some help with that?"

His words were fuzzy in my mind, and his face blurred for a second. Did the brown-haired boy with the prettiest green eyes I'd ever seen just ask me if I needed help hanging the laundry? Surely, I must be dreaming.

Coming to my senses as quickly as I could, I looked around for anyone watching before facing Micah.

"Uh, no…but it sure is nice of you to offer—none of my brothers ever have," I said, turning back to the work.

As much as I wanted his company, I wished he'd leave. If Father or Mother caught him talking to me, I'd be in trouble for sure. Especially with everything so mixed up with our families and all. Oh, if only Noah had never gotten involved with Constance. He hadn't taken my advice, and now we all were paying the price—especially me.

Micah chuckled softly and said, "My mother and sisters trained me well." He paused and took a wet work shirt from the pile and began hanging it. "Actually, I don't mind helping you at all."

I quickly grabbed the garment from his hands and tugged. "You mustn't do that. Someone might see, and then questions will be raised."

Micah was strong, and he wouldn't let go. He pulled the shirt back and argued, "There is nothing wrong with me assisting you. I hardly see why anyone would complain."

Nearly frantic, I glanced around and yanked hard. The rip was loud, and I didn't need to see the shirt to know a seam had split. The material came loose from his hands, and I stepped back.

My cheeks felt warm when I said, "Now look what you've gone and done. You're supposed to be building a fence with Peter. And with all the trouble brewing, you should be happy that Father invited you to do so."

Micah must have lost his mind, I thought, when he came forward and whispered close to my face, "If you hadn't refused my help, that wouldn't have happened. Besides, the only reason my father allowed me to come over here at all was to spy."

I felt light-headed and ignored the possibility of others watching us.

"What are you talking about?"

Micah did a quick scan of the area and said, "I shouldn't have said anything, but I don't guess you'll tell anyone. You used to talk to me and smile sometimes, and now you won't even glance my way. Is it because of your brother and my sister?"

Sighing, I said, "Of course, silly. I'm not sure why we became friends, but the things that your father has said about Noah and my family have made it impossible for our friendship to continue. It wasn't proper, anyway. I'm going to begin courting Edwin."

His hand shot out and grabbed my arm. The heavy feel of it made the blood drain from my face. "What...?"

"Are you crazy, Sarah? You don't even like him."

"Course I do. And who are you to say so?"

Micah leaned in and said with a sureness that made me believe him, "'Cause you like me, that's why. Things will settle down soon between our families. Don't do something that we'll both regret."

He left me and went back to the fence across the yard. A part of me wanted him to come back, but the other wanted him to stay far away. He was dead wrong about our families. When the bishop announced Noah and Constance's separation on Sunday, it would get worse.

Wiping the wetness from my eyes quickly, I went back to work. I had to get Micah Schwartz out of my mind.

He was nothing but trouble.

4

Sam

Rubbing the sleep from my eyes, I stared at the ceiling. Why the hell did I have to get dragged into my family's shenanigans? How did Summer manage to get me to do whatever fool thing she wanted? It was beyond me, but I was looking forward to the day when the honeymoon phase ended, and I could think straight again.

"Come on, Sam, Dad's downstairs and about to pop a blood vessel. He wants to get moving," Justin said, peeking in the doorway. He was too smart to come all the way in and risk my early morning wrath.

"If he only knew, he wouldn't be in such a damn hurry," I mumbled into the pillow.

Justin risked a step in but kept his hand on the door. "What did you say?"

I opened my eyes and stared at my little brother. He'd grown a couple of inches over the summer and was nearing my height now. At some point, my intimidation tactics might not work on him.

"Are you so tied up in your fantasy military world that you don't notice anything going on in the here and now?"

Justin thought for a second, before saying, "I know everything going on. You're the naive one, thinking I'm clueless. That's what makes me smarter than any of you."

The smug expression on his face made me sit up straighter and narrow my eyes at him. Could he possibly know about Rose? I was suddenly suspicious that he might.

With a speed that surprised even me, I was out of the bed and through the doorway. I tackled Justin to the floor in front of Rose's room. The kid might be sneaky, smart and growing, but I still held the superior strength. Thank God.

Near his ear I whispered, "You better tell me exactly what you know, or I'm going to sprain your hand and you won't be able to hold your controller for weeks."

"You wouldn't. Dad's in the kitchen," Justin whined quietly.

"I don't care where he is. I'll do it and then I'll lie to him about what really happened...you know I will."

The extra pressure on his wrist did the trick. Justin puffed out, "All right, ease up." He lowered his voice and said, "Rose is pregnant."

The volume wasn't low enough, though. Rose was standing in the doorway. I caught only a glimpse of her pale, shocked face before she stepped back into her room and slammed the door.

Rolling off of Justin, I sighed loudly, "Now you've gone and done it, you idiot."

5

Noah

Elijah's cold, hard look sent a shiver through me, but I didn't turn away. The man's anger was thick in the air even though he'd remained silent during the announcement of the wedding's cancellation. I can't say that for the rest of the community, though. The gasps and fervent whispering had to be quieted by Aaron. He quickly jumped into reciting the rest of the morning's news, obviously trying to calm the situation.

Father sat staring straight ahead. He didn't meet the hostile looks coming from the Schwartz men. Father was a formidable and respected man in the community, yet I knew that he was worried about the situation. His fear about the future had settled over me like a heavy blanket in wintertime. If he was afraid, then we all should be.

The ball of tightness in my stomach became too much for me as we left the Schrocks' church building. I had to get away now. Moving past Marcus Bontrager and several others stalled in the aisle, I pushed the sliding door open and stepped into the cool morning brightness. The warm-up we'd had in April had been tempered by colder air in May. Ruth's line of pink peonies was still blooming, but their petals were drawn up tight, as if they were attempting to shield themselves from the harsh wind that pricked my own skin.

I didn't button up my vest, thankful for the cold, stiff breeze. It cleared my head.

The hand on my shoulder didn't surprise me, and the voice close to my ear was expected.

"What's going on? Have you lost your mind?" Timothy whispered.

I glanced back, and seeing that Matthew was close behind him, I signaled both of them to follow me toward the stable.

Once through the doorway I turned and faced my friends, knowing they were completely loyal to me. The Troyers would side with Father if it came to an open contest between us and the Schwartzes in church, but I wasn't so sure about the Weaver family. Mervin Weaver, Matthew's father, always had his own agenda.

"It's about Rose."

Timothy rolled his eyes and leaned against the stall door with a groan. Matthew's jaw dropped, and he stared at me with wide eyes.

Before either of them could speak, I plowed on. "Her brother wrote the letter saying she'd quit me—not her. She didn't know anything about it."

"How did you find this out?" Timothy asked. His voice was calmer and his face serious.

"It's a long story. Basically, Sam had a moment of clarity. He must have felt guilty about his father's lies. At first when he told me, I didn't believe. But after a torturous night of running it through my head, I realized he must be telling the truth. Rose would never have left me like that. She'd have talked to me at least, explained things in person."

I sat down on a bale of hay. Timothy and Matthew followed suit, taking the bales across from me.

"I was angry with myself that I so readily believed Doctor Cameron's story, and abandoned my girl." I looked up and met their steady stares. "I had Mr. Denton take me to the city. He found out her address on the computer when I told him the names of her aunt and uncle—the people she was staying with. We went there that next day, and Mr. Denton left me."

Matthew continued to watch me, hanging on my every word, but Timothy closed his eyes and thudded his head against the barn wall. Timmy was a whole lot sharper than goofy Matthew.

"You didn't," Timmy said.

After a pause, I met his gaze. "I did. It was incredible to have her in my arms again. All the feelings came rushing back. I'd never stopped loving her. I never will."

"Your father let you dump Constance to be with Rose? How is that ever going to work?" Matthew exclaimed. "Is she going to become Amish?"

"Shhh, someone might be listening." I leaped up and went to the door to look out. When I turned back, I said, "No one knows the particulars yet, and I'd like to keep it that way."

The soft voice from inside the darkened stall to my left made my heart stop dead away.

"Sorry, but you're a little late for that."

Suzanna's blond head peeked over the divider. She smiled sheepishly. Miranda's face soon joined hers.

"Aren't you girls ever where you're supposed to be?" I groaned and shot a warning look at Timothy and Matthew, whose faces told me instantly that they were as shocked as I was.

The cold, damp air in the barn seemed to warm a bit as the girls left the stall to join us in the hallway.

Timmy stood up and went to Suzanna. "What are you doing, Suzanna, spying on us like that?"

Suzanna placed her hands on her hips and frowned at her boyfriend. The look made him take a step back.

"What kind of fools go into the barn to have a secret meeting and don't even check the stalls to make sure they're alone? Huh, tell me that," Suzanna hissed and I knew it was useless to argue with these girls about anything.

Matthew wasn't so smart. He looked at Miranda, his own girlfriend, and asked, "I thought we didn't keep stuff from each other, Mirn—what's going on?"

His voice had a whinelike quality, and I wasn't surprised when the usually quiet girl blurted out, "I'm not doing a thing wrong, or worth telling you about. We came in here to talk for a few minutes in private before we went to help with the lunch sandwiches."

When Miranda paused, Suzanna jumped in, saying, "It's not our fault that you ran your mouth before checking if the stable was occupied. I'd have thought you would've known better."

I nodded. "Yes, you're right. I've been torn up all morning because of Elijah. He isn't going to let this thing go."

Suzanna came closer. She whispered, "How's Rose? Is she all right? Are you two really getting back together? Is she coming back to live among us?"

I put up my hands to stop her bombardment. The motion silenced her, but her light blue eyes sparked with more questions. I sighed, knowing I wouldn't be able to escape the barn without sharing some information with her. Suzanna and Miranda were Rose's friends, after all. It was understandable that they'd want to know what was going on.

"All right, slow down. Rose is fine. Yes, we're back together, but it isn't common knowledge yet, so don't go gossiping."

"You know we wouldn't. Anything you tell us will never leak out. I thought we've proven ourselves to you," Suzanna huffed.

Looking into her eyes and seeing her determination, I knew she meant what she said. I relaxed further and continued, "Rose is coming back to Meadowview today, but she's not going to be Amish straightaway. I guess the only reason her father is all right with her coming back to the area is that she's convinced him that she's over me. She's finishing out the few weeks of school to prove to him her intentions."

"Not more lies. Haven't you two learned your lesson well enough? After the incident with that letter you were talking about and all, I'd think you'd want to be in the open with your love," Suzanna said.

I shook my head. "You're not thinking it through. We can't be together just yet. She's still only seventeen. Her father wouldn't allow her to come back if he knew about us. And, my father has asked that we stay away from each other for some months to let the trouble with the Schwartzes die down. When Rose turns eighteen in late November, enough time will have passed for the community to again accept our union, and her father won't be able to stop us, either. We'll marry soon after and begin our life together in the Amish world."

Timmy scratched his chin and nodded his head slowly. "That sounds like a good plan to me. If you and Rose got back together immediately after you canceled the wedding with Constance, you'd be frowned on by the entire community."

"And, Elijah would be after you all the more," Matthew added.

Suzanna picked up Miranda's hand and pulled her toward the doorway. She stopped before she stepped out and said, "You're just plain dumb, Noah, to think that it will work out that smoothly. Something unexpected always comes up to ruin well-laid plans—especially if you're going to be dishonest once again."

A second after she disappeared, she poked her head back in and said, "I'm happy that Rose is coming back, though. You tell her I expect her to contact me straightaway. We have a lot of catching up to do."

The gust of air hit me for a couple of seconds before the girls had the door pulled shut.

Suzanna was right. But what could I do, except try to make it work out properly? As much as I loved Rose, I still didn't want to hurt Constance's feelings any more than necessary. She was a good girl, and the only thing she'd done wrong was fall in love with me. Mother had given me sound advice when she'd suggested that Rose and I wait awhile before we went public. Maybe over the summer, Constance would begin courting another, and her heart would be healed. His daughter's happiness could soften Elijah once again, and all would be right in the community.

I tried to convince myself, but when I looked at Timothy and Matthew and saw the doubt and worry etched on their faces, I knew I was fooling myself. Nothing had gone right ever since I'd first laid eyes on Rose, and I reckoned this would be no different. But I'd try not to worry until something came up. After all, I'd get to be with her tomorrow, and that's all that I wanted to think about.

6

Rose

"Hold up, Summer," I said as I stopped and squatted beneath the pine trees.

My stomach rolled, and I tried to swallow down the nausea. It didn't work. Hot juices rose in my throat, and I threw up. My body heaved, and I clutched my stomach when the spasms didn't stop.

"Here, let me get your hair out of the way," Summer said, kneeling beside me. She rubbed my back and murmured soft words that didn't mean much to me. I just wanted the bubbling feeling in my gut to quit.

The week after I'd discovered I was pregnant, I'd felt perfectly fine and decided that the pregnancy thing wasn't so bad. I had even been able to pretend in my mind I wasn't pregnant, that maybe all the tests had been wrong. When I'd said as much to Summer, she'd laughed and told me to wait awhile, I'd be feeling it soon enough. She'd assured me that she'd seen it happen to her stepsister and another girlfriend firsthand. Then, bam, yesterday morning the sickness had hit with the force of a raging hurricane. It didn't just happen in the morning, either. The rocking in my belly and throat had been almost constant since it began.

Finally, after another minute of gagging and spitting up yellow liquid that must have come from the pit of my empty stomach, I sat back against the tree trunk.

Summer handed me a tissue from her pocket and said, "Somehow, you're going to have to pull yourself together or Noah will know for sure."

"How? I can't go an hour without being sick. He'll see right through me."

Summer placed her hand under my chin and forced it up. I looked into her bright green eyes and calmed instantly.

"Now, you listen to me, Rose. You're a strong girl. You can do this. I have faith in you."

"No, I can't. He'll figure it out...and then what'll I do?" I sniffed back the tears that were almost falling again.

Summer's strawberry-blond hair bobbed on her shoulders as she shook her head. "You and your baby's entire future depend on this. Noah can't find out about the pregnancy until you've made up your mind for certain what your future is going to be—Amish or English."

"I want to be with Noah. I don't care where we live."

Summer's voice was harsher than usual, and I gazed at her, wishing that I wasn't pregnant at all.

"A week ago you told me and Sam that you didn't know what you wanted. You told us that you had reservations about raising your baby Amish. Don't go changing your tune now. If Noah isn't willing to go English to be with you, then why should you give up everything to be with him?"

The shadows under the trees were growing, and I shivered as the cooler air settled beneath the green canopy. Summer had a very good point, and my head agreed with her...but not my heart. Now that I was having his baby, I wanted to be with Noah even more. I needed him to help me through this. He'd probably be fine with the pregnancy. But then why was there still a tickling of doubt deep down inside me? What had changed?

"All right, you might be happy enough marrying Noah and being Amish, but what about your child? Will he or she? Maybe there will come a day when that little person growing inside of you will be mighty upset at the choice you made."

The fixed line on Summer's mouth proved how serious she was, and maybe she'd hit the matter on the head. Could I really make such a decision for my child? Was it even fair?

"You might be right— Here, help me up."

Once I was standing, the queasiness settled for a minute. I closed my eyes and took a deep breath. When I opened them again the forest came into sharper view. The sun was low in the sky, and I realized that we didn't have a lot of time.

"Do you have any gum left?"

"Sure do." Summer pulled the pack from her back pocket and handed me a piece.

I turned and started up the barely recognizable path. Summer came up beside me and bumped my shoulder with hers.

"Are you going to be okay?" she asked.

I continued walking and didn't look her way. "Yeah, I'll survive, but I'm not making any promises. I'm not sure if I'm going to tell Noah about the baby."

Out of the corner of my eyes, I saw Summer nod wearily in acceptance.

When we reached the boulders, Summer climbed onto the nearest one and sat down.

"What are you doing?" A shimmering of panic spread through me as she gazed down at me.

"You're on your own with this one. It's your life."

"That's it—you're going to abandon me now?"

"I'm doing no such thing. I'll be sitting right here when you're finished." She paused and glanced away, then back again with more compassion. "I don't want to make you do something...or not do something that you'll regret later. It's your life and you have to decide. Neither Sam nor I can tell you what's best for you in this mess you've gotten into."

"There probably isn't a best thing to do."

I sighed.

"Probably not."

Without glancing back, I moved past the giant rocks and picked up speed as I pushed through the last of the branches and brush. My belly was calm, and with a sudden longing to be in Noah's arms, I hurried across the clearing and up the rickety old porch steps.

When I opened the door, the darkness inside was complete. There wasn't even a cheery fire to greet me.

"Noah, are you in here?" I whispered into the blackness.

The silence chilled my insides, and I zipped up my jacket. After a few seconds of hesitation and looking over my shoulder as twilight descended on to the forest, I walked in, using my hands to feel the way to where I thought the chairs would be.

I sat down on the first one I bumped into and folded my arms tightly around me. Goose bumps spread along my skin, and I shivered again, sucking in a breath. Could Noah have forgotten me?

My insides tightened at the thought as my eyes adjusted

to the darkness. Several of the chairs and buckets were turned over and lying haphazardly around the floor. The fireplace had a few old ashes in it and no fresh logs beside it. It dawned on me that no one had been in the ramshackle cabin since the time I'd been here with the girls many months before.

Thinking back to that night, I couldn't help but smile. I'd whacked Timmy in the head with a two-by-four when he'd snuck in on us. Noah had been so surprised to see me. He'd hugged me until it almost hurt. But, oh, how wonderful it had felt. That was when things were easier. I'd just joined up with the Amish and had been learning their ways. What a gift it had been that the others had arranged for me and Noah to be together.

I'd still been a virgin then—and that's just the way Noah had wanted to keep me, until our wedding night. Now it was gone forever. One night of passion after we'd been kept apart for so long by our families, we'd let ourselves go, and here I was pregnant.

My head began pounding, and I clenched the sides with my hands. *Do I tell Noah?*

"Rose?"

His whisper pierced the cold, dark night air. I sniffed back the tears and stood up.

"I'm here."

A second later he had me in his arms, right where I wanted to be. The warmth of his body pressed against mine, and the scent of horses and leather on his skin made me melt against him. I couldn't stop the tears from falling. For the first time in a month I felt safe again.

I couldn't lie to Noah. I loved him too much.

"I thought you said Summer was coming with you," he said in a sharp voice that brought me from the fog.

"She's at the boulders. I think she wanted to give us some privacy."

He nodded and relaxed. "That makes sense."

He sat down, guiding me to his lap. I wrapped my arms around his neck and stared at the little I could see of his face in the darkness.

"I was beginning to wonder if you were going to show up," I said softly.

He took a breath and said, "The singing was canceled, and some of the adults had a meeting. Father was tied up there, so I took Mother and Naomi home before I could make it out here."

"What kind of meeting? I don't remember the singing ever being canceled before." Uneasiness spread through me, and I sat up straighter.

"Never has been as far as I recall, but there are some important issues that needed discussing, I reckon."

He said the words in a nonchalant way that pricked my interest all the more. Telling Noah about the pregnancy could wait a few minutes. I had the odd feeling that the special meeting had something to do with me. I pressed my hand on to his chest to hurry him along with the news.

"Well...Elijah Schwartz isn't very happy that I've called off the wedding to his daughter. He's making things difficult for me and my family."

My inner lioness rose, and I blurted, "What's he doing?"

"Nothing yet—the meeting will give us a better idea of how far he's willing to take the matter, but you don't need to worry your pretty head about it."

He stopped talking and brought his mouth against mine. The feel of his lips distracted me, but not completely.

I broke away from the kiss and said, "Have you talked to Constance?"

"No, she wasn't at church service this morning. I haven't seen her since our fathers spoke."

The way he said the words, like he was feeling bad for her, made me suddenly jealous. After all, he had asked the girl to marry him. He must have really liked her to do such a thing—and he must have kissed her. I closed my eyes quickly, trying to erase the image that made me suddenly feel sick again.

Swallowing carefully, I said, "Let's just forget about her for now. There's something more important we need to talk about."

Before I could continue, Noah hugged me tightly, pressing his face against my chest. His voice was muffled when he said, "Yes, we certainly do."

He pulled back, and with moonlight shining through the doorway, I could see his face better. His mouth was smiling and his eyes were content.

Gathering my courage, I opened my mouth to speak, but he placed his finger on my lips and shushed me.

"I've got it all figured out. My folks support us getting back together. They're going to give us a couple of acres on the far side of their property that we can build a small house on. The adjacent land is owned by Marcus Bontrager, and he's willing to sell about twenty acres, so we'll have that option as time goes on."

"But, Noah..."

"Hush now, and listen. Now that you're back in Meadowview, we can arrange meetings like this. It won't be so bad if my parents are in agreement. Your father is gone most of the time, anyway. But, Rose, there's one little hitch to the plan that I'm going to need your help with."

"What do you want me to do?"

"Wait. That's all, wait. We need some more time to make this happen. Father and Mother think we need a while to announce our engagement. If we do it straightaway, it will enrage Elijah all the more. I understand their worry. It would be unfair to Constance for us to be formally together so quickly."

Without breathing, I asked, "For how long?"

"Until after your birthday—what's that, about six months away? It will give Father enough time to iron things out with the Schwartzes, and maybe Constance will have a new beau by then. I'll continue to work and save money to start our life together. Your father will be thrilled that you'll be finishing up your last year of schooling, and he won't have any reason to think that you're going to become Amish when you're legally an adult and marry me. It will work out perfectly this way."

The intensity and speed of his words beat into my head as I repeated them over again in the silence. Wait six months—it was impossible. Anger rose in me.

"So you're okay with us being apart for that long, having to put our lives on hold once again to accommodate everyone else—and now Constance?"

"Don't go getting jealous. What I've done to her is terrible, and I can't just go on without taking her feelings into consideration. It would be wrong to do so. Besides, I just listed off all the reasons it's in our best interest to wait. For once we need to follow the course of patience and faith, Rose. We've made such a mess of things in the past. Let's do this the right way and begin our life together in the best light."

My heart was breaking. Now, even Noah was keeping us apart.

When I didn't speak, Noah's voice came out quiet, his words apprehensive. "Unless, there's some other reason to hurry things along? Is that the case, sweetheart?"

I heard Summer's voice in my head, and then I thought about Noah's desire to protect Constance and her feelings. The fact that the community seemed more important to him than me woke me from the deep sleep I'd been living in for the past week.

Noah didn't want to hear the truth. He wouldn't be happy to know that his well-laid plans were about to go up in smoke. For the first time I had an excuse to lie.

"No reason at all."

As Noah tilted my chin and began covering my face with featherlight kisses, I sighed and let him love me.

At that moment, I felt no guilt, and I wondered if that was even worse than the lying part.

7

Sarah

As I untied Juniper, I felt the tingle of being watched and turned to look around the dark interior of the barn. When Micah stepped out from behind the wooden post, I wasn't surprised. His brazen behavior was getting worse, and secretly I loved it.

He smiled and said, "Do you need any help hitching up your horse?"

Unable to keep my foot still, I pushed at the shavings on the ground with the toe of my black shoe. "Thank you very much, but I'm fine." I placed my attention back on Juniper's head.

"I knew you'd refuse me."

Catching the slightly raised pitch of his voice, I glanced back and met his green-eyed stare.

Lowering my voice, I said, "You really must stop this."

"Why?"

"We've already gone over it. It's better if we don't talk anymore, because of the situation brewing between our families."

"You didn't pay any attention to Edwin during volleyball. What does that mean, then?"

I sighed. Micah was so different from Edwin. If I didn't

make eyes with Edwin or start up a quick exchange of words, he was too shy to approach me. I had to do all the work or nothing would ever get done with the boy. Micah was the opposite. He was forward to the point of rattling my nerves.

"Again, it's none of your business what happens between me and him. I wish you'd just leave it be."

"I caught you looking at me several times during the service."

My face reddened with the heat that suddenly flamed my cheeks.

"I only turned your way because you were so rudely staring at me. I'm surprised the entire community didn't notice."

"It wouldn't be so bad if they did."

"You're being silly. Please excuse me while I take the horse to the buggy."

Shocking me, Micah blocked the back of the stall. If I continued to nudge Juniper in that direction, he'd get trampled.

"Why isn't Noah assisting you? Where is he, anyway?"

I wasn't supposed to know where Noah was, but deep down I had my own suspicion why he'd hurried off to take Mother home, completely forgetting about me and Rachel. After listening from behind closed doors several times this week, I was fairly certain Rose was involved.

Part of me was happy for him, knowing in my heart all along that she was the girl for him—even though she was born English. But I also feared the trouble that would be stirred when it came to pass.

"Since my father must attend the meeting called by yours, Noah took Mother home. Now if you'll kindly step aside, I'll be on my way, too."

He stepped out of the way and motioned widely with his

arm. I ignored the frown on his face as my heart raced. I wanted nothing more than to talk to him longer, even if it wasn't the most pleasant kind of talk. As much as I tried to push Micah away, I felt myself growing closer to him each time we came together.

"Thank you," I muttered, not looking up as I passed by him.

Before I cleared the doorway, he raced up behind me and tapped my shoulder. His touch made me catch my breath, but I stopped and glanced back, anyway.

"Wait. There's something I want to give you. It isn't much—I made it the other day when I had a little free time."

He handed me a soft, tan strip of leather. When I turned it over, I gasped as I read the engraving of my name.

"It's a bookmark," he said quietly.

I looked up and met his gaze. When he smiled and shrugged, my heart melted, and I knew that I was lost to him. All the anxiety I'd carried before vanished. As if my eyes were opened for the first time, I saw the young man before me...and I knew he was mine. The contentment that filled me was sweeter than honey, and I returned his smile.

"Sarah, what are you doing?" Jacob's voice boomed from the barn opening. I quickly tucked the leather beneath my apron and tugged on Juniper's reins. Micah moved swiftly by without looking at me or my oldest brother and left the barn.

"What was that all about?" Jacob said as he stepped in front of me. His eyes flashed accusingly, and I was suddenly angry.

"Only me getting Juniper ready to harness—there was no need to startle me so."

"I'm not blind. I saw that you were talking to Micah."

"And what if I was? It isn't against the rules to say hello to someone passing by in the barn, is it?"

Jacob smoothed the small amount of hair on his chin down in a movement very much like Father before he said softly, "I'm not giving you a hard time, Sarah. I just don't want you to get hurt."

"Whatever makes you think that I'll get hurt?"

"Elijah Schwartz will never allow one of his sons to become involved with a Miller. Not after what Noah did to his daughter. There are too many other eligible young men for you to court around here. Don't go after something that is only going to cause you grief. Take the lesson learned from Noah and his disastrous choices."

From somewhere deep within me, defiance grew, and I met Jacob's stern gaze. "My situation is nothing like Noah's. There is no reason that our heavenly father would work to keep Micah and I apart if we chose to be together. We share the same faith, beliefs and community. Elijah Schwartz has no right to interfere."

The smile that rose on Jacob's face was unexpected. "You looked a whole lot like Father when you said that." Chuckling, he took the reins from me and turned to take Juniper to the buggy. As he walked away, he said over his shoulder, "I reckon Elijah might have met his match."

How did I go from not wanting anything to do with Micah Schwartz to defending a relationship that hadn't even begun with him to my oldest brother, and all in the matter of some minutes?

I didn't know the answer, but for the first time I was the one in the family having some excitement.

And, I liked the feeling a whole lot.

8

Sam

I set the bowl of ice cream down to answer the door. Who the hell would be knocking at this late hour? I wondered. When I looked out the window and saw that it was Hunter, I relaxed and opened the door. With Rose's situation, I was always ready for the worst.

"Hey, bro, what's going on?" I asked Hunter as he slid past me to stand in the foyer.

"Is Rose home?"

I ran my fingers roughly through my hair while I quickly thought of an answer. I certainly wasn't going to tell him that she'd been knocked up by Mr. Suspenders and was off on some sneaky liaison with him that Summer had hatched. No, the less Hunter knew, the better, but I was still majorly bummed that things hadn't worked out between him and my sister. Hunter was a good guy, especially now that he'd quit drinking.

"She's out with Summer, doing some girl thing."

"Do you mind if I hang around for a while and wait for her?"

He didn't exactly sound like he was begging, but his eyes were for sure. Damn, under the current circumstances, having Hunter in the house when Rose returned could be a national disaster in the making.

"Uh, man, I don't think that's such a good idea. She just got home last night and she's still settling in. You know how temperamental she is."

Hunter smiled. "Yeah, I do, but I don't mind if she has a meltdown. I need to talk to her."

Part of me was becoming aggravated that the guy wasn't listening to me, but the other part had to respect his persistence. It was just a shame that he didn't have a chance now.

"Look, it's your skin that's going to get chewed up and spit out if she comes home in a mood."

Hunter followed me into the family room, and we'd barely sat down in front of the TV when Summer and Rose came through the door.

Summer shot me a look that gave me the heads-up that she was upset with me, but Rose didn't even take the time to look my way before she began her barrage.

"What's *he* doing here? Are you insane or just stupid, Sam?"

"Hunter's my friend, and he can come by whenever he wants."

"Oh, is that so? Even with everything going on, you'd do that to me?"

I glanced at Hunter's look of shock and Summer's narrowed eyes. I was screwed no matter what I said.

"So, I guess things didn't go so well with your meeting?" The words tumbled out of my mouth without much thought. I really just wanted to get back to my bowl of ice cream and the episode of *Swamp People,* but it was unlikely that would be happening anytime soon the way Summer was glaring at me.

"Can you ever just keep your mouth shut?" Summer growled.

Rose turned and ran from the room. Summer paused long enough to shake her head at me and mutter something that was mostly unintelligible, except for the word *idiot,* before pursuing Rose. Their stomping feet could be heard going up the stairs before a door slammed shut.

"That didn't go well, did it?" Hunter asked quietly.

I thought for a second and said, "Actually, it could have been much worse."

"The night isn't over yet," he said as he walked past the couch toward the stairs.

I leaped up and followed him.

"Where are you going?"

Without slowing to glance my way, he replied, "I'm going to talk to Rose."

"Are you nuts?"

"No, I'm perfectly sane, just in love."

I grabbed Hunter's shoulder as he began climbing the stairs, stopping him.

"You couldn't possibly fall in love so quickly," I argued.

"Some people do. It might not be your thing, but give me a break here."

"Trust me, I am. You don't want to go up there."

"Just try and stop me."

Hunter's eyes held a cold glint that I hadn't seen before. The dude was dead serious. I lifted my hands in the air and backed down the step.

"I warned you."

I returned to the couch but purposely left the door open. Hunter was still my friend, after all. I was expecting to have to rescue his ass in a few minutes, anyway.

9

Rose

"What is he doing here?" I demanded of Summer, knowing full well that she was as clueless as me.

"Maybe he came by to see Sam. They are friends and all," Summer suggested as she flopped onto my bed.

I shook my head. "No, there's more to it than that. Hunter won't quit. He won't accept that I'm with Noah again."

"How do you feel about that?" Summer asked quietly.

I took a deep breath and sighed. "It doesn't really matter now, does it? I'm pregnant and I have to marry Noah."

Summer sprang off the bed and grabbed my arms. "Whoa, you have options. Life isn't over because you're pregnant."

I rolled my eyes and sat down on the bed.

"You never did tell me how Noah reacted," Summer said as she joined me. She placed her arm around my shoulder.

Staring at the ugly wallpaper adorning my walls, I quickly thought about what I should say. Even though she hadn't come right out with it, I knew Summer was already against Noah. If I told her what he'd said, she'd really get down on him.

"I took your advice. I'm going to wait a little while longer before I break the news."

"What made you change your mind?"

"From the first moment I laid eyes on Noah, I've acted impulsively...and look where it got me. I'm going to take things slower from now on and really think everything through before I make a decision."

Summer pulled me into a tight hug and said, "That's a girl. You're not alone, either. Sam and I will be there with you every step of the way."

I sniffed back the tears and returned her hug. The smell of her flowery shampoo tickled my nose, and I was suddenly very grateful to have her by my side.

The soft knock at the door separated us. Summer's face scrunched into a frown, and she said loudly, "Go away, Sam, I'm busy with Rose."

There was a silent pause before Hunter's voice called out.

"It's me. Rose, can we talk for a minute? I promise if you hear me out, I'll leave when you ask me to." Another pause and he said, "Please, Rose."

Summer's frown disappeared, and she looked at me thoughtfully, shrugging her shoulders.

"Maybe you should listen. What harm can it do?" Summer leaned in and whispered.

A whole lot, I thought, but instead of trusting my instincts to keep distance between me and Hunter, I reluctantly nodded.

"If you need me, give a shout. I'll be right downstairs." Summer squeezed me one more time and then hopped off the bed.

When Summer opened the door, Hunter smiled thankfully at her as she held her arm out, allowing him to pass.

She quietly shut the door behind her, and I was alone with Hunter.

I couldn't look at him. Too much guilt. Noah was the love of my life, but Hunter had touched my heart. He'd been there when I'd needed a friend...and he'd accepted me unconditionally. His willingness to change colleges to be close to me flooded my memory, and sometimes I wondered if I'd regret someday not picking him over Noah.

He moved across the room swiftly and sat where Summer had been. Touching my chin, he lifted it, forcing me to face him.

"Please, don't ignore me. I hate this awkwardness between us. Have you forgotten how you used to talk to me—and laugh with me?"

When my eyes met his greenish-hazel ones, I was once again mesmerized by the little brown flecks in them. He flicked his head slightly when a few strands of his blond hair fell over one of them. The action reminded me of so many other times he'd done the same thing, and I relaxed a bit.

"I remember, but it can't be like that anymore. I'm with Noah, and I'm afraid that you won't let up and accept it."

Hunter sighed and looked straight ahead. When he spoke, his voice held a tone of defeat that made me suddenly sad.

"I'm sorry I've pushed you to be with me. I just couldn't help it. I've had this feeling all along that we're meant to be together— Guess I was wrong. I won't bother you anymore if that's what you want."

My heart was greedy. Even though I knew it was wrong to keep Hunter on standby, I didn't want to lose him. When

I glanced at the side of his face looking so depressed, I needed to comfort him.

Reaching out, I touched his cheek lightly with the back of my fingers and said, "I'm so sorry. I never meant to hurt you."

Too quick for me to pull away, he turned and wrapped his arms around me. He did no more than hug me tightly, and the warmth and security of his hold felt good.

Letting him continue to embrace me, I pressed my face against his chest.

"I know you didn't mean to make me fall in love with you. It was my fault that I ever thought I could rid your mind of Noah," he said quietly.

I pulled back to look up at his frown and felt a sharp sense of loss myself.

"I do have feelings for you, Hunter. I don't want you to think I don't. It's just that it's not the same as what's between me and Noah."

When he sighed, I looked at him, and he said, "Are you happy to be back in Meadowview?"

Was I happy? I didn't even know my own feelings anymore. The fear of being pregnant was even worse now that Noah wanted to wait before bringing our relationship out in the open. I could understand his reasons, even though I didn't like them. I didn't have room to be worrying about Constance's feelings. I couldn't afford to be generous at this point in my life, not with a baby to think about.

The pressure inside of me began pushing outward, and I suddenly felt as if I couldn't keep it in any longer. Hunter had helped me get a grip on my emotions before—maybe he could do it again.

"It doesn't really matter where I live now," I whispered, staring straight ahead.

"I thought you'd be ecstatic to be so close to Noah."

I hesitated and remained silent.

"Look, I'm not mad or anything. I really want you to be happy...and I hope we can remain friends."

Hunter's voice was sincere, and when I glanced at his face, I couldn't keep the secret any longer.

I blurted out, "I'm pregnant."

Hunter's eyes widened, and his mouth dropped open. I watched him turn away and take a breath before he faced me again. Seeing that his expression was neutral gave me confidence that I hadn't made a mistake telling him.

"What is Noah going to do about it?

Realizing that I'd just told Hunter about the baby before Noah, I felt a stab of guilt. But the slight tremor of anger toward Noah for proposing to Constance still heated my insides, and I pushed aside the troubling thought.

"He doesn't know yet."

"What? How come you haven't told him? You shouldn't have to deal with this alone," Hunter said harshly, his voice rising.

"Shhh, my dad doesn't know about it, either. Just Sam, Summer and Justin." I paused, catching my breath. "Justin figured it out on his own, but Sam and Summer were with me when I took the tests."

"You still haven't told me why Noah doesn't know yet."

I fidgeted for a second, worrying what Hunter would think about my relationship with Noah when he knew the truth.

"I was going to tell him tonight, but I just couldn't. He

has our future planned out in his head, and a baby isn't part of it right now."

"What do you mean? I'm sure he'd be thrilled if you're pregnant. Then he has you trapped forever."

Fire swelled in me. I sat up straighter and said, "I'm not trapped. I can still make my own decisions."

Hunter groaned. "That may be true to an extent, but Noah's part of the equation, and he'll use the situation to make sure you never leave him." He stared at me with a deep frown and said, "How could you let this happen? Now you have no choice but to become Amish."

I wanted to be with Noah, more than anything. Even if I had to become Amish to do it. But then why did what he'd just said make my belly do a somersault? Were my choices really gone?

Reading my mind, Hunter's voice softened when he said, "I guess you don't have to become Amish if you don't want to. You don't even have to raise the baby. There are other options."

I looked at him questioningly, and he said, "My cousin gave her baby up for adoption."

The subject of other options for my pregnancy hadn't come up with Summer or Sam. I think they just assumed that I would keep the baby...and so had I. I understood why some girls would choose to go that route, but the thought of giving the child I created with Noah away made the bile rise from my already queasy stomach.

I swallowed down the hot juices and muttered, "I'm keeping my baby. How could you suggest such a thing?"

"I hate to think of you in this situation. You're still important to me and this pregnancy changes everything." He paused and lowered his voice. "You're going to have to tell your dad about this. It's too important not to."

"That's what Sam says."

"He's right. I'm sure you're afraid to and all, but he's a doctor. He'll understand better than most parents."

I shook my head. "He'll be devastated...and he'll probably ship me back to Cincinnati to live with Aunt Debbie. I need to get some things straightened out with Noah before I tell Dad."

"When do you plan to let Noah in on it?"

"Sam thinks I should do it right away, but Summer wants me to wait. She thinks that I need more time to decide about the whole Amish thing...and to be honest, I'm not sure that I want to be Amish anymore."

Hunter was quiet for a minute and so was the house. I listened for any sign that Summer and Sam might be arguing, but heard nothing. The only noise was the wind rattling the window every so often.

"If you aren't absolutely certain about the course you want your life to take, then give it a little more time to decide."

"You really think so?"

Hunter put his arm around me and squeezed my shoulders softly. I rested my head in the crook of his arm.

"If you decide to take care of the baby on your own, you'll have support from your family and friends. And, from me—It doesn't make a difference that it's Noah's child. I'll be there for you one hundred percent no matter what you decide."

As I listened to his heart beat against my cheek, I was more confused than ever.

10

Noah

Marcus Bontrager shifted on his feet uneasily as Father and I watched him. When he wouldn't meet my gaze, instead looking down at the ground in front of the Yoders' barn where the church service had just been held, I knew that I wasn't going to like what he had to say.

"I'm really sorry, Amos, but Elijah already put money down on the land. It's sold."

Father's face turned red, and he tugged his beard before saying, "Its Sunday, Marcus, and I frown upon talking business, but you assured me weeks ago that Noah had the option on the acres. What changed, my friend?"

Marcus glanced up at Father and me for an instant. His voice lowered, and he said, "When it was announced last week that the wedding plans had fallen through, I reckoned you Millers wouldn't be interested in the property. Elijah visited me some nights ago and made me a good offer."

"Since your land joins mine, we won't be able to find such an arrangement elsewhere." Father paused and leaned in, placing his hand on Marcus's shoulder. "Please, reconsider."

Marcus shook his head, saying, "It was never my intention to breach our trust, but a man must look after his own interest. The amount Elijah offered couldn't be ignored." He turned to me and added, "I wish you the best of luck, Noah. It's not personal."

After Marcus had walked off, Father sighed heavily.

"I can hardly believe that Elijah would go so far as to spend his own money to go against us."

Jacob, who had been holding back, exclaimed, "That isn't the half of it, Father."

Father lifted his eyes to the sky and took a deep breath. "What else do you know of?"

"I just heard talk that Elijah has befriended Mervin Weaver."

Any patience had left Father's voice when he motioned with his hand for Jacob to spit it out. "Where is this gossip coming from?"

"Katie overheard her parents discussing the matter last night. They want to call a vote to keep Rose from rejoining the church, and Elijah has asked Bishop Abram to not allow their wedding to take place within the community."

I burst out, "He can't do that."

Father put his hands on each of our shoulders and hustled us farther away from the barn as people were leaving the service.

"Hush now, Noah. There are prying ears everywhere. No, I don't believe that Elijah will be successful in the endeavor. Both you and Rose have many friends among our people. But the man's persistence is troubling."

"What can we do?" Jacob asked. My older brother stood straight and tall, and he appeared ready for immediate action.

Father shook his head and said, "For now, we wait. Once the sting of the wedding cancellation lessens, I'm hoping that Elijah will become preoccupied with other things."

"And if that doesn't happen?" I said, suddenly worried that the feud could go on for years. I wasn't waiting that long to be with Rose.

"We'll take that day when it comes, and not a moment sooner. It is not our way to fuss over the choices of our children. Elijah's actions are not being dictated by scripture or law of God. His own pride is corrupting him." He glanced between us and added, "This should be taken as a good lesson for the two of you. Our people are not our enemies and should never be treated as such."

I couldn't help the aggravated sigh that escaped my mouth. Father grasped my arm and warned, "Noah, be vigilant nowadays. You and Rose will be joined in due time, but this storm must settle before that happens. Please, for once in your life, take heed of what I say and control your emotions."

Reluctantly, I said, "Yes, Father."

He was right, and I knew it, but it was more difficult than ever to be kept from Rose. All I wanted to do was to have her by my side and begin our lives together, but everyone under the sun was working against us.

Father and Jacob left together to hitch up their horses, but I lingered at the fence line watching a newborn foal as it punched with its nose at its dam's udder for milk. A beautiful sight, but I was thinking about Rose, wondering what she was doing on the warm, sunny morning.

I ignored the sound of the buggy's wheels crunching on the gravel behind me until I heard my name called out.

Micah Schwartz stepped out of the buggy and walked the few steps to reach me.

His hair curled out from under his hat, and I was thinking to myself that he needed a haircut when he said, “Constance wants to speak to you.” He nodded toward the buggy, darting his eyes back and forth to see if anyone was watching.

“It isn’t proper for me to be alone with her. Your father would have my hide.”

Micah nodded with understanding, and I suddenly realized that he was a likable fellow.

“Father and the rest of the family have left, but I’ll stay close to the buggy in case questions are raised.”

My heart stilled. The last thing in the world I wanted to do this morning was to talk to the girl whose heart I’d broken, but seeing the determination in Micah’s eyes to make it happen, I knew I couldn’t refuse. I owed Constance that much.

When I climbed into the buggy, I avoided her gaze at first and sat as far from her on the seat as possible. Since the space was small, we were still closer than I wanted.

Her voice was petal soft when she spoke, and I finally glanced up at her oval face. She really was doll-like with her pale skin, dark eyes and auburn hair. She’d have no problem finding a new suitor, I thought. She was too pretty a girl to be left alone for long.

“Even for all the embarrassment this meeting causes me, I still needed to talk to you about it. I don’t understand and wish that you could make me see your side of things.”

Her mouth frowned slightly, but her face did not look at me with the hatred I would have expected. Constance really was a good girl, and I regretted even more that I'd hurt her at all.

"I want you to know that when we were together I was absolutely sincere in my feelings for you. I cared deeply for you, and I still do. But my love for Rose consumes me. She is the woman I'm supposed to be with, and I realize that now."

"You told me that you were over her, that she wasn't right for you. Why change your mind?"

I glanced at her but couldn't look into her staring eyes for long.

"It wasn't our fault. Her father and brother wrote a letter basically saying that she was moving on in her English world. I was heartbroken, but let her go, thinking that it might be best for both of us. After I learned the truth and saw her again, I realized that she was the only woman for me. I'm sorry that I got you involved in our troubles."

Her voice changed, and there was a hint of coolness in it that I'd never heard before.

"You asked me to marry you, Noah. That's a very serious thing. Now I see that you never loved me at all but, instead, were trying to erase your hurt feelings about the English girl by using me. As a Christian woman, I will forgive you, but I'll never forget what you've done to me. You deserve to suffer a little before you find your happiness in life…just as I will do."

I was shocked at her words. I would have expected Ella, the crazy Amish girl who'd been obsessed with me since we were children, to make such a proclamation, but not the timid Constance who'd thawed my heart after I'd thought

Rose had left me. Knowing more about her father, I really shouldn't have been so surprised, but I still was.

I sighed heavily. "I'm sorry, Constance…truly I am."

Micah peeked in the doorway and said, "Noah, you need to leave now. It's been long enough to raise suspicions."

I stepped out of the buggy without another word to Constance.

After the buggy pulled away, Sarah appeared beside me and asked, "What did Micah say to you?"

Her question pulled me from my own heavy thoughts.

My sister's eyes were wide and bright, and her face shone. She looked different, and after a second of concentration, all my own problems disappeared for an instant.

"Are you interested in Micah?"

When Sarah blushed and looked down at her feet, I had my answer. Good God, the girl didn't have a clue what she was getting herself into.

Lowering my voice, I told her, "Don't even go there, Sarah. That family is nothing but trouble. Elijah Schwartz will never allow his son to court you after what I did to his daughter."

Her voice prickled when she said, "It's none of your concern or Jacob's which boy I show favor to." With a kick at the gravel, she added, "At least he's one of us. Surely, things will be easier for us than they will be for you and Rose."

The words slapped me, and I stepped back. Her face suddenly became remorseful, and she followed me and said, "I'm sorry. I didn't mean to say that. I'm just upset that you echoed Jacob's own sentiment." She mumbled, "Now I understand how you felt when you couldn't be with Rose. Why is the world so unfair?"

I stopped, suddenly feeling closer to my younger sister than I ever had. We really did have something in common.

"God willing, in the end I'll be with Rose and you'll be with Micah, if you choose him."

Sarah smiled and nodded. As we walked back to the barn to get the horse hitched, I worried that God might have other plans for my sister and me.

A feeling of uneasiness pinched my soul as I watched Sarah carefully back Oscar from the tie stall. She was such a sweet girl, and the thought that my actions were causing her grief darkened my mood even further.

Out of all of us, Sarah deserved happiness the most. I was bound and determined to make sure that she had it—even if it meant putting my own life on hold for a while longer.

11

Sarah

A million butterflies fluttered in my belly as I played volleyball. Each time I glanced toward the net where Micah was, he'd be looking straight at me and I'd turn away quickly.

His brazenness awakened my spirit, and I'd found myself thinking about him constantly. It was difficult to get my chores done properly when visions of his bright green eyes and lightly tanned face would pop up unexpectedly. It had become more difficult over the past couple of days to concentrate, and my mind had been filled with remembering each and every word he'd ever said to me. I'd replay all of our meetings, analyzing his comments to the point of exhaustion.

Mother thought I was sick and had offered to allow me to return to bed. My younger sister, Rachel, had mocked me for being an old woman with hearing problems when I'd ignored her while we'd hung the laundry together.

My thoughts drifted back to this morning when I'd talked to Noah. I really did understand how he felt. The longing to be with someone could cause a person to do silly things. I'd already been thinking of opportunities to speak with Micah again, but hadn't come up with anything even remotely promising.

"Sarah, snap out of it. You're missing every ball that comes your way," Suzanna scolded.

Wisps of her pale blond hair fluttered around her face in the evening breeze, and her cap was slightly crooked.

The game stopped when I reached over and felt along the top of her head to pull out the pin. Suzanna stood still for me to set the cap back on straight while I answered her.

"I'm sorry, I didn't see them."

"And you didn't hear me calling you?" She gently shook my shoulder and said, "Are you sweet on someone, Sarah Miller?"

Of course, Miranda was standing in Suzanna's shadow, and pudgy Maretta had appeared beside my elbow. All the girls stared at me, waiting for an answer.

I nodded slowly, heat rising on my face. All eyes widened and Suzanna grabbed my arm, ushering me away from the nets. She settled on a grassy spot some distance from the games and pulled me to the ground. Miranda and Maretta followed suit, and I found myself sitting in the middle of their gawking faces.

"It's Edwin, isn't it?" Maretta muttered.

"Oh, Lord, I hope not. He's so boring," Suzanna put in.

Miranda cleared her throat and said, "Hush and let Sarah tell us herself."

All eyes looked at me expectantly, and I whispered, "Do you swear to keep it to yourselves?"

They nodded vigorously as I expected. Feeling a rush of giddiness, I said, "Micah Schwartz."

The looks on the girls went from interest to pure shock in an instant.

Suzanna glanced around and then said, "Are you crazy? Since Noah quit Constance, Micah is off-limits to you."

Miranda, the most thoughtful of the group, must have pitied me when she chastised Suzanna, giving me a bit of hope. "I don't see any reason why they can't be together. Noah, Constance and Rose have nothing to do with Micah and Sarah. They're both of courting age and members of our church. Once Mr. Schwartz settles down about the whole business, it will be fine." She reached over and patted my hand.

Suzanna stayed silent, but Maretta jumped and smiled. "Are you sure you don't want Edwin, Sarah?"

"I'm sure...why?"

"I've always liked him. I think I'll make eyes at him and see what he does." She scowled at Suzanna and added, "I don't think he's boring at all."

I watched her jog away toward the nets with a deep sense of rightness. Maretta was meant to go after Edwin all along. She had just been waiting for me to make a decision about him. Now, she was free to pursue her heart.

I was smiling broadly when Suzanna said, "I have to admit the two of them are perfect for each other. He'll never have to talk with Maretta around, and that will suit him just fine." Then her face became serious, and she said, "Have you and Micah discussed a courtship?"

"No, not exactly, but he gave me a gift. Do you think he likes me?"

"What did he give you?" Suzanna asked.

I pulled the soft leather strap from my pocket and showed the girls. They each leaned in, and Miranda ran her fingers down the engraving of my name.

"It's very pretty," Miranda murmured.

"If he made this himself, then he definitely likes you," Suzanna said with sureness.

Her words made me feel lighter, but the worry was still present in my heart.

"I'm afraid to say a word to my parents about it. They're so worked up over the matter with Noah and Constance that I don't want to burden them further."

Suzanna flicked her hand. "Two people falling in love shouldn't be a burden. Old man Schwartz is overreacting if you ask me."

After another quick search of the area and seeing that the games were over and the boys were taking down the nets, I said, "Have either of you spoken to Rose? I do miss her so."

Suzanna and Miranda shook their heads, but even as darkness was setting in, I could see the twitch of excitement on Suzanna's face and I was suddenly very worried.

12

Sam

I tried to kiss Summer, but she wiggled out of my arms and said, "Where's Rose?"

"She's upstairs, clutching her puke bucket to her chest as usual. She's managed to hide the fact that she's always sick from Dad—probably because he's never around. She even convinced him to let her finish up her classes online so she doesn't have to do the few weeks until the end of school here in Meadowview. You know, I'm close to the point of taking matters into my own hands."

Summer's face tightened, and she pointed her finger at me. "You wouldn't dare. You promised to give her some time to know for sure."

I left Summer in the foyer and went into the family room, saying, "I'm just worried about her health."

I wasn't surprised that when I flopped on the couch, she was right beside me.

"This is serious. Rose needs to be checked out by a doctor. Dad needs to know. Hell, Noah should know."

"You don't even like Noah," Summer nearly shrieked. She was cute when she got riled up. I just wished what we were discussing wasn't so damned important.

"He's still the father, and he needs to step up and help Rose out." It made perfect sense to me, but whenever I broached the subject with Summer, she always went into hysterics.

Summer's eyes narrowed, and she lightly punched my arm. "You better not say a word to Noah about this, Sam, or..."

I cut her off. "Or what? It will be over between us? Please, don't throw that one at me. You're stuck with me and you know it. Besides, you're way off base on this one."

Surprising me, Justin, who I thought was in a video game haze in front of the TV, spoke up quite clearly, "You're both wrong."

"Spit it out, kid. What do you mean?" Summer asked, focusing her anger on the back of Justin's head.

"It's Aunt Debbie who should be told. She'd know what to do to help Rose, and she can keep a secret, so none of us would be breaking our oath to not tell Dad or Noah."

I looked at Summer, whose face was scrunched in thought. When her gaze met mine, she shrugged and said, "What do you think?"

Never a day went by that I didn't think about Mom and wish that she was still alive, but this was one of those moments when I really wanted her to walk through the door and take charge of the hysteria that our lives had become. But that was impossible, and the next best option was her sister, Aunt Debbie. She was more of a free spirit than Mom, but she still had a commanding way about her. I trusted her to handle a family crisis like this one.

"As usual, you surprise me, little bro. We'll give Rose a few more days and then make the call."

The knock at the door brought me and Summer quickly

back into the foyer. It wasn't very often that we had company after dark, living in the boondocks.

I hadn't gotten the door open more than twelve inches when Summer squealed and pushed me aside to open it more quickly.

There was a flurry of drab-colored dresses and white caps bouncing around for a minute before things calmed down.

I recognized the blonde girl who'd flirted with me the night on the road, but not the slender girl with the black eyes and pale skin. The healthier-looking girl with the brown hair and lighter eyes of the same color seemed familiar.

"I didn't think you ladies were allowed to go visiting your non-Amish neighbors after dark." I couldn't help smirking, even though Summer shot me a look that would have killed most men.

The blonde answered with a tilt to her head, "We're sorry to come by unannounced. We'd like to visit your sister, if we may."

For a second I was without words. All that could be heard was the tapping of Summer's foot while the girls looked expectantly at me. I wasn't used to girls asking me before they did something. At that moment, I could almost understand Noah's insistence on staying Amish.

I was careful not to look at Summer's face, but I had the feeling she was glaring when I said, "Sure thing. Stay as long as you want. She's upstairs. You know the way."

The girls brushed past me, following closely behind Summer.

It was an odd sight, and Justin obviously agreed when he finally roused from his gamer chair and peeked around me to watch the girls heading up the stairs.

"Ever since we moved here I've felt like I'm caught in the middle of an insane reality show version of *Little House on the Prairie,*" Justin said before he turned and disappeared back into the family room.

I mumbled to myself, "I couldn't have said it better myself."

13

Rose

I was expecting to see Summer walk through the door, but when Suzanna, Miranda and Sarah followed her in I leaped from the bed right into Suzanna's arms. In turn, I hugged Miranda and then clutched Sarah even more tightly than the others. A couple of minutes later, the five of us were all cross-legged on the bed.

"I still can't believe you shot Levi," Suzanna exclaimed.

"And jabbed his eye out," Miranda added with a look of awe on her face.

The mention of Levi brought a flash of images through my mind that I didn't want to see or think about. I shrugged and gazed out the window into the dark.

Sarah must have sensed my reluctance to speak of it. She coughed lightly and said, "We're relieved that you're all right, Rose. I envy your strength. If I'd been in the same situation, I wouldn't have been so brave."

Turning to Sarah, I had to admire her subtle beauty. Her brown hair with its golden highlights was similar to the rest of the Miller kids, but her wide-spaced eyes were a lighter brown than those of her siblings. Those eyes were deep pools that seemed sad most of the time. Noah's sister always spoke kind words in a soft voice. I wished I was so naturally nice.

"I'm sure if you were faced with a life-or-death situation, you'd be able do the right thing, too," I said quietly.

Sarah nodded and then reached over to squeeze my hand.

I looked at Miranda with reservation. She was Levi's sister, although she certainly had no reason to love him after the sick things he'd done to her when she was younger. But still, I'd nearly killed Levi when he'd come to Cincinnati to attack me. Could she really forgive me for doing such a thing?

"Miranda, I'm sorry about what happened with Levi, but he left me no choice."

Miranda scooted closer and hugged me. "Don't you dare apologize—he would've killed you for sure." She whispered into my ear, "I've been taught the way of grace, and I forgive Levi...but I'll never forget what he did to me. He deserved the punishment you served on him."

When she pulled back, her eyes were moist, and she hurriedly wiped them with the back of her hand.

In an attempt to lighten the dark mood that had descended on the room, Suzanna giggled. "Have you heard, Rose—we all have suitors now."

"Hush now, that's not true!" Sarah exclaimed with wide eyes.

Summer finally woke from her silence and said, "Whoa now, did Sarah finally tell that Edwin dude how it was going to be?"

I was surprised when I saw the clear distress on Sarah's face. Her voice rose to a level I'd never heard from her when she nearly shouted, "It's not Edwin—it's Micah!"

Summer and I exchanged a confused glance. I said, "Who's Micah?"

The amused smirk on Suzanna's face contrasted greatly with Sarah's worried frown.

Sarah murmured, "Oh, just a new boy in the community."

"Not just any boy, either." Miranda paused and looked to Suzanna for approval of what she was about to say. When Suzanna nodded, Miranda added, "He's Constance's brother."

Hearing Noah's ex-fiancée's name spoken sent a ripple of instant anger coursing through me.

"When did you begin dating him?" I asked, trying to keep the level of my voice calm.

"Oh, we aren't official...and we probably never will be, anyway."

Sarah shrugged. I saw the glint of moisture in her eyes before she turned away.

My heart suddenly went out to her, fearing that I might be the cause of her problems.

"Why would you say such a thing?" When Sarah wouldn't meet my gaze, I looked at the others. Suzanna and Miranda both shook their heads sadly, and Summer gave me a knowing look.

After a long, uncomfortable silence, Sarah finally said, "Elijah Schwartz doesn't want his children mingling with the Miller family in the future."

Suzanna and Miranda exchanged unsure glances when Sarah looked straight at them.

"I guess you girls already know about Rose and Noah being together again, right?"

My heart stopped, and I held my breath. I didn't think anyone besides Noah's parents knew.

Suzanna breathed a sigh of relief. "We learned about it by accident." She looked at me and smiled. "Your guy is kind of dumb about being secretive. We overheard the news. I couldn't be happier for you."

"I came down to the kitchen late one night to get a drink when I noticed the lamp on. I wasn't being sneaky or anything, but I didn't want to intrude, either. When Mother spoke of it to Father, I heard. Looks like we'll be sisters, after all," Sarah said as she patted my leg.

A roll of nausea passed over me, and I swallowed. I wondered at Sarah's words—would we really be sisters one day? Then I thought of the baby inside of me, Sarah's own niece or nephew. What would Sarah think if she knew about my pregnancy?

"Reckon, it's better we get it out in the open, so we can move on to other drama," Summer said. She turned to Sarah and asked, "So you can't date this Micah guy you have the hots for, because Noah broke it off with Constance?"

Sarah nodded.

"That is a sticky situation. I'm sure in time, it'll all sort itself out and his family will be fine with it," Summer said.

Sarah muttered, "I hope so."

Hearing the depression in Sarah's voice, I realized that this was yet another reason for Noah and me to delay being together. If we hooked back up right away, it would make it even worse for Sarah and Micah. Maybe this was another aspect of the situation that Noah was considering when he'd told me that we needed to take our time.

My heart felt lighter, and the angst I'd been carrying toward Noah disappeared. There were more people being affected by our decisions than I'd known. Glancing at Sarah's worried face, I was determined to do whatever I could to make sure that Noah and I didn't ruin her chances at being with the guy she loved. Of all people, I could never do that to a friend. I understood too well how awful it was to be kept away from the person you wanted to be with.

I picked up Sarah's hand and said, "Noah and I are doing things differently this time. I promise we'll be discreet and keep our relationship hidden until you work things out with your Micah."

Summer cleared her throat and said, "Ah, do you think you can do that?"

I shot her a warning look that would have wilted most girls. Not Summer, though. She sat up more confidently. "Because I'm not so sure."

"Yes, I can." Staring into Summer's green gaze, I knew she was talking about the baby. I said, "Especially with the help of my friends."

Summer shook her head and looked away.

But her aggravation was worth the wide smile that Sarah's face now held.

"Oh, Rose, I don't know if it will work or not, but it's worth hoping for," Sarah breathed with renewed life.

"And, since we are your good friends, we'll make sure you and Noah get some alone time, in secret," Suzanna promised.

Not being able to see Noah would be hard, but until I told him about the baby, being around him might be even more difficult.

"It won't be easy to get us together. Everyone will be watching extra closely now," I said.

"Don't underestimate me. I've got a plan for everything."

Suzanna grinned. "Like right now, I've already got your next meeting arranged."

I raised my eyebrows, suddenly weary.

"Friday night at the benefit dinner and auction," Suzanna said.

The prospect of seeing Noah again so soon made my heart race. I was beginning to feel the tingle of excitement about Friday when I caught Summer's deep frown. Suddenly, I was fearful all over again. I'd be seeing the Amish people I'd left behind months ago when my father had kidnapped me and relocated me to Cincinnati. I wondered if Ruth and James, my foster family, would be happy to see me and what I would do when I faced Ella—or, worse yet, Constance.

With a fresh surge of bile in my throat, I rushed out of the room to the bathroom. Maybe going to the Amish event was a bad idea, after all.

14

Noah

The line of buggies down the fence row was the most I'd ever seen. There were a lot of families from neighboring communities in attendance at the benefit, and I smiled thinking about the money our church would be pulling in for the schoolhouse.

The day was overcast but warm, and I undid my top button now that Mother was too busy with the other ladies in the kitchen to notice. As I watched three English teenage boys walk up the hill together wearing their comfortable jeans and T-shirts, I felt a bit of envy seep in. I loved my way of life, but I wasn't fond of wearing the clothing, restricted to button-up shirts, sturdy trousers, and suspenders.

Seeing the curious stares of the boys as they passed by me, I turned away angrily. I hated being gawked at, and lately I'd noticed it more than usual.

"Why the sour face?"

Timothy looked worried. With all the craziness in my life nowadays, I understood his hesitation.

"Ah, it's nothing—just the usual staring eyes of the outsiders."

"Yeah, I hate that." With a sudden burst of energy, Timothy exclaimed, "Did you see the black Saddlebred buggy horse that the Yoders donated to the sale? She's a beautiful mare and Joshua says completely road trained."

I smiled, picturing the horse. Throughout the day, I'd found myself back in front of her tie stall several times to admire her.

"I'm planning to bid on her. I need a new buggy horse more than anyone in the community at the moment. I hope the others will keep the price down for me to get her."

"Will your father help out if she goes higher?"

"He said he would—but not a large amount." Seeing Suzanna and Miranda approach, I teased, "Here comes trouble."

Timothy's smile made me think about my feelings for Rose and how I'd love to see her walking up to me. Unfortunately, we'd have to wait awhile longer for such a display. I purposely hadn't mentioned the dinner and auction to her. It would be difficult to deal with my emotions in front of everyone in the community if she was nearby—especially the Schwartzes. I shivered at the thought of Rose and Constance coming face-to-face.

"Hello there. What are you boys up to?" Suzanna said as she stopped a couple of feet away from us. She was careful not to touch her boyfriend or say anything that could be overheard as being inappropriate. As usual, Miranda stood quietly staring at the ground. Even when Matthew, her own boyfriend, was beside her, she rarely spoke.

"We're just talking. Judging by your wicked smile, I'm almost afraid to ask what you're thinking," Timothy said with a tight face.

Suzanna's grin turned into a full-blown smile as she

looked at me. "You don't have to worry about a thing, Timmy. It's Noah we came to talk to."

"What now?" I asked with a sense of dread.

"Rose is here."

My heart skipped, and I caught my breath. I was both elated and terrified at the same time.

"Where is she?"

"She's eating dinner with her younger brother at the tables. She'll meet you in her truck when darkness falls." She pointed to the area where the cars were. "It's parked in the back."

I didn't want to be rude, given her obvious excitement at having helped arrange a meeting between me and Rose, and I smiled back and said, "That's wonderful news. Thank you."

But inside I was reeling.

15

Rose

My eyes darted around nervously. I couldn't eat any of the food on my plate for fear I'd throw it up in front of the entire community. Instead, I nibbled a bite here and there and pushed the mashed potatoes around with my fork.

"You really should eat something. The chicken is excellent," Justin said as he shoved a forkful into his mouth.

I whispered, "You know why I can't, so stop bugging me about it."

In a very matter-of-fact way, he said, "You'll die if you don't eat." He lowered his voice and added, "You need to for the baby's sake, you know."

"Shhh." Frustration pricked my insides, and I took a deep breath before I whispered, "I do eat, just not very much at a time and certainly not around a bunch of snoopy people."

"How long is this going to take? I have friends coming over tonight."

I looked at my little brother sternly. His eyes were puffy from lack of sleep, and his skin was pale. Normally, when he got out of the house into the fresh air, he was a good-looking fifteen-year-old, but today he was suffering from some serious Xbox fatigue.

All of our lives had changed so dramatically since Mom's death. She'd never allowed Justin to sit around in front of a TV all day gaming, and she'd never have put up with Sam's arrogant, bossy ways, either. Most importantly, if Mom were here, I wouldn't be pregnant—my life would be completely different right now.

But she was gone, and our lives were upside down.

"You promised if I bought you those pizzas for later, you'd come with me tonight."

"Yeah, I did and I'm here, but we didn't negotiate how late we'd stay," he said with a sly grin.

I rolled my eyes. "I already told you, until after dark." Glancing up at the pale sky, I figured the sun would set in a half hour or so, and suddenly my heart began pounding like crazy that I was about to see Noah.

A soft squeeze on my shoulder brought me around. Ruth Hershberger stood above me with a huge smile on her chubby face. The swell of emotions was too great, and even though I'd rehearsed this moment in my mind several times already, tears began streaking down my cheeks.

When I rose, she pulled me tightly into her cushy body and stroked my hair, which was loose and free. I was suddenly self-conscious that my hair wasn't beneath a cap, and I smoothed it down when she released me.

Ruth's eyes were shiny with moisture, but she smiled. James, Ruth's husband, stood a few feet behind her. He was in quiet conversation with another Amish man, but he paused to look my way and nod at me. My chest tightened at the quick acknowledgment.

Ruth took my hands into her warm ones and said, "How are you, Rose? Have you settled back into your old ways?"

The questioning look in her eyes couldn't be mistaken. There was hidden meaning in her words.

I glanced around, noticing several pairs of eyes dart away when my gaze passed over them. Everyone in the community was aware that I was here—and they were all waiting to see what happened next.

Nervous energy filled me when I said, "I'm planning to come back. I have to wait until I turn eighteen in the fall, but that's what I want to do."

I was partially aware of Justin's eyes narrowing, but I ignored him to watch the look of shock pass over Ruth's face. I understood Justin's feelings, but I couldn't worry about him right now. I had too much going on in my life.

"My dear girl, I wasn't expecting you to say such a thing. I thought that being in your old life would have changed your mind." She paused and searched around, before lowering her voice and leaning in. "Especially now that you aren't courting Noah Miller...unless there's something else you'd like to tell me."

Her probing eyes brought me to my senses. Ruth was too sharp for her own good. I wanted to do this Noah's way and help his sister out in the process. The last thing we needed was for the older women to be gossiping about our business. As much as I respected and cared for Ruth, she was still one of authority.

Thinking quickly, I said, "Oh, no, there are no secrets these days. I'm going to do as my dad wants and give my world another chance before I make a definite decision."

She nodded and brought me back into a quick hug. She whispered in my ear, "You're always welcome to come back. If you need anything at all, you can trust me."

"You better let loose of her, Ruth. We all want to talk to our Rose."

The sound of Mrs. Miller's voice warmed my insides, and I turned to her and got another bone-crushing embrace. As Noah's mother patted me on the back, I wished I could tell her that she was going to be a grandmother, but then I spied his fifteen-year-old sister, Rachel, peeking out from behind her, and I came to my senses. She smiled and said, "We've missed you."

Maybe the pregnancy made me even more emotional than usual, but from the time I was in Rebecca Miller's arms until I was sitting on the bench closely beside Katie Miller, Noah's sister-in-law, I held in a lot of tears.

I was amazed at how welcoming all of the women were being. Even the bishop's wife, Martha, had joined the reunion with a brilliant smile and a warm hug. The reception I received from the women who I'd only been with for some months touched me deeply, and I began imagining how wonderful it would be to be a part of that kind of comradeship again.

When a group of young boys asked us to vacate the table so that they could take it down, we moved into the building and everyone's voices continued to fill the air. The sun had disappeared, and only a soft gray light colored the sky. Justin had escaped the barrage of women a while ago, probably to hang out with the boys who'd befriended him the year before, and I anxiously searched the crowd of both Amish and English people for Noah.

My desire to see him had been building throughout dinner. Being around the women and feeling their support gave me hope that maybe I could be happy being Amish. The auctioneer's voice calling out numbers mixed with people talking and moving about the open area of the schoolhouse. Standing on my tiptoes, I scanned the dimly lit room, receiving many startled glances from members of the community who recognized me, even in street clothes.

Seeing that darkness had settled on the churned crop land beyond the window, my heart sped up. It's time, I thought. Smiling, I muttered to Katie and Ruth that I needed to find my brother, and moved away through the crowd before they could stop me.

It was strange how my experience at this benefit dinner was so different than the one I'd attended the previous year. I was more confident as I squeezed in between the men with their long, scraggly beards and black hats and the women in their white caps and polyester dresses. They weren't a scary, mysterious bunch any longer. Many of them I called friends, and I had a deep respect for the hard work they did and the simple and honest way they lived.

When I caught sight of Amos Miller, Noah's father, I slowed. Sure enough, Noah was standing beside him, along with his brother, Jacob. They were near the large doorway opening with a group of men, next to a tall, black horse. Its coat was shiny even in the darkness, and its exquisite head and fine bone structure made me stop in my tracks.

The auctioneer's voice rambled numbers, and I sucked in a breath when I thought I heard four thousand and saw Noah's card go up. Mr. Miller leaned over to Noah before they both quickly looked across the room.

For a second I pictured Noah racing through the field on Rumor, and I imagined that, in his younger days, the black horse had probably looked a lot like the beautiful mare he was bidding on now. A lump formed in my throat, and I swallowed down the acidy bile when I remembered the last time I'd seen the horse. He'd been lying on the roadway, broken and dying from the impact of the semi-truck that had nearly killed Noah. His suffering whinnies still haunted me to this day.

Forcing the horrible image to leave my mind, I followed their gaze until I spotted the lanky Amish man raise his hand and nod to the auctioneer. Before I turned back to the Millers, my sight settled on the young woman beside the man bidding against Noah. She wore a lavender dress, and the small amount of hair I could see in front of her cap was auburn. Her face was pretty and doll-like. My stomach tightened.

Constance.

I'm not sure exactly what told me that the girl was Noah's ex-fiancée, but I knew with certainty that she was. In a very odd moment of acknowledgment, she looked over at me. Her features suddenly changed from tranquility to irritation as her eyes widened and her mouth opened slightly. The look only lasted for a second before her features went calm, and she glanced away.

It wouldn't surprise me if Constance recognized me. The other girls would have told her all about me.

I sighed, knowing that I had to deal with the jealousy of another one of Noah's admirers. Well, I had to admit, Constance was more than just that. She'd been engaged to him, after all.

When the auctioneer called out the last bid, I watched Mr. Miller and Jacob both shake their heads, and Noah dropped his. The man beside Constance, who I guessed was her dad, smirked and nodded in the Millers' direction. The look on the man's face was anything but Christian and reminded me of the same twisted expressions Levi would direct my way. This was not a nice man, and he was obviously holding a grudge against Noah.

I pushed through the crowd trying to reach Noah, but he didn't see me and instead disappeared through the doorway into the night. Changing directions, I ducked behind a group of Amish women and avoided coming face-to-face with the other Miller men.

The guys in Noah's family had always been polite to me but distant and aloof at the same time. After living among the Amish, I learned that this was the way all the Amish men treated women who weren't their wives or blood relatives. They were always careful not to do anything that could be misconstrued by others in the community. I was used to it now, having learned to avoid them as carefully as they did me.

When I reached the side door, I pressed it open and stepped into the cooler night air. Because the schoolhouse was on a hill overlooking the parking area, I spotted Noah instantly as he walked in between the parked cars, making his way to my red pickup truck.

I'd barely left the building when a hand reached out and touched my shoulder, giving me quite a jolt.

When I turned around, I was shocked to see Ella's oval face staring at me.

"Stop, Rose. I need to talk to you."

"You've got to be kidding. Haven't you caused me enough trouble?" I spat out. I really hated the girl, and the fact that she was one of Noah's admirers wasn't even the reason. Ella Weaver was truly the wickedest girl I'd ever met.

"Wait, please, hear me out," Ella pleaded.

There was a softer expression to her face than I'd seen before, and for a second, sheer curiosity got the better of me.

"What do you want?"

She took a deep breath and looked away for a few seconds, leaving me in suspense, before she turned back to me.

"I'm sorry. I never meant for things with Levi to go the way they did. He is a troubled boy, and I pray each night that God forgives me for talking to him."

I searched her eyes and was unsure. I liked to believe in the goodness of people, but it was proving difficult with this girl. She'd given me a lot of grief over Noah, and the fact that her friendship with Levi Zook had nearly gotten me raped and killed made it almost impossible for me to turn the other cheek.

"You better keep on praying, because you're going to need it," I said quietly.

Ella's face showed shock before her eyes narrowed, and she said, "You won't forgive me?"

"Really, it's not my place. Now, if you'll excuse me, I have other things to do."

When I turned to leave, I was glad I hadn't let Ella off so easy. People like her were good at acting nice, but the sentiment had never touched her hazel eyes.

"You're making a mistake, Rose," Ella whispered loudly.

I ignored her and kept walking. I'd had enough of her games.

When I reached the truck, Noah wasn't there. I looked

around the other side and then opened the driver-side door. On the seat was a folded piece of paper.

I picked up the note and read.

Rose,
Meet me in your barn loft at midnight.
Love,
Noah

I leaned back against the seat in disappointment. I'd have to wait several more hours to be in Noah's arms.

Spotting Justin at the edge of the parking area where we'd planned to meet up, I started up the truck and pulled out. Suddenly, a wave of nausea hit me, and I had to open the door to throw up. I was getting more used to puking and had the door shut again quickly.

Wiping the wetness away from my mouth with a tissue, I became more determined than ever to tell Noah the truth.

For good or bad, I couldn't do this without him any longer.

16

Noah

The heaviness of disappointment hung over me as I climbed the stairs to the barn loft. I couldn't believe that Elijah had bid to forty-five hundred dollars for the horse. Father had mumbled that the man was a "damned fool" when the last bid had been taken, but I was all too sure he was anything but foolish.

Elijah Schwartz was a man of his word. And he'd told me and Father that I'd made a mistake, and without having to say it directly, he'd made it clear that he was going to punish me for my sin.

It wasn't just that I'd lost the horse. There were other geldings and mares out there that would make fine buggy horses for me. The fact that he was the only man who'd bid against me after the reserve bid had been made said a lot. The other men in the community knew how much I missed Rumor and were happy to see me get excited about this particular mare, but not Elijah. When he'd seen the longing in my eyes, he'd become determined to keep the horse from me. He would have gone to ten thousand dollars before he'd let me have her. Father had been right when he'd stilled my hand. If I was going to start a life with Rose, I couldn't go wasting my money overbidding on a pretty horse.

The other thing that worried me this night was that several of the men in the community had stood beside Elijah in the bidding, including Mervin Weaver. The men hadn't thrown their own bids against me, but just the fact that they were beside the man showed their support of his actions.

I'd noticed Abram shake his head before I'd left the sale. There was nothing he could do to curb the bad will that was growing within the community. A line was being drawn, and men were taking sides. Father believed it would blow over in time, but I wasn't so sure. Some men held the fire of a grudge that never was extinguished.

The difficulty of it all was wearing on me. The gatherings weren't so nice anymore, and I began to wonder what good the Amish way of life was if there wasn't peace within the community. The community was our entire way of life.

Rose was the only thing in my life that gave me any joy these days. Just the thought of seeing her this night had kept the ill feelings at bay. In my excitement to see her, I'd arrived a half an hour early, but to my surprise, Rose was already sitting on the hay bales in the corner of the loft. She must have been as anxious to see me as I was her.

Taking long strides I covered the distance and had her in my arms a second later. She clung to me even more tightly than usual, and I bent down and placed my face beside hers.

For a minute we stayed like that, hugging in silence. Her warm floral scent triggered my memories, and I thought about the many times I'd held her this way. When Rose was pressed against my chest, nothing else in the world mattered. She was my girl and I loved her.

She pulled back a little and looked up at me. The shards of moonlight piercing the gaps in the barn's wall shone on her face, and I saw moisture there. Using my thumb to wipe away her tears, I said, "Rose, sweetheart, are you all right? Why are you crying?"

She sniffed and drew me down to the hay. When we were seated, she rested her head on my shoulder and replied, "I hardly get to see you…and I miss you."

Her hesitation brought me to attention, and I became nervous.

"We saw each other just a few days ago. You know I want to be with you. I'm always thinking about you—don't ever question that. In the course of our lifetime, waiting a few more months is nothing to us."

"It's not even like we're a couple now. Here we are, sneaking around again. I'm tired of it," Rose said, her voice rising.

I took her hands in mine and tilted her chin to me. "We're together now. Can't we just enjoy it?"

Leaning down, I pressed my lips to hers, and after a few seconds of not responding, her mouth opened. Tasting her mouth's salty wetness made me forget everything else. Kissing Rose was the only thing I wanted to do.

Her mouth began moving on mine more aggressively, and her enthusiasm heightened my desire. Before long, she was lying on the hay with me on top of her. I was careful to keep all my weight from pushing down on her, but she had her arms around my neck and was guiding me closer.

Images of the times I'd made love to her in her bedroom came alive in my mind, the touch of her soft skin against mine, her long hair brushing my face. The feelings were about to consume me when I rose back into a sitting position, pulling her with me.

Tucking her under my arm, I said, "Rose, my precious Rose, I want to make love to you again, more than anything, but we can't risk you getting pregnant." After a pause, I added, "That would be the worst thing in the world to happen to us right now."

I felt her body tense against me.

Her voice carried a sharp edge when she said, "Sometimes it feels like we're going to wait forever to begin our lives together."

"No, not at all— When you turn eighteen, I promise. But right now the community is divided, and it's causing more trouble than you can imagine."

"Does the black horse you were bidding on have something to do with all this?"

I nodded, grateful that she was beside me and I could tell her my problems and fears. Somehow, having her near made me stronger.

"Her name is Fancy. I've had my eye on her for weeks, ever since I learned that the Yoders were donating her for the auction. Christian Yoder figured that it was a done deal that I'd end up with her, but…"

Rose interrupted me. "But Constance's dad outbid you."

"How did you know that…? Did Suzanna or Sarah point them out to you?" I said, not trying to hide the surprise in my voice.

"No, I figured it out on my own. They were the only people I didn't recognize, and there was something about the way Constance reacted to seeing me that made me certain."

Slowly I asked, "She recognized you?"

"I think so, unless nearly fainting when she looks at a person is normal for her."

"That's not good. Elijah doesn't need any more fuel for his anger. He'll take you being at the auction as another slight against his daughter." Seeing Rose's wide-eyed and worried look, I sighed and said carefully, "Is that why you were crying? I've told you already that I never loved her. You're the only girl for me."

"That's not why I was crying at all. Actually, I kind of forgot all about her." She paused and glanced at me before looking ahead again. "It's interesting, though, how quickly you started up with another girl…and got engaged and all."

"You did the same thing with Hunter." I tried to keep the contempt out of my voice when I said his name, but probably failed.

"I wasn't engaged to him! That's a big deal."

"I know, I know, and I'm truly sorry. I was trying to heal my broken heart over you. It was the stupidest thing I've ever done."

I had to smile in the semidarkness when she snorted and bobbed her head. Her tears were definitely dry now. It still fascinated me how she could jump from emotion to emotion so quickly. The way she kept me on my toes was one of the things I loved about her.

"I'll never let you leave me again. I promise that. Just be patient on this. Let's not do anything to upset the Schwartzes any more than they are. We have all the time in the world."

The barn loft was silent while I held Rose tightly against me. I could feel the beating of her heart against my side, and for a few minutes I was at peace.

Out of the darkness, Rose whispered, "Time may not be on our side."

Too afraid to ask her what she meant, I kissed the top of her head and said nothing.

17

Sam

"You're going to what?" I said, grabbing Hunter's arm as we left the exercise room.

"Ask Rose to the senior prom," he answered, daring me with his eyes to argue.

Of course, I was up to the challenge.

I waited until the last of the guys walked past us to the shower room, and lowered my voice. "I can't go into details or anything, but you've got to let go of this infatuation you have for my sister. It's never going to work—especially not now."

Hunter met my gaze and said calmly, "I know why you're saying that, and I think you're wrong. There's still a chance for me and her. She doesn't have to be with the Amish guy just because she's pregnant."

The last part settled on my mind for a few seconds. Trying to figure out how Hunter knew was not important—what he thought he could do about the situation was.

Not missing a beat, I said, "Really, man, you're an idiot if you think she wants to put on a gown and go out dancing. She has more important stuff on her mind."

Hunter nodded. "Yeah, I hear you. But she's still a

seventeen-year-old girl. Her life doesn't have to stop. Maybe a diversion like a dance will do her a lot of good."

"You really are persistent. Why are you so dedicated to Rose, anyway? You two only dated briefly, and you know she's in love with another guy and having his baby. I don't get it."

Hunter sighed loudly and said, "I don't really know myself, except that from the first time I met her, it felt different than any other girl. It was as if I'd known her all my life. Hanging around her is comfortable and fun. I've never met anyone like her before."

I had to admit I felt sorry for him. "You need to move on, bro. There are plenty of nice girls around here. Go find one and be happy, 'cause I'm telling you, Rose is a train wreck for you. She's just going to get married to Noah and probably join the Amish."

"I'm already in too deep to give up all hope. A heart can only be broken once, right?"

He turned and left me standing alone in the hallway.

I shook my head. No, man, a heart could be shattered until it was completely unrecognizable. Seeing the path that Hunter was determined to take, I was betting his would be powder when Rose was through with him.

I wished that Summer was sitting closer to me, but instead she was all business, looking out the window and rambling on nonstop. Trying to tune her out was useless. Each time I went another place in my mind, she'd swat me with her hand like I was a naughty child.

Why do I put up with it?

Glancing over and watching her animated face almost as red with frustration as the hair on her head, I knew the reason. I was falling for her. Of course, I'd never let her know that. I could only imagine the power she'd wield over me if she was aware of how crazy I was about her.

"Are you ignoring me again?" Summer blasted.

"How much more is there to say? If Hunter wants to ask her to a dance, who am I to tell him he can't? You're the one who keeps telling me that it's not a big deal and that she can pretend she's not pregnant until she decides to break the news to the world."

"The last thing she needs to deal with is Hunter being all sappy around her. She likes him a lot as a friend, and she'll feel terrible turning him down."

"Maybe she won't."

Summer's eyes turned a menacing dark shade of green, and I glanced away, focusing on the roadway.

"Don't you dare go saying something like that, Sam Cameron! Rose loves Noah, and there's no way she's going to agree to go out dancing with Hunter in her condition."

"What condition?" I was pushing my girlfriend's buttons, but I couldn't help it. Rose was my sister, after all. I had as much of an opinion as she did.

Summer growled the words out. "I never argued that Rose has an important condition, just that she has a little time to convince Noah to..."

She suddenly stopped talking, which in the heat of an argument was unlike her.

Feeling confident that I was about to get an earful, I said, "Convince Noah to what? There's no doubt that the guy will marry her, so what does she have to convince him?"

Summer breathed out angrily and said, "Oh, all right. I thought it was pretty obvious, but you guys are so one-track.

Rose has to be sure she wants to be Amish again. It's a huge decision...maybe Noah will change his mind and go English. Rose is taking some time to figure it all out."

"Noah isn't going to become English. He's already made it clear that he wants Rose to join up with him and live the simple life. Now that she's knocked up with his kid, I don't see that she has an alternative."

"What are you saying?" Summer shrieked.

"Rose has to marry the guy and follow his rules. Before she was pregnant, she still had a chance to escape and live a normal life, but not now."

I didn't need to look at Summer to know she was incensed. Her fury was sparking the air around me when she said, "What a pig you are! She certainly has choices. She can raise the baby herself and remain English, she can marry Noah and they can both be English, she can become Amish if she wants...it's her damn choice, not yours or Noah's."

For the first time I was seriously angry with her. "Of course, Noah has a say—it's his baby. Just because it's in Rose's body doesn't make her the only interested party."

"I can't believe that you're taking his side against your own flesh and blood," she raged.

"I'm standing up for what's right. And you know what? If Rose doesn't get a grip on all this and tell Noah, then I'm going to. He has every right to be involved in deciding what's best for everybody. Rose already made her own dumb decisions. Now she has to deal with the consequences."

Summer slid as far from me as possible and muttered, "You guys always take up for each other."

Actually, I was thinking the same about women. The fact that I was going to have a talk with Noah was probably inevitable. He had a right to know, and Rose needed him to help her through the pregnancy—I just hadn't decided if I should tell Dad first.

18

Sarah

Mixing the lemonade, I paused in front of the window and enjoyed the warm spring breeze on my face. I was especially happy and could barely keep from smiling. But I tried hard to, worried that someone would see right through me and guess that I was sweet on Micah Schwartz.

Slipping a hand into my pocket, I touched the cool smoothness of the stone that Micah had placed there earlier in the day. I'd been surprised to see him and several members of his family at the Hershbergers' farm helping to bring in the first cutting of hay. Mr. Hershberger had put his back out a few days earlier, and several families had gathered to help him with the chore.

Luckily, Micah's father hadn't come along, and besides a few tense moments when we'd first arrived, the day had passed in relative peace. When I'd walked by him on the way to the house after I'd brought the first pitcher of lemonade out to the field, he'd lingered longer than the other boys and given me the stone when no one was looking.

Still touching it, I remembered its beautiful golden-brown color and his words when he'd tucked it into my pocket—*It's the same shade as your eyes.*

Blushing, I looked around at the other girls and women in the kitchen and was relieved that no one was paying me any mind at all. That was until Suzanna's voice sprang up behind me, saying, "Gracious, Sarah, anyone with a right mind will know you're lovesick if you don't wipe that silly look off your face."

"Hush now," I chastised her, feeling too giddy to be irritated in the least.

As Suzanna leaned against the sink smirking, Constance came over and asked, "Would you like me to make this trip to the field?"

Her voice was hesitant, and I suddenly felt a strong pang of sympathy for the girl. Noah had done her a nasty turn, and even though I was happy that he'd be with Rose again, like I knew he was supposed to all along, I was still ashamed of his behavior.

I looked at the girl whom I had wished to call sister one day, and was about to say yes, but before I could, Suzanna blurted out, "Constance, Sarah has it covered. You can help with the sandwiches."

I frowned at Suzanna before turning back to Constance and saying, "If you'd like, you can help me. We'll walk together."

"No, that's all right. I see where my place is. I won't be bothering either of you again."

Suzanna lowered her voice to a harsh whisper and said, "Oh, please. Don't go acting all sweet and naive. You stood by and let your father raise the bid on that horse to an amount Noah couldn't dream of paying. His own horse, Rumor, that he'd raised from a foal was the same shiny black color and died in the accident that almost killed him. You all should be ashamed of yourselves."

Constance's eyes had widened during the onslaught, but when she spoke her voice was still the same wispy sweetness it always was.

"I don't control what my father does, the same as both of you." She turned to leave, paused and looked back over her shoulder to add, "I wish we'd never moved here."

There were too many people in the kitchen for me to chase after her and apologize for Suzanna's behavior, but I almost did just that before Mother appeared and grasped my arm.

"Leave her be, Sarah," Mother said softly.

I looked into her dark eyes and saw the same sadness I felt.

"How can you say that? Aren't we all God's children?"

Mother pulled me into a hug and murmured, "Yes, of course, dear, and I'm proud of you for holding it to your heart, but the situation with Constance is going to get worse before it gets better."

When she pulled back, Mother gave Suzanna a stern look that sent her bustling out of the room. Mother picked up the other pitcher and motioned me to follow her through the door. We walked together through the yard in silence for a minute until we'd passed the children playing and the older women spreading the cloths on the picnic table.

Once we were completely alone, Mother slowed and said, "Elijah Schwartz outbid your father on a house that he'd already been asked to build. He also offered Matthew an amount of pay that Mervin Weaver wouldn't refuse, so we're now short a worker on the crew."

I stopped and said, "Matthew's working with the Schwartzes? How can that be possible?"

"Mervin has had issue with us since Noah turned down Ella. He only stayed in line because of the union of Katie and Jacob, but now that he has the backing of Elijah, he's becoming an arrogant man."

Hearing Mother speak with anger in her voice was rare, so I took her words to heart.

"What will Father do?"

"He'll do what he always does, the right thing. God will sort this mess out in time for us, but until then, the less you have to do with the Schwartz young'uns the better."

Mother saw it in my face, I know it. Her eyes were kind, but her mouth was tight, when she went on to say, "Do you understand what I mean, Sarah?"

"Yes, Mother, I do."

As we finished our walk to the hay field, I hardly noticed the bright sunshine or the warmth on my skin from it. The horse nickering in the nearby pasture seemed a million miles away. My life had gone from joy to misery in a matter of minutes.

If Mother was warning me away from Micah, then I had no choice but to obey. She would never lead me wrong, and I trusted her wisdom in all things.... Still it broke my heart just the same.

19

Rose

"Rosie, is there something wrong?"

I glanced at Dad for a second and looked away. I wanted to tell him, really I did, but the fear that gripped my insides wouldn't let me do it. I wouldn't be his precious little girl anymore— He'd hate me.

Spreading the butter lightly on the toast, I wondered how long it would be before I could keep something other than bread and butter in my stomach. Luckily for me, Dad was too busy with his hectic schedule at the hospital to notice my eating habits lately. He was a doctor, after all; if he spent a lot of time around me, he'd figure it out.

"No, why do you ask?"

"You seem a little off lately. I thought we'd agreed that in the future you'd be open and honest with me—no more sneaking around."

"I'm not sneaking," I said.

"You're becoming distant again, Rosie, and I'm just trying to nip it in the bud before it becomes serious. You've put your old dad through a lot this past year. I'm worried about you."

Still avoiding his gaze, I replied, "I know, and I'm sorry.

Really, there's nothing wrong. It's hard to get settled into living in the middle of nowhere again, that's all."

"Do you want to go back to Aunt Debbie's?"

"No!" I said it too fast and with an amount of emotion that raised Dad's eyebrow high.

Looking at him had been a mistake. He was more suspicious than ever.

I wracked my brain for a diversion and grabbed on to the first thought that came to mind. "Hunter...I don't want to move away from him."

The lie flowed out of my mouth too easily, and I felt a stab of guilt. As much as I liked Hunter as a friend, any romantic feelings I'd developed for him had been erased when Noah and I got back together. Unfortunately, he was the only option I had to get Dad off my back for a while longer.

Dad smiled and said with a lighter voice, "So, you've been spending some time with him, have you?"

"Uh, yeah, he came over the other night. We talked for a while. It wasn't a big deal or anything."

"Hunter is a nice boy. You should give him a chance."

"I'll take that under advisement, Dad."

Hope's barking alerted us both to a visitor, but Dad was the first to the window to look out.

"Well, speak of the devil," he said.

"You've got to be kidding."

Dad was quick to pick up his briefcase and head to the door.

"Justin's still sleeping, and Sam will be home from work this afternoon. It's a beautiful morning. Have a good time."

Dad winked, and before I could respond, he had the door closed behind him.

I folded my arms on the counter and dropped my head on them.

This can't be happening....

20

Noah

"Why don't you head over to the Camerons' home and ask David if he has any odd jobs he'd like done this week," Father said as he paused from his work on the disk. Barney, the larger of the two Belgian horses hitched to the plow, tossed his head in irritation at having to stand still while Father freed the large tree root that had gotten stuck in the blade.

His words shocked me for a few seconds, but I finally answered, speaking slowly to make sure there wouldn't be any misunderstanding.

"It would be all right with you if I went there?"

"I know where your heart is, son, and I appreciate that you've been patient with me and the situation with Elijah. I've asked quite a lot of you to put off having Rose by your side, but I don't want you to feel punished. It would be a good thing for you two to see each other for a short time, given that you restrain yourself and keep in mind our goals. Besides, now that I've lost the Tarry building contract, work will be slim pickings for a few weeks."

Anger flared inside of me. "Does the man have no shame? How can he so blatantly go against us?"

Father wiped the sweat from his forehead and sighed. He

said, "I'm trying hard to not let his actions blacken my heart toward him. Elijah feels that he's been wronged by us. But I believe in time, he'll move on and let go of his grudge."

"But what about Matthew? Even if you get another job lined up, we'll be short one man."

Father reached out and touched my shoulder. It pained him as much as me to lose Matthew from the crew. Not only was Matthew one of my closest friends, he also had a jolly spirit that helped the work days go by more quickly. I still couldn't believe that after five years, he wasn't with us any longer.

"It will be difficult without Matthew, but one day he might be back, and there are other young men in the community who'd be happy for the opportunity. God has a plan in everything, and this is no different."

The smell of the plowed ground was strong in my nostrils, and I gazed out at the land that Father had already loosened. The dark brown dirt stretched down to the roadway, and I felt a deep sense of satisfaction that the work had been done by horse and man, instead of tractor. He still had several acres to go, but within a couple of days the field would be ready for corn seed.

With a groan, Father had the root free. Barney snorted, letting Father know that he was ready to continue, but before Father climbed back on to the seat, I stopped him with my hand.

"What will we do if Elijah doesn't quiet down? We can't continue living on in a community where some of the people are working against us. Already it's cost us a paycheck, a horse...and my ability to marry Rose in a timely fashion."

"Son, I pray each night that God will lighten Elijah's

heart. We must have faith that it will happen sooner than later. There are other horses for sale and houses to build." He paused and looked at me intensely with his blue eyes, making sure I was listening before he went on to say, "As far as Rose is concerned, you'd have to wait until she turns eighteen, anyway. Her father has made it clear that he will not tolerate you being with her while she's underage. We must respect his wishes. You must be patient."

Feeling as if Father were treating me as a grown man, I became brave and told him my fears.

"I worry that the community won't accept a union between me and Rose now."

Father brought his foot down from the plow, and he asked with hesitation in his voice, "What are you saying?"

"Rose and I might have to find another place to live." Seeing his mouth begin to open in protest, I surged ahead, wanting to get my troubles off my chest. "It's difficult enough to live our ways, without dealing with members of our own church causing us grief."

Father nodded slightly and said in a firm voice, "Yes, we have chosen a difficult path, but the troubles we work through make us stronger men and Christians. God will not put more on our shoulders than he knows we can bear."

"It isn't a sin to join another church. You and Mother left your community in Pennsylvania and came here when Jacob was a baby."

"True, but not because of issues with members of our church—we chose to begin our life as a family in a less crowded place. A place where we had more opportunities and land was cheap. But know that we were torn on the decision. We left behind friends and family, and that wasn't easy to do."

"But you did it and have fared well here in Meadowview."

"We felt guided here by our Lord— We weren't running away from any discord."

I walked over to Barney and patted his tan neck. He turned his head to me, blowing warm air on my arm.

I took a deep breath and asked, "Has there ever been a moment in your life when you considered leaving the Amish altogether?"

Surprising me, Father smiled slightly. "Of course, haven't we all at some point?"

Never had I heard Father speak so candidly on the subject, and I was relieved for his willingness to talk about it without anger.

"What stopped you, then?"

Father breathed and gazed out at the untilled earth ahead of the horses. Stretching out his arm, he pointed and said, "Right there is one of the reasons—the simplicity of working the land with a team of horses. I love this way of life and wouldn't trade it for all the modern conveniences that the outside world offers. I have also prayed on the matter and feel deep within myself that we are doing what God has instructed us— He smiles down on us."

"Do you think as Abram and the others do, that the outsiders are living in sin and being disobedient to God's wishes?"

Father didn't answer straightaway. I watched as his face became conflicted before he turned back to me with a frown. "You aren't considering leaving our ways, are you, son?"

I could hear the worry in his voice and didn't want to give him more grief than he was already dealing with. But recently the thought had plagued me. In the past, there were times when I'd longed to watch an old Western movie on Mr. Denton's TV, or drive his old pickup truck myself, breezing along the highway on my own. But those desires were of the flesh, and I felt the press of sin against me when my thoughts strayed in those directions.

Lately, though, the idea of being forced to see the likes of Elijah Schwartz and Mervin Weaver, and being under their control and authority, had me undone. Living within an Amish community meant surrendering self-will to the group, and I wasn't about to put my life and livelihood in the hands of those who were hoping to see me fail.

For the first time ever, I wondered if a life in the Meadowview Amish community would be best for me and Rose and our children.

"I don't know, Father. Some of the members of this community aren't following the way of grace and forgiveness. I'm not sure if I can forge a life for my family in such a place."

Father nodded solemnly. "I understand, but I hope that the ill will we're experiencing does not push you away from our beliefs and customs. The dangers to the spirit in the outside world are greater than anything we face being Amish."

"But isn't it a stronger character who is tempted, but rises above it?"

"Right and wrong become muddled out there, and all actions become justifiable." As if Father was suddenly uncomfortable with the conversation, he climbed onto the seat and gathered the reins in his hand. He said, "Let go of these thoughts for now. Go next door and see if you can drum up some business. If you're lucky, you'll get to see Rose."

"I never dreamed of a day that you'd be encouraging my relationship with an English girl."

Father smiled sadly, and his expression stung my heart. "Hopefully, one day she'll be Amish alongside of you. That's what I pray for each night. It feels like providence that the two of you should be together, and who am I to argue with the will of God?"

21

Rose

Standing like a statue, I listened to the knocks. Could I get away with pretending that I wasn't home? Not likely. I was pretty certain Dad would have gone out of his way to say something friendly to Hunter before he drove away. And then there was my little red pickup truck sitting in the driveway. Nope, escape wasn't feasible, either.

My irritation grew with each rap on the wood. Gathering courage and swallowing down the tightness in my throat, I opened the door.

I tried to ignore his wide smile and said in a businesslike way, "Sorry, but Sam's not here."

"I didn't come to see your brother." He looked to the side in obvious nervousness and then back again.

"Hunter, we already went over this. I don't want to see you anymore. It's better for both of us."

"I don't agree, but just put that aside for a minute. Can we talk?"

Nodding my head, I went through the doorway and onto the porch.

"I have to let Lady out and clean her stall. You can talk while I work."

Hunter eagerly followed me down the steps to the walkway. I tried to forget the happy expression he'd worn when I glanced his way as we left the house. He was fooling himself if he believed that he could say anything at all that would change my mind about being with Noah. Hunter was sweet and good-looking, and maybe in another lifetime I'd have fallen head-over-heels for him but not in this one. I loved Noah and was pregnant with his child—there was nothing to talk about.

Hunter watched silently while I led Lady from her stall to the pasture and turned her loose. He didn't clear his throat until I had the wheelbarrow in the stall and was scooping up the manure.

"Ah, why don't you let me do that for you?"

"Why? Do you think because I'm pregnant I can't clean a stall?"

I stopped to stare at Hunter with narrowed eyes feeling conflicted about his offer to help. The fact that he was being so nice bugged me all the more.

"Well, kind of, yeah." He lowered his voice to a whisper and added, "Working with the horse might not be the safest thing for you."

"You don't know anything. Pregnant women do all kinds of work and athletic activities. You should have seen Emilene raking the leaves in her yard last year or feeding the cows. She stayed busy right up to the day she gave birth to her twins."

The thought of Emilene erased Hunter's confused face from my mind for a moment. I remembered her bloated body struggling in pain to give birth to the boys and how I'd had to call Dad at the last minute to help out.

I winced and looked back at Hunter.

"That might be true and all, but I feel really uncomfortable watching you work while I'm standing here doing nothing." He held out his hand and said, "Please, let me do that for you."

The pleading sound to his voice and the fact that I was feeling especially tired this morning made me hand the shovel to him.

He quickly got to work while I leaned against the grain box in moody silence.

"How've you been feeling?"

"Besides vomiting several times a day, I'm fine."

He nodded his head and said quietly, "Have you told your dad...or Noah yet?"

The question hit a nerve, and I hissed, "It's none of your business who I tell. And you had better keep your mouth shut about it."

"I wouldn't tell anyone, I promise you that. I can only imagine what you're going through. It would be bad enough to be pregnant, but keeping it secret would be even worse in my opinion."

I gazed out the barn door, my eyes wandering to where Lady was munching on the grass beneath the oak tree. The birds were chirping, and the cool dampness of morning was being dried away by the bright sunshine. It was the perfect day...except for the fact that I was pregnant. If Hunter hadn't shown up, I could have pushed the knowledge to the back of my mind and pretended I was an ordinary teenage girl enjoying the warm weather.

But as irritated as I was with Hunter at the moment, I couldn't deny that having him to talk to was probably a good thing.

"I know you'll keep the secret. Besides, it's not like I have a lot of time before everyone knows, anyway."

"That's why I came to talk to you today."

I glanced up to see the eagerness on his face and suddenly felt very wary.

"What do you want from me?"

"Actually, I want to do something special for you." Seeing my frown, he quickly went on to say, "Wait, Rose, please hear me out on this. You're right, in a few months everyone will know that you're pregnant and then your life will change forever. You'll probably marry Noah and spend the rest of your life as an Amish wife and mother. There will be so many things that you're going to miss out on, things you won't ever be able to do."

His words made my heart drop into my stomach. I'd thought a lot about how becoming Amish and having a baby would change my life. What he was saying was like an arrow of truth through my chest.

Sniffing back the emotions, I said, "Did you come here just to upset me, because that's what you're doing."

He took a couple of steps closer and looked down on me with wide eyes. "No, I'm not trying to hurt you. I want to give you a memory that you'll have for the rest of your life. Something that I know you'll love. Please, say yes."

"You haven't even told me what you're talking about."

"I'd like you to accompany me to my senior prom."

A million feelings rushed through me. He wanted me to go to a school dance with him? For a moment, I imagined the fancy sequined dress I'd pick out and the flower corsage he'd put around my wrist. A night of twirling and sliding across a dance floor—it sounded like heaven.

Before the dream got too out of hand, reality sank in, like a bucket of cold water on my face. With effort I blocked the images out of my mind.

"Are you crazy? I can't go with you to a dance. I'm Noah's girl...and I'm pregnant. Pretending it isn't so won't erase the facts."

"Now, wait a minute, the ball is next week. You won't be showing by then, and as far as Noah is concerned, I'm inviting you as a good friend. I don't have a date, and I thought that the opportunity to do something like that would be fun for you—a special memory that you'll always have."

His eyes told me he was being sincere. Hunter might have ulterior motives, but he did want me to have some fun before all hell broke loose in my life. The temptation was so strong that I tried to rationalize why it was all right to do it. I even considered for an instant that I might be able to go with Hunter as friends and keep it from Noah, but only for a second. I'd never do something so dishonest to the man I loved. A dumb dance wasn't important. I felt guilty for even allowing the thought to cross my mind.

"I'm sorry, but..."

The clip-clops on the driveway caught my attention. Hunter and I looked at each other quickly before we left the stall and peeked out the doorway.

To my utter amazement, Noah was in an open buggy, being pulled up the driveway by a bay horse. My mind ran through all the possibilities as I began to go through the opening to greet him.

Hunter pulled me back and said, "Rose, will you go to the prom with me?"

Sadness touched my heart when I saw the emotions swirling around in his eyes. Hunter really did have deep feelings for me. But there wasn't anything I could do for him. At that moment of seeing Noah, even at a distance, I knew where I belonged. I would forever love Noah, and I'd never do anything to cause him pain intentionally.

"Thank you so much for the offer. You're right, it would have been very special for me, and you would have been the perfect guy to go to a dance with, but I can't. I'm in love with Noah...and I'd never do that to him."

Hunter's eyes darkened a shade to become brownish-green, but he slowly nodded his head in acceptance.

Hunter let go and stepped away, but too late.

Noah had seen us and drove the buggy right up to the barn doorway. I turned away from Hunter's dejected face to Noah's angry one. I knew how it must have looked to Noah, but I stood up straighter, feeling confident I hadn't done a thing wrong.

Noah jumped from the buggy and said, "Is everything all right, Rose?"

He stopped beside me and glanced between me and Hunter.

Hunter's expression changed to defiance, and I inwardly cringed, hoping that he behaved himself.

"Yeah, I'm fine. Hunter came by looking for Sam."

"So, you're Hunter?" Noah's voice was cool, but I worried that it was an act.

"Nice to meet you," Hunter said, thrusting his hand forward.

Noah hesitated for a second but, in the end, grasped it.

Seeing the two of them shaking hands was an odd and short-lived moment, when Hunter said, "You'd better take good care of her."

"Rose is none of your concern."

Hunter smiled slightly, and I remembered his persistent personality.

"That's where you're wrong. What happens to her will always matter to me."

"Whoa, guys. Let's keep this friendly," I pleaded as I pushed Hunter toward his truck with my hands. "You better get going, Hunter. I'll tell Sam you stopped by."

Hunter became solid rock beneath my fingers, not budging. I looked up and begged him with my eyes, but I knew immediately he wouldn't listen.

"I think I'll hang around awhile until he shows up. After all, the two of you aren't supposed to see each other without a chaperone. Or is it that you aren't even supposed to be together?"

Hunter's voice was sarcastic. Any sympathy I'd had for him earlier was erased, but I didn't have the chance to say anything about it.

Noah stepped forward and said, "Rose asked you to leave. That says it all."

The movement of Hunter's body was too fast for me to

stop. There was a blur as he shoved Noah hard. Noah lost his balance, but caught himself with his hand before his whole body hit the ground. He shot up and knocked his body full force into Hunter, and the two of them fell to the ground together.

"Stop it, both of you, please!" I begged, but it was no use.

They rolled around on the ground, striking and grabbing in a fit of mutual craziness. I barely noticed the sound of the dually truck as it accelerated up the driveway and came to a screeching halt a few feet from the wrestling match.

Sam was out of the truck in a heartbeat, and at the same moment was joined by Justin who was out of breath from sprinting from the house, barefoot and still in his pajama pants.

The two of them descended onto Noah and Hunter swiftly. Sam got a hold of Hunter and put him in an arm lock, while Justin struggled to pull Noah away.

My legs finally loosened, and I jumped in, helping Justin with Noah. When my hands closed around Noah's waist, he stopped fighting and leaned against me.

"What the hell is going on here?" Sam yelled. He continued to restrain Hunter for a few more seconds until his friend sagged in his arms.

"I heard you scream, Rose, and it got me out of bed in a hurry," Justin said in a calm voice that sounded strange above the heavy breathing from Noah and Hunter.

I pressed my hands softly into Noah's belly and asked, "Are you okay? Did he hurt you?"

"He was giving it right back to me," Hunter gasped.

"You're the one who started it," I shouted at Hunter, angrier with him than I'd been the night he'd gotten drunk and forced his kiss on me.

"Open your eyes, Rose. You're going to ruin your life with him—you can't even be yourself with him and tell the..."

Sam pulled Hunter backward and twisted with him at the same time, instantly quieting him.

"You need to be on your way, bro," Sam said. When Hunter began to protest, Sam talked over him and said loudly, "No, seriously, man, this is not the time."

When Sam reached Hunter's car, he shoved him into the driver's seat and then leaned in, mumbling some words I couldn't make out. Hunter met my gaze for an instant before he shook his head and slammed the door shut.

I had mixed emotions watching him race down the driveway and then peel on to the roadway. He'd been instrumental in helping me get over Noah when I'd thought he'd left me, and the time I'd spent with him had meant something to me; but he'd gone too far today. If Hunter couldn't accept that Noah was the only man for me, then we couldn't be friends anymore. I wouldn't risk losing Noah for Hunter—my feelings didn't run that deeply for him.

"I'm sorry, Rose. I don't know what came over me."

Justin took a step back and said, "It looks like my superhero skills are no longer needed."

As he passed by Sam, Sam growled, "A little girl could have done better than that."

"Sorry, I put more emphasis on my mind than my muscles. I guess that would explain your unusually low IQ," Justin said casually, but he began running when Sam faked him out with a chase.

"Damn, he's irritating," Sam said. He walked back toward us, and when I looked at his face, I was suddenly very much afraid.

"Why is Hunter so protective of you?" Noah asked me quietly.

"So, are you going to tell him, Rose, or am I going to have to do it?"

22

Sarah

During the entire youth dinner I'd tried not to look at him, but I couldn't stop my eyes from straying his way from time to time. To my chagrin, Micah was always grinning back at me.

It would be much easier for me to do as Mother asked and ignore the boy if he'd return the favor. I didn't have the ability to be outright rude to a person, especially when they were being nice to me. Leading Micah on any further was wrong, and I needed to do something about it before the situation drove me crazy.

The voices of the women while they worked to clean up the Schrocks' basement distracted me. As I placed the last dinner dish into the box, Martha Lambright's softly spoken words became suddenly distinct, and I paused to listen.

"I apologize for disagreeing with you, Ruth, but I believe the worst thing that could happen to our community at this time is for Rose to rejoin us."

Ruth Hershberger replied in a louder voice, and I noticed several of the other women had stopped working to spy on the conversation. I glanced over my shoulder to see Ruth take a step closer to Martha.

"You supported the girl before—what's changed your mind?"

Martha continued to fold the tablecloth neatly as she spoke. "I can understand Elijah Schwartz's concern over the matter. After all, Noah asked for his daughter's hand in marriage. That's serious business, in my book. Perhaps if Rose was out of the picture, Noah and Constance would find their way back together again, and the clash within the church would be mended."

Heat spread within me, and I couldn't help but turn around. For all of Martha's smiles and compliments, she was an intimidating woman. Being the bishop's wife carried with it a level of leadership that none of the other women possessed.

I said a quick silent prayer for the Lord to give me wisdom in my words before I interrupted the two, saying, "You're wrong on that account, Martha. Noah would never have Constance back, because he loves Rose. The only reason their relationship fell apart was by her family's doing."

Martha's eyes narrowed, and her face tightened for a second before it became soft and smiling again. That second was enough to give me goose bumps.

"It's nice of you to speak for your brother and your friend, but honestly, you are too young to understand the ways of the heart. If you really wanted what was best for your brother, you'd wish that he'd forget the English girl and patch things up with Constance. He'll find only pain with Rose."

Ruth snorted loudly and then said, "From what my James has told me, your own husband isn't in agreement with you on the matter."

"You know from experience, dear Ruth, that wives and husbands don't always see eye to eye." Martha paused and looked around at the other women gathered as she spread out her hands and asked the group, "How would any of you have felt if your beau was spirited away by a pretty English girl? The Schwartzes are not out of line in their feelings—we'd probably all feel the same way if such a thing was done to our daughter."

My eyes widened, and I glanced at Ruth who stood confidently facing Martha. Suzanna and Miranda, who'd paused from their work at the sink with everyone else, had silently moved to my side during the conversation. Suzanna's warm fingers squeezed my hand briefly in reassurance.

When I looked around the room, I wasn't so sure which way the crowd would go. Libby Weaver was grinning from ear to ear, obviously elated that Martha was stating her own thoughts exactly. It wasn't surprising since she'd been against Rose ever since Noah had refused advances from her own daughter, Ella. The Yoder women kept their faces neutral but were standing close to Libby, and that worried me. Christina Bontrager's face was pointed at the ground, and she shifted the weight between her feet, showing her discomfort with the entire situation.

"Whether we agree or not, it's still our place to side with our husbands on matters of the church. You, of all people, should know that. Besides, it's in God's hands now. But I would hope that if Rose ever does come back to us, you'll show her the warm kindness that you're known for," Ruth said carefully.

"Of course I will. If it's meant for Noah and Rose to be together, then it will work itself out in their favor." Martha turned and crossed the room, pulling me into a hug. I stood awkwardly in her arms, the strong smell of laundry detergent from her dress filling my nose. She whispered for my ear only, "I'm sorry to have upset you, Sarah, but if your mother were here, she'd have said so much herself. Just the other day we talked, and she spoke her mind. See, I'm not standing against your family's own wishes."

The false niceness in her voice and the pleasant smile didn't fool me in the least. Anger swelled inside of me, and I pulled away, saying, "Of course, Martha. I know you're a friend of my family."

I hurried across the basement with wet eyes, remembering my conversation with Mother. It was difficult to believe that Mother could be influenced by Martha's cunning ways, but perhaps she had been. Or maybe, she truly felt that Noah would be happier in the end with Constance instead of Rose.

Either way, it didn't matter. I still had to stop Micah from pursuing me. There was no way we could be together now. I would never go against Mother's wishes.

"Are you all right?" Suzanna asked from behind me with a worried frown.

I stopped and looked over my shoulder. "Yes, I'm fine. You go on and finish up. Don't mind me at all."

"What you said was right, you know. Noah will never be separated from Rose again." Miranda nodded agreement.

"I wish others would mind their business where Noah and Rose are concerned. Haven't they done enough damage as it is?" I asked my friends, feeling that the world was spinning out of control.

Suzanna lowered her voice and looked around before saying, "They should stay out of your business, as well, if you want my opinion."

I reached for her hand. "I agree with you. But they won't,

you know. Even though I'm not English like Rose, because of this mess between our families, Micah and I can't be together."

"Don't you say that— Trust me, it'll work itself out in time. You have to be patient and not let the will of others pull you away from him." She moved closer and added, "You've always been the best of us, Sarah, the good girl. Yet you never judged me and Miranda or gave us a hard time the way the other girls have. Even though we were rebellious, you never turned your back on us. You deserve happiness. Please don't let them take that away from you."

Her conviction startled me, and I found myself saying, "I'll remember your words."

"You better. We'll meet up with you in a bit," Suzanna said before she returned to her duties. Miranda lingered for a second more and smiled sadly.

"Don't give up hope. Even when life seems darkest, there's always hope," Miranda said in her whispery way and then followed Suzanna back to the sink.

Susanna and Miranda's encouragement made me brave. Smoothing my hands down my hunter-green dress, I searched the basement and found Micah leaning against the far wall with a few of the other guys.

His gaze immediately locked on mine, and I raised my chin slightly pointing toward the door. When he nodded almost imperceptibly, I breathed again. He understood. I only hoped he'd be discreet about following me.

Before I could escape, Rachel appeared at my side and asked, "Where are you going? Mother told us it's our turn to help put the benches up."

Rachel was two years younger than me and had darker

hair and eyes than I did. Out of all the Miller children, she was the only ill-tempered one, constantly upset about something. The frown she was gracing me with told me she was in an especially sour mood at the moment. Whether she'd overheard the exchange between Martha, Ruth and me was anyone's guess.

But I was still her senior, and answered with authority. "Surely you can handle it on your own with the others. I have…something to check on in the barn."

Rachel's face grew suspicious, and she said, "What do you have to check on?"

Leaning closer to my sister, I whispered fiercely, "It's none of your concern. Now, get back to work and leave me be."

Rachel's mouth lifted into a smirk that made the hair on my arms rise.

"Be good, Sarah. Mother would be disappointed if you weren't."

She turned and left me standing alone. The two of us had been closer when we were little ones, having enjoyed each other's company when we played dolls or rode our ponies together, but lately, my sister always wore an angry scowl when she looked my way. Perhaps she was jealous that Mother was more lenient with me, but that was only because Rachel was so lazy about doing the housework and chores. It got on Mother's nerves something awful. Besides, Father had not been shy about showing his favor for Rachel when he'd invite her to go hunting with him and the boys or tag along on trips to the stockyards.

I tried to dismiss the encounter with Rachel and pushed the door open. The drizzle falling from the dark clouds dampened my mood even more as I lightly stepped around the puddles to reach the stable. The smell of hay and leather greeted me when I entered the dimly lit interior of the barn.

Being extra careful, I made my way to the stall where Father's horse, Strider, was tied and pretended to check his hoof for a stone.

Just as I had the weight of the hoof between my hands, Micah's voice whispered from behind, causing me to drop it.

"You wanted me?"

I could only look at his smiling face for an instant before I locked my gaze on the ground.

"Oh, well, not exactly...wanted you. I mean...I wanted to... talk to you is all," I stammered out, utterly embarrassed.

Micah glanced around before taking a step closer. My back was against Strider's warm shoulder, so there was nowhere for me to go.

"It's all right. I understand what you're saying. What do you want to talk about?"

My mind went blank as I met Micah's stare. After a moment of absorbing his sandy-brown hair, high cheekbones and full lips, the thought occurred to me that he truly was handsome.

I suddenly didn't want to tell him to go away forever and forget me.

He must have seen something pass over my face. His brows lifted, and the smile disappeared.

"What's wrong, Sarah?"

Mother's words echoed in my head, *the less you have to do with the Schwartz young'uns, the better.*

I was torn, desperately wanting the opportunity to be with Micah, but not wanting to disobey Mother.

The sides battled inside of me, and for the first time in my life I felt utterly alone in the world.

"I don't know what to do," I said softly as a tear began falling from my eye.

Micah moved swiftly, and before I knew what was happening, his lips were on mine. At first I was so surprised that I didn't respond, but after a few seconds of feeling the pressure of his mouth, the shock disappeared and I relaxed.

I was aware that I was sinning but pushed the knowledge aside. Micah's soft touch had ignited a flame inside me that had made all rational thought leave my mind. I liked kissing him, and by embracing me, he'd struck away the loneliness in a heartbeat.

His arms tightened about me and his lips opened slightly, covering my mouth. The movement caused a tingle in my belly, and I responded by opening my mouth farther. I felt his smile against my lips, and I was suddenly relieved when he ended the kiss. He was being respectful, and that made me sure that he was the boy for me. Gently he guided my head to his chest as he held me close. Hearing the rhythmic beating of his heart, I closed my eyes.

"What's going on here?"

The booming voice shattered the moment as Micah and I separated, yet still stood side by side.

"Father, please listen. It's not what you think...." Micah implored, but he wasn't able to finish the sentence.

Elijah Schwartz's face was red and held a tight scowl. The anger pushed off of him like heat blasting from a roaring bonfire. Fear made my insides go cold, and I couldn't have spoken if I'd wanted to. But in that instant I did catch a glimpse of Rachel's face in the doorway. Her wide eyes locked on mine in solid support. She was gone in a blink, and I was finally able to take a shallow breath, knowing she wouldn't leave me to deal with the angry man on my own.

"I know exactly what this is, boy—a mistake, a huge mistake. I will not allow you to tie yourself up with that family. Who knows what mischief this girl has in mind...she's probably no better than her lying brother."

"Don't you dare say such a thing about Sarah—she is not her brother!" Micah shouted.

"I'd listen to your son, Elijah, he speaks the truth of it." Father's firm voice was music to my ears. Even though I wanted to flee the stall and run into his arms, I stood my ground beside Micah, not wanting him to take his father's wrath on his own.

The storm that was brewing around Elijah suddenly changed direction as he turned to Father.

"Just the fact that your girl is out in the stable playing with a boy shouts the truth to the world," Elijah said with more control to his voice than he'd used with Micah.

His words struck home, and I bent my head in shame without meeting Father's eyes.

"I will deal with my daughter as I see fit. You have the responsibility of controlling your own son," Father said.

"Agreed." Elijah motioned to Micah to come out of the stall.

Micah glanced at me before he joined his father in the aisle. The look had been brief, but it spoke volumes—he wasn't giving up on us, and he didn't want me to, either.

When Elijah and Micah were gone, I finally had the courage to face Father. He shook his head and frowned, but his arms spread wide.

I ran into his embrace, letting his protection tighten around me.

"I'm so sorry. I never meant for it to happen, I didn't," I cried into his shirt.

He murmured, "I know, I know. You must be strong, dear child, and stay away from Micah."

Before the tears blinded me, I saw Rachel standing behind Father. Her face held only pity for me as she lowered her eyes and shook her head sadly.

23

Noah

The look that passed between Rose and Sam chilled me to the bone. What was he talking about?

"No, Sam, please, don't. I'll do it. I'll tell him myself."

"You promise?"

Rose nodded her head as she glanced between her brother and me.

He wagged his finger at her and said, "You better. This has gone on long enough."

When he'd left, Rose held out her hand, and I grasped it. She avoided my gaze, leading me to her barn. I followed along, very nervous about what she had to say.

When I was seated on a hay bale in the loft, I watched her pace back and forth in uncomfortable silence for a minute or so before curiosity overcame the worry, and I blurted out, "Rose, come sit down and talk to me. Please."

She stopped and looked at me with her own fear clearly showing. The loft felt very different in the brightness of late morning than it did in the dark of night when we'd met before. Somehow the light beams shining through the gaps in the wood made the moment feel more real…and frightening.

With reluctant steps, she approached, stopping in front of me. I spread my legs and pulled her forward into a hug. Breathing in the lovely lavender scent, I tried to relax. Rose needed my strength now.

She whispered against my cheek, "I'm pregnant."

I wasn't shocked. Deep down, I'd known all along, although I'd been afraid to face it. I should have asked her that night when we'd met in the cabin.

I wrapped my arms around her for a long minute. My heart calmed. The thought of my precious Rose having our child warmed my heart. Sure, there were things to worry about, but I pushed all ill thoughts away and instead focused on what was the best thing to say to prove to Rose that I was ready to be a father…and husband.

Pulling Rose onto my lap, I took a deep breath and looked into her blue eyes that reminded me of the summer sky.

"It's wonderful news, sweetheart. I can't wait to hold our baby. I just wish I'd talked to you about it a long time ago."

Rose's face brightened, and her mouth dropped open for a second.

"I thought you'd be upset. That's why I kept it from you. You said you wanted me to be patient and wait for things to settle down in your community—that we couldn't be together."

Understanding flooded my mind and anger at my own self along with it.

"I'm sorry. I never meant to make you question my intentions. Of course, if I knew you were with child, nothing else would matter."

"I was so worried," Rose said as she leaned her head against my shoulder and let out a long sigh.

With the most conviction I'd ever felt in my life, I said, "You don't ever have to worry again, sweetheart. I'll tell my parents, and we'll arrange for a quick wedding before you even begin showing." As an afterthought, I said, "Just think, our baby will be born not too many months after Katie and Jacob's. They can play together as they grow."

"Katie's pregnant—really?" Rose pulled away and looked at me in surprise.

I nodded my head, happy that her face had lost the thoughtful frown. Everything would be all right.

"How are you feeling? Have you been sick?"

"It's been awful. I throw up at least three times a day. I can hardly keep any food down at all."

Seeing my worried look, she rushed to add, "But other than that, I've been fine, really. Summer babies me like I have a rare disease, and Sam and Justin have actually been pretty helpful."

With some hesitancy, I said, "How is your father taking it?"

"He doesn't know yet."

A sudden rush of adrenaline pumped through me. "What— Are you serious? Does this mean you haven't been checked out by a doctor yet? How could you keep such a secret from him?"

I watched a variety of emotions battle on her face, before she said softly, "I almost told him this morning, but I was afraid to. I don't want him to hate me."

"He won't hate you. You're his daughter—he's proven the lengths he'll go to protect you."

Rose rolled her eyes, and her words spoke her doubt. "How would your dad feel if Sarah told him she was pregnant?" When I didn't immediately answer, she said, "Huh, tell me."

"That's completely different."

"How so?" Her voice became sharper, and I knew I'd said the wrong thing. "Oh, I see. It's because I'm English and you think it's all right for a girl like me to get knocked up."

"No, that's not what I meant at all. Gosh, Rose, you have to stop taking everything I say so personally. It's like you always have a battle going on between our cultures that I don't know about." Softening my tone, I continued, "I meant that your father is a doctor. He understands things better, and he's more experienced to handle such a situation. Besides, I've been trying to marry you for a year. Your father knows that I'll be a committed husband and provider for our children. Sarah isn't even courting."

The huffing noise that Rose made sidetracked me for a second.

"At least, I don't think she's courting anyone."

Rose met my searching gaze straight on and nodded.

"Who?"

"Do you know a guy named Micah?"

I thudded my head back against the hay bale behind me, saying, "Oh, great, they're moving a lot faster than I ever guessed they would."

"Don't tell me that you're going to give her a hard time after everything we've been through." With a sharp warning, she said, "Don't even go there, Noah."

"It's not that at all. Micah is a great kid. I like him a lot, but he's one of Constance's brothers."

"I get it that her family is upset, but it shouldn't matter. Sarah and Micah are not you and Constance."

"Regardless, it's going to be a lot of trouble for them, and unfortunately, I'm to blame."

"I know. You were pretty dumb to get hitched to her."

The abrasive sound to her voice made me wary of the direction the conversation had gone. I had just found out that she was pregnant and was still dealing with shock of it; the last thing I wanted to do was argue with her about my bad choices.

Pulling her to my chest, I murmured into her ear, "Sweetheart, you're right. It's the dumbest thing I ever did. I'm so sorry."

I could feel her body soften beneath my hands, and I continued to hold her in silence for a minute more before I asked, "What do you want to do?"

She tilted her head and looked up at me with raised eyebrows.

"You're asking me? I thought you'd already have a plan."

I couldn't help but smile. Rose really was naive.

"Ah, this news changes everything, of course. I'll tell my parents the truth of it, and I'm sure they'll support a quick wedding...but, what I meant is how you want to go about informing your family. You're still underage. Your father may not allow it."

She looked up with such a horrified expression that worry suddenly filled me. What could we do if David didn't give us his blessings on the union?

"Could he keep us from being together if I'm pregnant?"

"I don't right know, but we need to be in agreement about what we're going to do if he interferes."

She sat up straighter and asked, "Would you run away with me? We can go anywhere—it doesn't matter where."

All my well-laid plans went straight out the window when I gazed into her fear-filled eyes. The only two things in the world that mattered were Rose and our unborn child—and it would be less than a year before she turned eighteen and we'd be away from the community. Surely my parents would understand.

"Yes, Rose, we'll leave this place together if your father is unreasonable about our marriage. Your family won't keep me from you—especially now."

She nodded her head and smiled before she leaned in and kissed me. The crazy desire in my gut that I always felt when our lips met flared to life. My mouth moved on hers rhythmically, and I knew everything would be fine.

In the back of my mind another thought crept in, and I let it go quickly, not wanting to mention it at that moment. *If we had to leave, we'd go far away to another Amish community and stay there until Rose comes of age.*

Somehow, I didn't think those were the words she'd want to hear.

24

Sam

"Where's your sister?"

Dad took a sip from his glass of milk, set it down and unbuttoned the top of his shirt.

I felt a momentary pang of guilt that I was about to screw up his evening in a major way, but I used my superior ability to stay focused on the task at hand and plowed straight in, anyway.

"She went into town with Summer."

"I'm glad she got out of the house. She's seemed a little off lately. Do you know if she's been talking to Noah in secret?"

Leave it to Dad to get right to the point. Maybe this conversation would go more smoothly than I thought.

When I nodded my head, he shook his and slumped into the kitchen chair.

"I hate to snitch on Rose, but you should know what's going on." After taking a deep breath, I blurted out, "Noah came over here today to see her."

"Dammit, I had a feeling. That's why I was afraid to bring her home in the first place, but she was so adamant about moving on and wanting to be with her family for her senior year."

"Rose is a good actor," I said, before sitting across from Dad.

"How long has this been going on?" Dad asked.

"Longer than you want to know. But that's beside the point."

With an aggravated voice, he said, "No, Sam, if she's seeing that boy again, that's the only point that matters to me."

"Sorry to burst your bubble, but things are a whole hell of a lot worse than you think."

"Watch your mouth with the language and just say whatever's on your mind."

"Rose is pregnant."

Watching Dad's eyes widen in shock and his face instantly pale was not pleasant, but seeing Justin's accusing eyes in the doorway to the foyer was even worse.

"You are such a loser," Justin said.

Dad finally came out of his coma and sputtered, "You... both...knew?" He leveled a hard stare at me and added, "Are you absolutely sure?"

"Definitely, I was there when she took about ten home pregnancy tests in a row. Summer's been helping her out, and Justin and I went along with her wishes to keep it a secret for a while longer."

"You are such a traitor. You made an oath to Rose that you'd let her tell Dad," Justin spit out.

"Shut up, Justin! This is too damn important to keep from Dad. This is real life, not one of your Xbox fantasy games. Rose was going to tell Noah this afternoon, anyway. Basically, I did her a favor—Dad has a chance to calm down about the news before she has to deal with him."

"She's going to hate you," Justin said with surety.

"Cut it out, you two." Dad looked at Justin and said, "I should have been told immediately. Sam's right about that." Then he turned back to me and whispered, "My God, is it Noah's?"

I had to admit, at that moment I was overwhelmed with confusion. I even glanced at Justin to see the same frown on his face that I probably held.

"Of course—who else could it be?" I said the words slowly.

Dad stared out the window as a small spray of light came through from the setting sun.

"I guess I was hoping that if such a thing had really happened, Hunter was the father. After all, they'd dated for a little while, hadn't they?"

Funny, Hunter had never even entered my mind the terrible day I'd learned about the pregnancy. But I could see how Dad's mind would have grasped that straw.

"Sorry, Dad, it's inevitable now. Rose will be Amish," I said.

"Like hell she will be." He stood abruptly, and his chair knocked over backward. After taking a breath, he added, "There are many options available. Rose will not be forced into that backward society because of a pregnancy."

The force of his voice made me lean back in the chair. In my mind, it was a done deal, but obviously Dad had other ideas.

Squirming in my chair, I asked tentatively, "What do you have in mind?"

"That's none of your concern, Sam. When she gets home, I'll discuss the matter with her, and we'll make a decision."

"Man, if I were you, I wouldn't be looking forward to that discussion," I said.

"He doesn't have long to wait— Here she comes." Justin

pointed out the window at the headlights of Rose's truck as she parked.

"You boys get out of here. I want to talk to her alone."

For once I was glad not to be included in the action. Standing up, I followed Justin from the kitchen without a backward glance. When Justin darted into the TV room, I waited beside the door for the girls to enter.

One look at Rose and I knew from her red-rimmed eyes that she'd been crying. Summer had her arm gripping Rose's shoulder, and her own face looked grim. I hesitated for a minute before saying, "Dad wants to talk with you. He's waiting in the kitchen."

The change to Rose's face made me take a step backward.

"You didn't," she said.

When I lifted my shoulders and looked away, she told me, "I'll never forgive you for this one—never."

She hugged Summer and left us in the foyer as she walked with a straight back and slow strides to the kitchen.

Summer looked up with angry eyes and said, "How could you rat your sister out like that—especially after you made a promise?"

"This isn't all black-and-white. We gave Rose a few weeks to make a decision and tell Noah and Dad. They both have a right to know, and I was getting the feeling that she'd let it go until her belly grew big. She has to make plans now."

Summer shook her head and reached for the doorknob. "You are so arrogant. All Rose asked was to have some time to think about what she really wanted to do, and tell her boyfriend and Dad the news on her own. The really sucky thing is that she was going to talk to your dad tonight, anyway."

I took a step closer to stop her from leaving and said, "Then what's the big deal?"

"You've robbed her of the chance to do it on her own."

Summer was quickly through the door and strutting down the stone walkway. With only a second of thought, I ran out of the house in my bare feet and grabbed her arm to stop her.

"Come on, Summer, please don't be upset with me about this. I was only doing what I thought was best for my sister."

Summer sighed and softly shook her head. "When are you going to learn that some things aren't up to you to decide?"

When I shrugged and put on the sorriest-looking face I could manage, she relented beneath my fingers and said in defeat, "I guess it doesn't really matter, anyway. She's already made up her mind about her future."

"What's she going to do?"

Summer smiled and lifted an eyebrow, saying, "You'll have to wait to find that out yourself. Unlike you, Sam, I can keep a secret."

25

Noah

Darkness was almost complete when I rode up the driveway on Maisy. After I'd left Rose, I'd immediately saddled up the horse and headed to the fields across the road. I needed time by myself to think and make plans—and deal with the fact that I was going to be a father.

Before, when I'd thought about the chance of Rose being with child, I hadn't been too worried about it, but now that it was a reality, my head was spinning. The fact that we weren't married was at the forefront of my troubled thoughts. My folks knew of the possibility, but how would the community take the news? I figured it wouldn't be well received, especially with all the problems Elijah Schwartz was already stirring up among the church members.

After spending hours riding through the plowed fields and along the hedgerows, I was certain of one thing—no matter what Father, Mother or my community said, Rose and I would begin our lives together, even if it meant moving away to do so.

Peter and Isaac running toward me caught my attention and I reined the old mare to a stop.

Peter blurted out, "Better not go in the house if you know what's good for you."

A tingling sensation of worry ran along my arms as I asked, "Why?"

"Father told us to go to the Yoders for the evening—we're heading that way now," Peter said.

Looking up, I spotted Rachel leaving the house with little Naomi's hand in hers. Daniel wasn't far behind them.

"He asked all of you to leave?"

"Except for Sarah," Peter replied.

When the others reached us, Peter nudged Daniel with his hand, and the two raced away down the driveway with Isaac running after them, struggling to keep from falling too far behind.

Rachel slowed, and I looked at her questioningly.

"Sarah's gone and gotten herself into trouble with that Micah boy," Rachel said with her usual tone of judgment.

The sound of her voice instantly angered me. Not that I wished it on her, but I was willing to bet that someday the girl would have her own heartache to deal with, and then she wouldn't be so smug.

I ignored Rachel's frowning face and spurred Maisy into a canter to cover the distance to the barn quickly. Rachel had the fine features to be far prettier than Sarah, but her personality dampened her beauty. Whereas Sarah's kind ways made her shine more brightly than most of the other girls in the community. It was a shame that Rachel hadn't been born with a gentler spirit. She'd have the pick of the boys in the community if she wasn't so surly all the time.

Once Maisy was back in the pasture, I walked in the dark to the house. The last thing Father and Mother needed was confirmation of Rose's pregnancy on top of Sarah's issues, but I had no choice. There wasn't any time to lose.

Pushing the door open, I quietly took my boots off in the mudroom and went to the kitchen. I wasn't surprised to find the three of them seated at the table beneath the gas lamp that let off a duller light than the electric lamps that the English used.

The room became quiet while I washed my hands. Only when I was drying them did I turn around and risk looking directly at Father. He sat in his chair with a slight slump that was uncharacteristic of the strong man. He appeared defeated, even before I'd given him my own troubling news.

"Noah, you need to leave for a while, maybe go visit Timothy for the evening," Mother said softly.

"No, Rebecca. I believe Noah should be here for this discussion. After all, Sarah's problem stems directly from his actions."

I cringed at his words but took the seat beside him nonetheless.

Sarah's sniff into a tissue brought my gaze up, and I smiled reassuringly at her tearful face. These kitchen table conversations with Father and Mother were nothing new to me, but if I had to guess, I'd say it was her first. Father could sure be intimidating when he was riled up over something.

"It isn't Noah's fault. The blame should be on that horrible man, Elijah Schwartz," Sarah said as she wiped another tear from her eye.

Father nodded in agreement but said, "That may be the right of it, but Noah does play a part in this mess."

"I'm already paying the consequences." Pushing aside my own problems I glanced between Father and Sarah and added, "What's happened to cause Sarah to be crying and the both of you to be looking at her with dread?"

Father sighed loudly and said, "Elijah caught Sarah and Micah kissing in the Yoders' barn this evening after the youth gathering."

The words boomed in my head for a few seconds before I accepted them as truth. The world really was upside down if good-girl Sarah was doing such a thing, but the fact that Father was as calm as he was even more surprising.

Sarah sucked in a gulp of air and cried out, "It was the first time. I promise it was."

"That's neither here nor there at this juncture." Father looked steadily at Sarah and continued, "I know you're a respectable young woman and that that you've learned from this incident. As God says in 2 Timothy 2:22, 'So flee youthful passions and pursue righteousness, faith, love, and peace along with those who call on the Lord from a pure heart.'"

Mother reached over and patted Sarah's hand, saying, "If Micah has pure intentions, he will be patient and wait for you."

Father's eyes strayed to me, and I glanced away. This was not a good night to tell him that Rose was pregnant.

"But his father will never allow us to be together. It's hopeless." Sarah began to cry in earnest and was quickly pulled into Mother's embrace.

Father's hand came down hard on the table, and he said, "Elijah has no good reason to keep the two of you from courting. The members of the church will not allow him to bully you both out of a relationship that would be God's will."

"He's caused so much mischief already, Amos. Some of the women in the quilting group hardly even speak to me now," Mother said, her voice slightly muffled as her mouth was against Sarah's cap.

Anger tightened my insides. Even Mother was suffering from Elijah's hatred of me.

"*Ach,* that's trivial business. I have faith that it will work out for the better good of the young ones and the community. We must be cautious in all that we do for a time as not to give Elijah more fuel for the fire he's created."

He turned to me and said, "That's where you have a part to play, Noah. You and Rose must be patient."

Carefully, I asked, "What exactly do you mean, Father?"

"Regardless of your wishes in the matter, you still will have to contend with David Cameron. So, waiting until autumn when Rose turns eighteen and can make a decision on her own about becoming one of us is the only way. You'll have to wait."

Remembering Rose's quivering lips and fearful eyes, my heart quieted, and I became brave. Facing Father, I said, "Rose's family is not your only concern."

Father shook his head lightly and replied, "No, it isn't. The community will not accept an engagement between the two of you at this point. Elijah has made sure to darken our people's hearts and cause them to question bringing an English girl into our community." Father leveled a hard stare at me and continued, "He can cause all kinds of grief for us if we aren't careful."

After silently asking God for strength, I said, "Rose is pregnant."

His eyes widened for an instant before his hand pounded

the table. Mother's sharp intake of breath was the only sound in the kitchen. I only glanced at her and Sarah long enough to see their shocked faces before turning back to Father, who seemed to have regained his composure somewhat when he asked, "Are you certain?"

"Yes, she's definitely pregnant."

"Oh, Lord, help us through this troubling time," Father implored.

"We need your help…and support, more than ever now," I said softly.

"Son, you've made a great many mistakes this past year, and your impetuous behavior has affected us all. But regardless of all of that, your mother and I will be there for you and Rose one hundred percent. You must take responsibility for your actions and marry her as soon as possible."

"What about Elijah?" I suddenly felt as if a great weight had been lifted from my shoulders. As long as I had help from my family, all would be well in the end.

Father shrugged and looked to Mother, who nodded her head reassuringly. Sarah still gaped, and I felt sorry that she'd been dragged into my problem and was suffering because of it.

"We will keep word of the pregnancy secret for now." He looked at Sarah, speaking to her, "You will not mention this to Katie, Rachel and especially not Micah."

"What about David? He'll have to go along with the wedding, won't he?"

Father's gaze met mine, and my stomach rolled when he shook his head with tight lips.

"What are his feelings about it?" Father asked.

"He doesn't know yet. Rose was afraid to tell him."

"There's no telling how the doctor will react to the news, Noah. By English law, I believe he still has a say in the matter. He may present more of a battle for you and Rose than Elijah Schwartz and his followers combined."

Just as I was about to respond, the loud rapping on the door turned all our heads. Father raised his eyebrows before he rose. I was surprised to see the bishop, Abram Lambright, come through the door.

"I'm sorry to arrive so late without notice, but there is a matter that I need to discuss with you, Amos. It's of utmost importance."

Father didn't seem surprised as he lifted his coat from the peg and picked up his hat to leave. I imagined they'd be in the dark barn within minutes.

As I followed Mother and Sarah out of the kitchen, Abram called out, "You best be coming with us, Noah. This pertains to you."

I stopped, my heart sinking.

Had Abram somehow found out about Rose's pregnancy?

26

Rose

A small part of me was glad that I didn't have to say the words myself. Of course, I'd never let Sam know it.

Once I sat down at the kitchen table, there were a few excruciating minutes of silence, with the exception of the distant, muffled noise coming from the TV in the family room and the rhythmic dripping of the faucet in the sink.

I focused on the sound of the drops hitting the porcelain as Dad stared at me grimly. What could he do? Ground me or scream at me, none of it mattered in the least. I was pregnant and that was that. For once in his life, Dad couldn't fix it.

Determined not to speak first, I gazed back at him, waiting. A strange sense of calmness passed over me. Having Noah's arms around me earlier had given me strength. I wasn't alone in this.

Finally, Dad cleared his throat and said, "Why didn't you tell me, Rosie?"

His voice was quiet and hurt. I caught my breath and found that I couldn't speak. The tears that I'd hidden from him for the past couple of weeks began to fall. It would have been much easier if he'd gone on a rant. Instead, his calm acceptance of the news made me feel awful that I hadn't trusted him in the first place.

In my blur of tears, Dad moved around the table and grasped my shoulders, pulling me up against him.

"It's all right, honey. I'm not angry. Disappointed and worried, yes, but never angry with you."

"I didn't mean for it to happen. I was stupid...just dumb."

Dad sat me back down and pulled his chair up close. He leaned in and said, "You made a bad decision and the odds fell against you, but it certainly isn't the end of the world. You have choices."

As usual, his voice was soothing and practical, and I found myself mesmerized by his words.

"Choices?" I whispered, suddenly very worried about what he was implying.

He nodded his head briskly and said, "Yes, of course. You made a mistake, but it doesn't have to affect your future. Have you thought at all about your options?"

I stared at him, suddenly afraid of what he was about to say.

"It's still very early. The pregnancy could be eliminated."

The words played over in my head a few times, and then my belly heaved. I jumped to the sink and threw up. The awful feeling of vomiting was welcomed. It woke me from the trance I'd been in since Dad had begun speaking.

Dad held my hair back with one hand as his other reached for the towel.

I snatched it from him and shouted, "I'm not having an abortion. You can just forget about that."

"Rosie, I didn't mean to upset you. Of course, it's your decision, but you need to know and understand all of your options. At this point the fetus is only the size of a thumbnail."

"I can't believe you'd suggest such a thing. This is my baby with Noah. It's your grandchild," I cried out, slapping his hand away as he tried to calm me.

"I won't apologize for telling you there's an alternative to you going through with this pregnancy. Dammit, your future is what's important to me. Why can't you see that?" he shouted.

I shook my head in defiance. "Nothing you say will change my mind, so don't waste your time."

Dad took a breath and said in a softer tone, "Have you considered adoption, then?"

It suddenly dawned on me that Dad didn't want this pregnancy to change me. If he had his way, nine months from now, the baby would be somewhere else, and I'd be graduating from high school and going away to college. Maybe I could take some classes at the local community college, but the university experience that Dad wanted for all his kids was impossible for me now.

Remembering that Noah had been happy at the news caused me to stand up taller and say, "We're keeping our baby."

"We're— Is that your plan, then? To marry Noah and become Amish, to throw everything away?"

Dad's voice finally rose to the level that I'd expected from the beginning. He was more upset about me becoming Amish than the pregnancy itself.

"You can't stop me."

"We'll see about that," Dad said. His blue eyes challenged me.

"Whoa, guys. I thought you were going to be discussing

this reasonably," Sam said in his usual arrogant tone as he walked into the room.

Summer was with him, and when her gaze met mine, she crossed the room in front of Dad and stood beside me. Her hand grasped mine, and I realized that even if I didn't have Noah, I still wouldn't be alone.

Justin strolled casually in and took the seat I'd vacated. He leaned back in the chair and smiled crookedly at me. He was with me also.

"This isn't your concern, Sam, nor you or you." Dad pointed at Summer and Justin in turn.

"It certainly is. That baby is my nephew," Sam said.

"Mine, too." Justin spoke more quietly, but with no less certainty.

My emotions were suddenly calm, and relief washed over me. Noah and I weren't alone. We might not have Dad's support, but I knew that my brothers and best friend would be there for us no matter what.

Dad knew he was outnumbered. He leaned against the sink and ran his hand through his hair, agitated.

"Just because you're pregnant doesn't mean you have to join that religious cult. You can keep the baby. We'll help you. I'm sure Aunt Debbie will be thrilled once the shock wears off."

"What are you saying?" I asked with hesitancy, expecting a trick.

"If you are adamant about keeping the baby, you can do it as a single woman. You can still go to college. I'll help you with the arrangements for child care. Your life doesn't have to end with this pregnancy. You don't have to become Amish."

I was still processing what Dad was saying when Sam put his two cents in.

"Why would you want her to do it alone when the father wants to take care of her and the baby?"

"Sam, you know as well as I do that, after a few years of living the primitive lifestyle, Rose will be miserable, but she won't be able to escape. By then, she'll probably have several children, and with no college education, she'll be trapped."

Sam shrugged and said, "Maybe so, but it's her choice. You can't protect her forever, Dad."

They were both right.

"Dad, I love you and you've spoken about some of the same doubts that I have about becoming Amish, but it is my choice."

"There is another way..." Summer whispered under her breath, but I heard her loud and clear.

I knew what Summer meant, and the time had finally come to talk to Noah about it.

As Dad began discussing his plans to contact Mr. Miller the following morning to arrange a meeting between the families, I wrapped my arms around my belly and said a silent prayer that I'd be able to convince Noah to consider my idea.

Somehow, I had to make him listen.

27

Noah

Neither Abram nor Father spoke during the buggy ride. We crossed over the darkened roadway in eerie silence at a fast clip, and I wasn't at all sure where we were going until we pulled into the Hershbergers' driveway. When I realized who we were going to speak to, my heartbeat sped up.

The gas lamp was burning in James's leather workshop, and that's where Abram parked the buggy. James was the only person in the building, and he was perched on a stool at the counter. He was tinkering with his heavy-duty sewing machine that could stitch both saddle and harness leather and barely looked up when we entered.

I followed Abram and Father to the counter and leaned against it, waiting impatiently for James to acknowledge us.

Finally James set the thick string down and sat up. He nodded and said, "I must say you got here right quick, Abram."

"These are difficult times that require immediate action."

James motioned for Father to come closer before speaking in a quiet voice.

I trusted the man. He'd always been a good friend to our family, and I knew he'd been kind to Rose during the months she'd lived with him and his wife, Ruth, as their foster daughter.

"I had an unexpected visit today from Elijah and Mervin."

"What did they want?" Father asked with reluctance in his voice.

James sighed heavily and shook his head. "I wouldn't have believed it of Amish men, even those two, if they hadn't come directly to me." James focused on Father and went on to say, "They are preparing the community for a vote against you, Amos. They want you removed as minister, saying that they have proof that Noah is secretly seeing Rose again, and that you are in support of the relationship. Now that the girl has gone back to her English world, she's off-limits for Noah, you know, and this business could bring our people down on you, my friend."

I'd held my breath while James was speaking but couldn't keep my mouth shut a second longer.

"What proof could they have?" I exclaimed.

"Ella…and your wife, Abram." James said the last part in almost a whisper.

Both Father and I swiveled to look at Abram's reaction. Unfortunately, he didn't seem surprised by what James had said.

Abram said, "Let's start with Ella—what's her involvement?"

"She told her father that she saw Noah slip into Rose's truck at the benefit dinner. That young woman is too interested in other people's business, if you ask me," James complained.

"And what of Martha, James—what does she know?" Father asked.

I fidgeted at the counter, only casting a quick sideways glance at Abram. The tall man was stroking his long, snowy beard thoughtfully. He held no hint of anxiousness or irritation at Father's question.

"She passed by the Camerons' place today and saw Noah making his way up their driveway. She reckoned that since it was broad daylight, the visit must have been sanctioned by you, Amos."

Father turned to Abram and said, "You knew of this?" When Abram nodded his head, Father went on to ask, "Then why didn't you ask me yourself of it?"

"The matters of our children can blur the path of righteousness in our eyes. Look what pride has done to Elijah and his kin— Caused a right mess in our usually tranquil community. He is blinded by anger, and he'll someday have to face his own sins…but you, Amos, are walking a fine line yourself when it comes to Noah and his obsession with Rose. I understand the difficulties that your family has endured this past year, and even I became quite fond of the girl, but as your bishop, I need to know now if the accusations are correct, so that we can act accordingly."

Before I had the chance to blurt out my own defense of Father, he spoke up himself.

"It is true, and I'm a better man for getting it out in the open." Father glanced my way with confidence and then turned back to the other men. "Abram, you advised me to keep the children apart until after Rose came of age and rejoined the church. I agreed with you wholeheartedly, except that I knew it would be impossible to keep Noah away from her. Instead of creating a situation where he would fall into sin, I decided to treat him as a responsible man. I felt that if he had the opportunity to spend some private time with her during their public separation, the ordeal would be easier for both of them to handle." He paused and gave me a stern look before saying, "But I had no idea the two planned to meet in her truck at the auction."

James nodded his head in understanding, but Abram's tight lips showed that he wasn't swayed.

"You can't change the rules of courting conduct for your child, Amos. That's unacceptable. I can see where Elijah's and Mervin's ill feelings are coming from. If each parent were allowed to set up their own courtship guidelines, our church would be full of all kinds of mischief and trouble. Our Ordnung allows the young people to begin courting only after they've joined the church. We have strict laws about this being a hands-off courting community where the couples are chaperoned at all times."

"Noah and Rose's predicament is not that usual for our children. They tried to do everything right, but others were working against them. Surely, you won't hold this against Amos's position within the church?" James said.

"There is no way around it. There must be a vote—the sooner the better, so that this matter can be settled once and for all, and we can return Meadowview to the peaceful community it once was."

I'd stayed silent long enough. As Abram was turning to leave, I grabbed his arm and stopped him. "Wait, Abram, please, don't hold my disobedience against my father. He's always done right by the church. Up until now, he's been one of the most respected men in the community."

Abram looked at me sadly, and I knew it was no use.

"I'm sorry, Noah. This has nothing to do with your actions. You were given permission from Amos to do something that went against our Ordnung by allowing you to see Rose alone, a girl who is not even a member of the church. He'll have to answer himself to our people on the matter." He looked at Father and said, "I'll take you both home now."

"It's all right, Abram, I'll drive them with my horse. I need Noah's help with some lifting here in the shop. My back is still giving me fits."

"All right, then." Abram tipped his hat toward us. "There's always a chance that a vote could go your way, Amos. Either way, I wish you find peace with your decisions and are able to move on from this business." As an afterthought, before he crossed the threshold, he turned back and said, "Do be careful tomorrow—there's supposed to be strong storms blowing in. Good night, all."

Once Abram had left, Father and James immediately got down to business. James pulled out a piece of paper and began writing names down in two columns. The two men talked late into the night, assessing which way each member of the church would vote.

I sat quietly listening to them but not really hearing their words. My thoughts were deep and troubled.

Even if Father somehow managed to win the vote, he'd still have a much larger issue on the horizon to deal with. Our people might understand him allowing me to sneak an occasional visit with Rose in, but they'd never forgive him for keeping Rose's pregnancy secret, which was a much more serious matter.

Father was doomed to lose his position as minister within

the church…and all because of me. I knew what I had to do, but just thinking about it tightened my gut into a knot.

There was only one way I could save Father—but it certainly wouldn't be easy on any of us, especially Rose.

Pulling back on the reins, I said, "Whoa," and parked the buggy. My uneasiness grew as my feet touched the ground. Father's hand on my shoulder didn't erase the ill feelings while we walked toward the house with Mother beside us.

It was all happening so fast. When David Cameron had called that morning, Father and I were tiredly climbing into the work truck. It had been the early hours of the morning when James had finally returned us to the house. Within minutes of the call, Father had instructed Mr. Denton to pick up Jacob and head to the building site without us.

This meeting between the Miller and the Cameron family was too important to put off. Even though I was relieved to be getting it over with quickly, I couldn't help being afraid of the outcome. There had been several times when Rose's father had been difficult to deal with. The man may have saved my life, but he certainly wasn't a fan of mine. I hoped in time his feelings would change and he'd come to accept me and Rose being together, although I expected it to be a long wait.

Looking up at the dark gray clouds building overhead, I remembered what Abram had said the night before about storms developing. It seemed appropriate that the weather was as turbulent as our lives, I thought as Father stepped up to rap on the large door.

Before his hand touched the wood, the door opened.

David said, "Hello," stiffly and motioned us to enter.

He guided us into the kitchen, and my heart sped up when I saw Rose already seated at the table. David's girlfriend sat close beside her. Tina's bright purple skirt suit contrasted wildly with the subdued powdery blue of the room, but I was glad to have her there. She seemed to have a calming influence over David, which, unfortunately, might be needed today. My eyes passed over the woman just long enough to feel her apprehension before settling on Rose.

She smiled but looked tired. Dark rings were visible beneath her eyes, and her skin was pale. I wanted to pull her into my arms and comfort her, erase all her fears, but I obeyed Father's instructions and didn't let my emotions show in front of David. But I did try to convey my feelings with a long gaze and reassuring smile in return.

"Would any of you like coffee?" David asked.

"Yes, that would be wonderful. Rebecca and I will each have a cup," Father said.

I shook my head and took the seat across from Rose. My stomach was too unsettled for coffee this morning.

A minute later we were all seated, and Dr. Cameron finally spoke again. "I assume you all know the predicament that our children are in."

Father nodded solemnly and said, "Yes, Noah spoke to us last night of it."

David chuckled, saying, "So you've been in the dark for as long as I have. That makes me feel a little bit better."

"I must admit, we're still getting used to the idea of this unexpected grandchild, but, God willing, Noah and Rose's path will be free of more hardships."

The tension in the room spiked after Father spoke, and

I shifted my gaze from Rose's wide eyes to David's narrowing ones.

When David spoke, his voice had lost some of the earlier friendliness.

"That's what we're here to discuss. Rose has informed me that she plans to keep the baby."

Anger took hold of me, and I said, "There's never been a question of that."

David faced me and wagged a finger. "Don't raise your voice with me, young man. Your thoughtlessness has caused this mess."

"Mess—is that what you think our baby is—a mess?" I said, beginning to stand. Father's hand caught me and tugged me down.

Tina placed her arm around Rose protectively, and rushed to say, "That's not what he meant, Noah. You have to understand that he's upset."

"I accept your anger, David, and I wish I could undo my son's actions, but I can't. We must begin making plans for the future now, and put the past behind us."

With a more controlled voice, David asked, "What are your plans?"

Father hesitated and glanced at Mother, who'd been quiet so far. Father usually took the lead in family matters, but sometimes Mother spoke her mind. Up until that point, she'd kept her eyes downcast and avoided the conversation altogether as she sat with her black coat buttoned up to her chin.

Now, she lifted her gaze and reached over the table for Rose's hands. She had her long, dark brown hair covered neatly with her white cap, and her head bobbed up and down a couple of times before she said, "My dear Rose, I hope you are feeling well. If there's anything at all I can do for you, please let me know. I have a recipe for a peppermint tea that helps chase away nausea. If you're in need of it, I'll bring a teapot over this afternoon."

Mother's words pushed the tension from the room. She was focused on the heart of the issue and understood how the arguing would affect Rose. Her offer was a way to tell Rose that she accepted the situation and would help her through it. My gut tightened, and I looked away, not wanting anyone to see how Mother's display had affected me.

"That sounds really good, Mrs. Miller. I could definitely use some of that tea."

David cleared his throat, and we all turned back to him.

"Of course, I understand your interest in the pregnancy, and I appreciate your kindness, but I think you might be mistaken about how things are going to be. Rose is not going to immediately run off and become Amish because of this pregnancy. I don't want her rushing into a serious commitment with your son."

"I see your concern, but as parents, the matter is out of our hands," Father said.

"Rose is still underage, and I won't give my approval for her to ruin her life. A baby is one thing...joining your culture is something altogether different. I won't be a part of her downfall."

Rose bolted out of the chair and shouted, "I want to marry Noah! It's our lives—why can't you all just leave us alone?"

Rose ran out the door with tears streaming down her cheeks. Before the screen door slammed shut, I was out of my chair, following her, but I stopped and turned to yell, "Why are you all making this so difficult for her...for us? I promise you, we'll be together, with or without your support."

A stiff, warm wind that was charged with energy touched my skin as I ran through the yard after her. She was heading for the barn, and I glanced over my shoulder, grateful that we weren't being followed.

When I reached the shaded interior of the barn, I found her leaning against the stall door with her face in her hands.

"Rose, sweetheart, don't cry. It'll be all right, I promise."

She came into my arms, and I held her tightly against me as I smoothed her hair down her back with my hand.

"It's hopeless. Why is everything so difficult?" She sniffed into my shirt as she spoke.

"Because I'm Amish and you're not."

Rose pulled back and looked up at me with glistening eyes.

"What are we going to do?"

I thought for a minute about the different ways I could tell her of the plan I'd come up with after meeting with James. A plan I hoped would save Father's reputation within the community and also hide us from her own father's angry intrusion in our lives. I was afraid, though, instinctively knowing that Rose wouldn't be happy about it.

After staring into her wide eyes for a few more seconds, I decided to just say it bluntly. With our need to hurry, there really wasn't time for coaxing.

"If your father doesn't come around soon, we'll leave together. We can go to my grandparents' community in Pennsylvania or maybe even Indiana. I have kin there, too."

She stared out the barn door, her face scrunched in thought for a minute before she finally spoke.

"If we ran away, would we have to go to an Amish community? I thought your family was the main reason you wanted to remain Amish. If we can't stay in touch with them, why be Amish at all?"

I wasn't surprised by her question, but my body tensed, anyway.

"There will be work for me, and we'll have lodging. You'll have women to help you through the pregnancy and delivery. Once your birthday arrives, we can come back here…or maybe we'll choose to stay in a new place. Heaven knows, I'm tired of dealing with the problems here."

"You'd leave your family forever? I thought that's the one thing you didn't want to do."

"It's not the same as being shunned, Rose. We'd be free to visit each other and have normal relations with our family and friends here."

"Is staying Amish the most important thing to you?" There was a hard note in Rose's voice that worried me.

"No, you and the baby are more important to me than anything else. I just don't want to make any more mistakes. I've gone against my parents' and the church's rules for too long. Only heartache has come of it."

Rose took my hand and held it to her belly when she said, "This is heartache?"

I shook my head and met her gaze solidly. "No, sweetheart, besides meeting you, it's the most wonderful thing to happen to me. I just wish we'd gone about it the right way. You know, us getting married and then having the baby."

"It's their fault. If everyone had left us alone, all the bad things wouldn't have happened. We could have dated like normal people."

I shook my head sadly at her naivete.

"It never would have been normal for us. We're different, you and I, from other worlds."

"But we love each other."

"Yes, we do, but that doesn't make it easier. Maybe it makes it more difficult." I paused and touched her chin with my fingers lifting it. "Will you go away with me to start a fresh life in another community?"

With steady eyes, she said, "Do you really love me, Noah?"

"With all my heart."

"I'll leave this place with you, but not as an Amish woman."

Her words boomed in my head, and I said, "You want me to go English?"

She nodded. "Just think of it, Noah, it will be so much easier for us. No rules about every little thing we do. We can be free to make our life together…and our child will be free, too."

I pushed a few stray locks of her brown hair off her face and whispered, "I can't do it, Rose. I'm sorry, but I can't do it."

28

Sarah

The clouds to the west pushed over the farm, quickly darkening the sky. The wind whipped the clothes on the line, and I hurried to pull them down, afraid that the storms Father had warned about earlier in the day were close to arriving.

As I pressed the boys' pants down into the basket, my mind raced back to the night before when Noah had said that Rose was pregnant. I was still in shock about it. A week ago I'd never have understood why they would have lain together before they were married, but after the kiss I'd received from Micah, I was able to imagine how such a thing might happen.

Rose was the same age as me, though, and I worried about how she was handling the pregnancy. As an Amish girl, I expected to be married by the time I was nineteen or twenty, but I knew that most English girls waited longer, finishing college and establishing a career before they became mothers. Rose seemed even younger than her seventeen years. Although I loved her dearly, she was spoiled and used to getting her way. Her life would change dramatically with a baby in tow, and I worried if she'd even know what to do with an infant. Of course, she'd have Mother, Katie and me to show her the way, and she'd spent some time with Emilene's twin boys, which was promising.

With the last of the clothes off the line, I picked the basket up, bending my head away from the hard wind that stung my face. Before I reached the door to the house, I heard the fast-falling clip-clops on the driveway. Setting the basket down, I jogged to the side of the house to see who it was.

Sucking in a breath, I clutched my hands to my chest. It was Micah.

Only Rachel and Naomi were at the farm, and if I was very lucky, they were busy enough cleaning the upstairs that they hadn't noticed the horse and rider. I said a silent prayer that the wind had muffled the sound of the hoofbeats on the driveway as I ran out to meet Micah.

When Micah saw me, he reined his Appaloosa gelding toward me and met me in the front yard.

"What are you doing here?" I spoke loudly to be heard over the gusting wind.

Micah grinned and said, "I thought you'd be happy to see me."

My face heated, but I suddenly felt lighthearted, and I shook my head and laughed.

"You're very sure of yourself, Micah Schwartz."

In a blink of an eye, he'd hopped off his horse and was standing beside me. I quickly looked at the windows of the house, wondering if Rachel was watching and whether I could trust her to keep a secret if she was.

"Are you crazy? Get back on your horse," I demanded.

"I won't get you into trouble again, I promise. I'm on my way to the Yoders' and saw you in the yard. I wanted to say hello, is all."

He wore a black knitted hat that covered most of his hair, but some of it curled out at his neck, and I absently thought that I should cut it for him.

"What are you thinking?" Micah asked.

His green eyes were curious, and again, I found myself laughing. "After your father caught us the other day kissing, I'd have thought you'd stay far away from me."

"No way—we just have to be more careful about our relationship."

I swallowed the butterflies down and met his gaze. His face was serious for a change. The look made my belly do a flip-flop.

"Relationship—is that what you're calling this?" I made a sweep of my hands.

"Absolutely, Sarah—you're my girl now, and everyone knows it."

He looked so sure of himself that the breath caught in my throat. Before I became lost in the emotions, a burst of wind nearly took my cap off, and I grabbed hold of it, repositioning the pin to secure it more tightly.

When I glanced back at him, standing in a position to block some of the wind from me, I realized that I wasn't so afraid anymore. Something about his confidence gave me hope.

"Is it true? Are people talking?"

He nodded, and the crooked smile returned.

"Your father will never allow it—especially not now."

"I overheard him and Ma talking last night. They were whispering, but I held my breath and risked leaning my head into their dark bedroom. Da said that he reckoned if I was as stubborn about you as I was with everything else, it was inevitable that the Schwartz and Miller families would be tied together in the end."

I couldn't believe my ears. Clasping his hand, I exclaimed, "He'll allow you to court me?"

"Eventually, yes, he'll give his blessing. But he's not there yet. We'll have to be patient."

"Oh, that's wonderful news. Noah will be free to..." I stopped abruptly and caught myself.

"I tell you that we'll be together someday, and you're thinking about your brother?" Micah raised an eyebrow.

Quickly, I tried to cover my slip by saying, "Of course I'm happy for us, but my entire family has been affected by your father's anger. If he can get past what Noah did to Constance, it's best for the community."

He frowned, and my excitement quickly dampened.

"It isn't all good news, is it?" I asked, already knowing the answer.

"Even if Da grudgingly accepts you, his bad feelings toward your brother and father may never disappear. He's just that way about things. Once he's been crossed, it takes an act of God to undo him."

"That's not very Christian-like if you ask me," I reprimanded, unable to keep my voice from rising. "My father would never hold such a grudge."

Another gust brought many of the new leaves from the maple tree we stood beneath down upon us in a pelting fury. Micah pulled me against him to shield me from the weather, and said into my ear, "Have faith, dear Sarah. We'll be together soon enough."

The quick brush of his lips on mine startled me, and I pulled out of his grasp.

"Micah Schwartz, we aren't courting yet, and I'll have none of that business until you've made a commitment to me."

"I expect no less from you."

His horse had been well mannered, standing quietly up until that point, but the last blast of wind had frightened him. Micah held the quivering gelding firmly as it tried to pull away.

"I best be going before it starts to rain." He mounted in a fluid motion and held the jumpy horse in check while he said, "Be careful...the sky looks awful dark. I think we're going to have us quite a storm."

I nodded and waved to him. For a few seconds he stared at me while the horse pranced in place, then he grinned and turned toward the road. Over the sound of the angry wind, I heard the cantering hooves pounding on the roadway as I made my way back to the house.

Grasping the door in both hands, I struggled to get it shut. The roar of the storm muffled my gasp as the screen door snapped away from my hands, hitting the side of the house and then lifting into the air.

Rachel screamed behind me, and I turned to see her face as white as a sheet. Naomi was clutching Rachel's leg, and when her light brown eyes met mine, I saw my own fear reflected in them.

I hurried over and scooped the four-year-old into my arms. "Hush, little one. It's all right, just a storm is all."

"I'll get the horses into the barn," Rachel yelled above the noise, but I grabbed her arm and held her close.

"No, we should go to the basement. This storm is dangerous. I can feel it in my bones."

As we ran to the stairs leading under the house, Naomi cried, "I want Mama, where's Mama?"

Cradling her head against my chest I said, "Mama went to the Hershbergers to help with Ruth's garden. She'll be fine there and home soon enough."

I grabbed the kerosene lamp off the hook as we went into the darkness of the basement and hoped that my little brothers were still at Katie and Jacob's house and hadn't left for home yet. I guessed that Father was safe in Mr. Denton's truck somewhere, but with a fearful stab at my heart, I remembered that Noah had left on Maisy a while ago, and I had no idea where he was.

Once the lamp was lit and giving off a dull glow, I put my arms around my sisters and hugged them close.

The rumble of the storm was growing louder, and with each crash and bang from the upstairs my pulse quickened. After several minutes of soothing words didn't stop Naomi from crying, I fell silent and just held her close. Rachel mumbled incoherently, but I knew she was praying.

I said my own silent prayer for the Lord to watch over my family...and keep Micah safe.

Even though I was afraid, I smiled into Naomi's soft brown hair.

Micah and I had a chance, after all.

29

Rose

The blast of wind spooked Lady, and she bolted sideways. I clung with my thighs and tugged on the reins until I had her trotting in a straight line again. Glancing up at the darkening sky, I wished I'd listened to Sam about the strong possibility of storms that afternoon.

I probably would have taken his advice if he hadn't been so bossy about it. In typical Sam fashion, he told me how stupid I was to go riding while pregnant. He even threatened to phone Dad at the hospital if I went, but I'd called his bluff and galloped away, anyway.

He'd shouted after me about tornado warnings in the area, but I'd ignored him, more intent on getting away to think than to worry about the weather. It had been several weeks since I'd been on my gray Arabian's back and at first the feel of the colder air hitting my face had been exhilarating. For a little while, I even forgot about the pregnancy, enjoying the freedom that riding a horse gave me.

But now, with Lady shaking beneath me, ready to bolt again, and the wind picking up even more, I started becoming afraid. To make matters more nerve-wracking, I worried that the fearful tightness in my body would fuel Lady's nervousness.

Of course I wouldn't even be out in the storm if it hadn't been for Noah. The way he'd shot down my suggestion that he go English was not really unexpected, but it still stung. I didn't want to be Amish in some faraway community. I'd have enough trouble surviving the lifestyle in Meadowview. At least here, I knew people, and my family lived just up the road. Even if I wasn't allowed to visit with them much, they would still be there—waiting for me.

I didn't want to leave Summer, either. She was my best friend and probably the only person who could keep me sane in the days to come. Her words of warning were also heavy on my mind.

"You know, Rose, if it's a girl, she'll be stuck living her life in the shadows of men. At least you made the decision to throw away your freedom...she won't have a choice."

Another thing that had been on my mind was wondering what Mom would have said if she'd been sitting at the table this morning with the rest of them. It was a dumb thought. If Mom was still alive, I wouldn't be pregnant. We'd never have moved to Meadowview and Dad wouldn't be dating Tina.

And, I wouldn't be in danger of being thrown into the mud of the newly plowed corn field in the middle of Ohio nowhere.

The flash of lightning was so close that it blinded me for an instant, but it was the boom of thunder directly overhead that caused Lady's legs to spread low to the ground before she gathered her muscles and took off.

My body was thrown back, but I held on, righting myself

in the saddle. Once I felt fairly certain that the mare wasn't going to buck, I began pulling on the reins to slow her down.

We reached the end of the field quickly, and I managed to turn Lady before we crashed into the darkness of the forest. The violent wind was pushing the trees downward, and all the leaves were flipped over. As Lady slowed to a trot, I heard wood splintering, and broken branches flying through the air bombarded me.

Lady snorted and tossed her head at the onslaught while I clung to her for dear life. I considered dismounting and leading her home, but was afraid I'd never be able to hold her. I wouldn't be able to forgive myself if my horse broke away and was injured in a mad dash to get back to the barn.

The rain began to fall lightly at first, but by the time I had Lady turned and heading back the way we'd come, the force of the drops had escalated to a heavy downpour.

Gripping the reins tightly, I rode through the driving rain, thinking about Noah and how upset he'd be if he knew what a foolish thing I'd done. I also thought about Sam and Justin and hoped that they were in the grimy basement of the old house waiting out the storm in safety. But mostly I thought about Mom, wishing that she were alive and waiting for me at home.

The force of the wind was nearly pushing me off the saddle, and I hunkered down lower over the horn. I said encouraging words to Lady as we approached the gap that led between a small stand of trees that separated the corn and hay fields.

There was a slight lull in the storm when we were about to leave the trees, and I exhaled in relief that I only had one more field to cover to reach the road. I might make it home before the worst of it hit, after all.

Suddenly a gale came up that was greater than any of the others so far. I braced myself in the saddle, fearing the worst, when the sky brightened with light once again and the air groaned around me.

I caught sight of the oak tree's large trunk bending abnormally, and then I heard the creaking and splintering of wood. The wind carried the treetop down in a blasting crash that landed only feet from where Lady and I were.

Even a nonspooky, well-trained horse would flip out over this, I told myself, as my mare leaped away, saving us from the heavy branches that were still falling. Her sideways movement was too much for me, and my tired muscles loosened. I lost my balance, and as her haunches dug in a second time, I separated from her body.

It seemed I was in the air an unbearable amount of time before the ground rose up, catching me with a hard jolt. I rolled once or twice, finally stopping in a clump of wet grass. Even though the world was spinning around me, I lifted my head a fraction to see Lady running at a full gallop through the hay field toward home.

I dropped my head back against the ground and looked up at the purple-and-gray clouds. The rain was lighter now, and I could almost count individual drops as they fell on my face. With effort, I moved my hand to my belly and began to cry.

My vision was fading, but I noticed how fast the clouds

were moving and I watched them in a hazy, dreamlike state until the blackness began to spread in my mind.

My last thought was of Noah...and how sorry I was that I'd ruined everything.

30

Sam

This is insane, I thought as I jerked the window down, stopping the beating wind that had already blown one of Mom's favorite paintings off the wall.

Hearing Hope's frantic barking, I yelled, "Justin, let Hope in! She's on the front porch."

I continued to shut the windows and met Summer at the bottom of the stairs. She gave me the thumbs-up and said, "The upstairs is in lockdown."

"I've never seen wind like this before. Damn, we might have a tornado, after all," I said as I looked out the old-fashioned pane of glass on the side of the door.

Only an hour earlier, it had been sunny with a few ominous clouds on the horizon. Now, with the blackened sky and driving wind, it appeared that the end of the world was near.

"What about Rose— You said she'd be back by now?"

Summer's voice was high-pitched, and I saw the fear in her eyes. I knew how she felt, but up until that point I'd figured my sister was smart enough to not get caught in the storm. I'd been expecting her to come through the door at any moment. The tightening of dread gripped my insides as

I ran to the front of the house and searched out the window for any sign of her.

"Dad just called. He said we need to go to the basement. A tornado was on the ground just east of town." Justin had Hope by the collar as he began unplugging his Xbox and throwing his games into a duffel bag.

"You've got to be kidding me. You're worried about your game system when there might be a tornado heading for us?"

"This house has been around for about two hundred years. I'm sure it's seen worse storms than this. I'm not too worried about it blowing down—but there might be water damage," Justin said as he tossed his remotes into the bag and looked back at me with only mild concern on his face.

The look must have bugged Summer. She shouted, "Rose is out there, you little turd."

Justin's eyes widened, and he glanced between the two of us, before he said, "Whatever for?"

I shook my head at his disconnect with the world around him. "When I got home from work, and you were in your gamer haze, she was freaked out about the powwow between Dad and Noah's parents. I guess it didn't go very well. She told me she was going for a ride to think."

"How could you let her leave—? She's pregnant and upset and there was a storm coming," Summer demanded with hands on her hips.

"Yeah, you idiot, why didn't you stop her?" Justin put in.

"I did try to stop her, but, unfortunately, even though I'm quite the athlete, I don't have the ability to outrun a damn horse."

The house creaked as the wind beat against it. Summer jumped at the sound and ran to me, throwing her arms around my waist.

"Oh, my God, the house just moved," she squealed into my shirt.

Justin went to the front window and gazed out, saying, "Have you tried to call her?"

"Of course, but no answer," I said with extreme irritation. Did he really think I was an idiot?

"Hey, wait—someone's coming up the drive on a horse," Justin shouted.

Summer and I ran to his side and peered through the windows that were now streaked with rain on top of everything else.

I tried to wipe the moisture away with my hand to get a better look. Disappointment hit hard when I saw that the horse was brown and not gray, like Lady.

"Who is that?" Summer asked as she pressed against me for a better look.

"It's Noah!" Justin exclaimed.

"Has everyone lost their freak'n minds—this is not a good time to go for a ride," I complained.

I left the window and grabbed my jacket off the back of the chair.

"Where do you think you're going?" Summer sprinted in front of me and held out her hand.

"I'm going to talk to Noah. Maybe he knows where Rose is." I paused and looked between Summer and Justin, absorbing their frightened expressions. Calming my voice, I added, "You both need to go to the basement right now. Don't leave there for anything."

"Oh, no, not without you," Summer replied.

She ran up to me, pulled my head down and kissed me on the lips and then whispered fiercely, "You'd better get your butt down in the basement in a few minutes, or I swear I'll come looking for you."

Without another word, she whirled and joined Justin. I saw them turn the corner together when I opened the door and stepped out into the storm.

It took all I had to close the door behind me and jog out to the driveway. The rain was beginning to come down harder, stinging my face.

"Is Rose around?" Noah's words were carried away by the wind, but I got the gist of what he said.

"She's not here—I thought she might have met up with you on the horse trails," I shouted up at him.

"Rose is riding that crazy horse of hers in this weather?" Noah asked. The worry was plain in his voice.

I nodded. "She left about an hour ago, heading toward the fields across the road."

Lightning streaked the sky, and thunder exploded above us a second later. Noah's horse jumped slightly at the sound but otherwise stood still. I noticed the whites of its eyes flashing, though, and suddenly realized that what Noah had said was right. Rose's horse would be downright dangerous under these conditions.

"I'll find her," Noah shouted into the wind, turning his horse and kicking its sides.

For another few seconds I watched him race down the driveway in the pouring rain until he disappeared into the darkness of the storm. I didn't think it would have made any difference if he'd known about the tornado warning, but still, I felt guilty that I hadn't pointed it out to him before he left.

But someone had to look for her, tornado warning or not, and I reasoned that he had a better chance at finding Rose on horseback than I did in my truck.

I only hoped that he got to her in time.

I ran back to the house, splashing through the puddles and trying to keep from falling as another gust of wind struck.

If the damn house did come down, Summer and Justin would need me.

Rose and Noah were on their own this time.

31

Noah

Squeezing Maisy faster over the muddy ground, I wiped the rain from my eyes and searched for Rose. The sudden turn of Maisy's head and the flash of gray—I spotted Lady running along the hedgerow.

My heart sank when I saw she didn't have a rider.

Turning, I guided Maisy in the direction that Lady had come from, spurring the old horse on to greater speed. The mare responded, sensing my urgency, and flew across the hay field. The sky had turned an ugly shade of dark gray, smeared with purple and pink that reminded me of the bruises on my face after the buggy wreck.

The wind still blew stiffly, but there was a slight calming of the weather that raised the hair on my arms. It was almost as if the angry sky was taking a deep breath to gather strength.

Scanning the tree line, I frantically looked for Rose. Fearing the worse, I whispered, "Please, God, protect Rose from harm."

A second after the words passed my lips I saw pink material on the ground beside a toppled tree. Maisy covered the distance quickly. I leaped from the saddle and dropped down next to Rose. Fear clenched inside of me when I saw her eyes were closed and her face as white as a ghost.

Pressing my head to her chest I stopped breathing and listened. *Please, don't be dead, please, don't be dead,* repeated in my mind until I felt the shallow rise of her chest against my face.

"Rose, can you hear me? Rose— Rose."

The rain had lessened to a steady mist, but she was still soaking wet. Pulling the handkerchief from my pocket, I patted her cheeks and forehead.

"Come on, Rose. Wake up for me…please, wake up."

Her cough and sniff were music to my ears. Pulling her into an upright position, I cradled her to my body and placed my hand on her stomach.

"I'm…so…sorry. I never…should…have gone for…a ride. Sam was right."

Hearing her speak coherently soothed my fears, and I chuckled in relief.

"Well, that's probably the first and only time I'll ever hear you say that about your brother."

She smiled and said, "You came to my rescue—how did you know where to find me?"

"I went to your place to talk to you. You were so upset when I left earlier that I was worried. I spent the rest of the morning thinking about what you said, and I guess you could say I had a change of heart."

"Really?"

I nodded. "We need to talk about our future, and I promise you I'll be more open to your wishes—you shouldn't have to give up everything while I give up nothing."

Her eyebrow rose, and she scrunched the side of her

mouth up in suspicion. The look made my heart explode with feeling for her.

"You aren't just saying this because you thought I was dead—are you?"

A flash of light tore across the sky at the same moment the thunder exploded, and the wind beat against us.

"No, silly, but this isn't the time to get into it. We have to get out of here. Can you ride?"

"Yeah, I think so."

As an even darker sky raced toward us, I pulled her up and supported her body against mine until we reached Maisy. The good old mare had stood stone still waiting for us, and now she continued to do so as I helped Rose into the saddle.

I flinched with each groan that Rose made, but she managed to fling her leg over the mare, and I reckoned that she didn't have any serious injuries.

Placing my foot in the stirrup, I mounted behind Rose, sitting on the mare's croup. It had been a long while since I'd ridden double, the last time being when Jacob's horse had gone lame while we were a couple of miles from home.

Taking the reins up in one hand, I placed my other around Rose tightly.

"Hold on to the horn," I yelled as I bumped Maisy into action.

The horse couldn't move as quickly with the extra weight, but she still managed a ground-covering canter over the short grass.

The wind grew stronger, and it took all my strength to keep Rose and myself on Maisy's back. The sky opened again, sending sheets of rain on to us, and the air lit up every few seconds. As we approached the road, the world was hazy and indistinct. The sky was a dark slate gray that only brightened with the neverending flashes of lightning.

Strangely, the floral scent of Rose's hair kept me focused and the fear at bay. My only thought was of getting her and our child to safety.

The loud swoosh of air hit us hard, causing Maisy to stumble. The horse went down on her front knees, and I slid off her back to keep her from going all the way to the ground while Rose clung to the saddle.

"She can't carry us in this wind!" Rose shouted, only to have her words snatched in the air and ripped away.

I braced my hand against Rose's side and tugged at the reins, helping the mare to her feet.

"Come on, Maisy, you can do it," I urged the horse.

The old horse found her footing and lurched forward.

Rose tried to protest, but I began to run with Maisy at my side. A low rumbling in the sky behind us stirred a terror in me that I'd never felt before and caused my legs to fly faster than they ever had. Hot air burned my lungs as I ran beside the horse up the hill and through the gap in the fence. When Maisy's hooves struck the pavement, I paused and turned.

The sky to our backs had lightened to a silver-gray, and in the middle was a wide swath of blackness that touched the ground. I'd never seen the likes of it before, but I knew instantly what it was, and every part of my body was screaming at me to run away. The tornado was close enough that I could see the churning debris on the edges, like smoke moving in a campfire.

"We're not going to make it!" Rose yelled.

Her voice loosened my limbs, and I turned around and judged the distances to each of our farms.

"Rose, listen to me—you have to stay on Maisy alone. She can run all-out with only you on her back. Turn her loose, she'll fend for herself and get you to your basement. You'll be safe there."

"I won't leave you."

She began to climb off the horse, and I grabbed her, holding her body to the saddle.

Looking into her blue eyes, I knew why I'd fallen in love with her so many months ago—she was the only person in the world who would complete me. My little Rose was brave and confident, where I was sometimes weak and afraid. Her spirit gave me life.

With my face against hers, I begged, "Please, do this for me and our baby. I'm going to try to make it to my house. The girls are there alone—they might need me."

Rose grew up in that instant. She nodded in understanding and quickly pressed her lips to mine. The feel of her mouth even for a second was enough to spread warmth to my cold and tired limbs.

"I love you, Noah," she said into my ear before she gathered the reins and leaned forward, kicking Maisy in a gal lop toward her home.

I wasted only a second to glance over my shoulder. The roaring funnel had grown and was close enough now that I could hear the explosions and crashes within it. Glancing one more time at Rose and seeing that she was nearing her driveway, I was hopeful that she had enough time.

Turning from the horror behind me, I ran with everything I had over the roadway.

Branches, boards and shingles rained down around me, causing me to dodge right and then left. The rain was gone, but the air was cloudy with dust, stinging my eyes.

The howling of the wind at my back intensified, knocking me to the ground. The hard pavement broke my fall. On bloody hands, I pushed myself up. I'd almost reached the long driveway that led to my farm when the rumbling noise began vibrating in my ears.

I knew the tornado was almost upon me when the gravel rose from the ground with such force that it pelted my skin, leaving agonizing welts. Something heavy hit my shoulder and crashed me to the ground once again.

I didn't even know if I screamed—the bellowing in my ears was so great. The pressure of the wind kept me on the road. I couldn't rise, and I realized with dread that I would have no cover when the storm passed over me.

A picture of Rose sprang to life in my head. She was smiling, and she motioned her finger to follow. She was encased in a soft glow while the storm raged around her. When she turned away from me, I found the strength to crawl after her. Scraping my arms along the pavement I moved in slow motion, trying to stay with her. I needed Rose—I couldn't live without her.

When she began to fade, my heart slowed, and I slumped in defeat.

Another object whacked into me, this time striking my back. Pain shot through me, causing me to look up.

A bit of white caught my eye, and hope flared to life.

Dragging myself, I aimed for the culvert as the air, thick with rubble, swirled around me.

The touch of the wet grass on my hands invigorated me,

and with one last surge, I pushed myself up and into the circular opening leading under the road. I was knee-deep in water, but at least I was out of the open.

Sagging against the cold cement, I chanced to look out. As the ground lifted and shuddered, the world exploded in black and gray all around me.

For all the trouble of trying to save myself, I realized I was going to die, anyway.

Closing my eyes, I accepted my fate. As long as Rose and our baby survived, nothing else mattered.

32

Sarah

"But I have to go pee," Naomi whined in my arms.

Stroking Naomi's back, I continued to hug her close and glanced at Rachel, who shrugged her shoulders. Sighing, I looked out the small basement window. The sky was still dark, but the rain had eased up. The wind had quieted, and for the past minute the house hadn't creaked and groaned from its force.

"Maybe the storm's over," Rachel suggested, standing up.

Worried, I met her gaze. Now that she thought the danger had passed, she'd be difficult to control.

Hurriedly, I said, "I think we should wait awhile longer."

"Aww, come on, Sarah. You're such a worrier. Do you want to clean up after Naomi if she messes on the floor?"

I looked down at Naomi and noticed that she had her ankles twisted tightly, and her face was bright red with her straining to hold it in. Poor little thing, I thought.

"All right, but be quick about it. Until the sky brightens, it's better we stay in the basement, I think."

Rachel blew out an agitated breath. "We're going to be behind in the chores for all this nonsense."

She stretched her limbs and then grasped Naomi's hand, tugging her away from me.

For a moment I continued to sit on the floor, my thoughts far away, up the road at the Yoders' farm. Micah had been so sweet to me earlier. Perhaps he was right about his father softening about the idea of a courtship between us.

But what if he didn't?

Rising up on sore muscles, I pushed the doubt aside. I'd have to put my faith in Micah.

And if the storm passed quickly, I might see him again at the softball game that evening. Unable to stop myself from humming, I made my way up the stairs and into the kitchen.

The opening where the door had been was glaringly obvious, and I smiled at the shock Father would have when he saw that it had blown away.

As I made my way to the doorway, I bent over and picked up the cloth and broken vase that had been whipped off the table when the door had been ripped off its hinges. Flowers were scattered around the floor, and using my foot, I pushed them into a neat pile.

A sudden gust of wind through the door blew the stems and petals everywhere, and a thousand knocks could be heard on the siding as branches from the oak tree flew into the house.

My heart rate began rising all over again as I ran to the opening and gazed out.

A wall of rain was moving through the fields across the road, obscuring the newly plowed fields and trees in the hedgerows. The trees that were visible were bent grotesquely in the direction of the house.

"Rachel, hurry up! There's another storm approaching," I shouted upstairs.

When she didn't answer, I grumbled and went to get my sisters.

Turning the corner in the upstairs hallway, I bumped into Rachel. Her wide eyes and frown froze my heart.

"Where's Naomi?"

She shook her head quickly and exclaimed, "I don't know. I led her to the bathroom, and then I went to make sure our bedroom window had been shut. When I came for her, she was gone."

Pushing past her, I went into the bathroom and pulled the curtain to the tub aside. Seeing it empty, I shouted, "Naomi Miller, come out right now!"

When only silence and the growing rumbling of the wind met my demand, I told Rachel, "Check the downstairs. She might have snuck by me. I'll search the bedrooms."

Rachel whirled away, and as I darted into the boys' room I could still hear her footsteps as she bounded down the stairs.

Naomi was a rambunctious child. She loved to hide and wait for us to find her. For a four-year-old, she had the uncanny ability to remain completely quiet and had caused us to be late on several occasions to places we needed to be. Father and Mother never scolded her too much, as she always emerged from hiding with a cheerful smile and hearty laugh at us all.

But now I wished the child had had at least one good spanking for her behavior—maybe then I wouldn't be frantically searching for her when we needed to be in the basement.

"Naomi, this isn't funny. You come out this instant!"

Things could be heard hitting the outside walls of the

house as I dropped to the floor and shimmied between Peter, Daniel and Isaac's beds, searching beneath them. Seeing that she wasn't there, I jumped to the closet and flung the door open. I bent and pushed aside the shirts and pants and, with growing fear, hurried from the room.

"Did you find her?" I shouted to Rachel over the pounding rain.

She answered immediately with a loud, "No!"

My heart was beating furiously as I entered the girls' room and began searching.

"Naomi!" I called over and over again as I checked the beds and closet.

The shuddering of the house brought me to the window, and I looked out in horror. Coming across the field, as plain as the nose on a person's face, was a black funnel that stretched from the billowing clouds in the sky straight down to the ground. It was enormous and well defined against the flashes of lightning around it.

I stood and stared, too afraid to move. My muscles were frozen in place, and the breath caught in my throat. The windows rattled, and the house creaked with the driving wind.

"Is that what I think it is?" Rachel said from across the room.

Her voice woke me from the terrified trance.

I left the window and grabbed her shoulders. "Go to the basement, now, Rachel, run!"

She let me push her down the hallway to the stairs, saying, "What about Naomi? We can't leave her!"

"I'll find her. Stay down there until it's over," I said firmly. "For once, please do as I ask!"

Rachel nodded her head and then bolted down the stairs.

The windows began shattering as I ran to Father and

Mother's room, the only one I hadn't searched. Wind burst into the house, ripping curtains away from the wall and sending knickknacks flying off the dressers. I couldn't help but glance out the opening where glass had been seconds before in my parents' room. The black mass covered the roadway, and its roar shook my entire body.

"Oh, God, please let me find her...please save my baby sister," I whispered fiercely into the pulsating air.

The house began coming apart, and I fled the room, heading for the stairs. Something inside stopped me, and everything calmed. I no longer heard the tearing noises of the wind and the snapping of wood. I couldn't feel the air hammering on my face, either. Peace and strength filled me as I turned and ran back into the room, going straight for the closet.

As I pulled the knob, I expected to see Naomi looking up at me...and there she was, huddled beneath Mother's dresses with her small arms held out to me. Her lips trembled, and tears washed down her face.

Time had run out. We'd never make it to the basement. I squeezed into the small space and covered Naomi's body with my own. Murmuring soft words, I stroked her head and felt the tension leave her body as she clung to me.

As the room exploded into a million pieces, and the ground disappeared beneath us, I asked God to shield Naomi from pain.

There was a flash of bright light, and then the world was silent.

33

Rose

Maisy wasn't nearly as fast as Lady, but she was quick enough to stay ahead of the storm. Leaning low over her neck, I clutched her mane between my fingers and tilted my face away from the pounding wind. The rolling noise behind me was similar to a train moving over tracks at high speed and loud enough that I couldn't hear Maisy's hooves striking the pavement.

With great relief, I turned into the driveway, pulling on the reins to glance back at the road.

Noah was gone.

He was athletic and strong. I hoped his legs already had him close to his own house, but I didn't dwell on the possibility that he wouldn't make it in time—I knew I had to get to safety to protect our baby.

As the air filled with dust, and the screaming noise of the tornado filled my ears, I bumped Maisy back into a run and closed the distance to the barn. Jumping off, I pulled the old mare through the doorway and found Lady in the aisle, soaked and shivering, but otherwise all right.

My horse trotted to me and touched her nose to my chest. Picking up her dragging reins, I wasn't sure what to do.

If I put the horses in the stalls, and the tornado struck, they'd be killed, but turning them loose, the way Noah suggested, frightened me even more.

With gathering speed, the inside of the barn darkened considerably. Wind smacked against the walls, carrying with it the sound of things crashing into the boards. Lady reared, and I stumbled backward into Maisy, who held her ground and didn't allow me to fall.

When Lady's front feet touched the ground, she whinnied, and the sound of terror rang with it. A swoosh of dirt caught me in the face, blinding me for a second. When I opened my eyes, they burned and watered.

The noise outside grew louder, and I was afraid to leave the building. Pulling the two horses close, I watched as the lawn chairs from the yard blew past the doorway, along with branches and other debris.

The thought occurred to me that the scene was eerily similar to the movie *The Wizard of Oz,* and I wondered if when it was all over I'd find myself in a faraway land full of little people.

With a shattering blast, the back wall of the barn lifted and broke apart, and Lady crashed into me, knocking me down. Somehow in the chaos, the rein had become wrapped around my hand, and with a second of terrifying understanding, I was yanked back up as Lady tried to bolt from the barn.

Out of nowhere a hand appeared and grasped the reins, pulling Lady to a stop. Frantically, I unraveled the leather from my fingers and let go.

"There's no time, turn them free!" Sam shouted.

I didn't question him and reached up and pulled the head-stall over Lady's ears. Sam and I jumped back as the mare tossed her head and ran back out into the storm. A second later, Maisy was also running out the door. I prayed they'd be safe.

"We have to get to the basement!" Sam shouted.

Sam put his arm around me, and together we charged into the furious wind. Things were hitting my body, and the air was thick with dust, but I kept my head down and ran with everything I had.

When we were almost to the house, the groaning sound pierced my brain, and I finally looked up. The tornado was on the road. Sparks shot through the rolling smoke as the electric poles snapped like Popsicle sticks.

Up until that point I'd only seen twisters on the television, and the reality of their destructive force had never registered before. Now it did.

We fell to the ground twice before we reached the door. Each time, Sam dragged me up and pulled me forward. If it hadn't been for his brute force, I'd never have made it to the house.

The door flew open and smashed against the bricks, but we didn't slow to see it blow away. The rumbling of the storm faded the deeper we went into the darkness of the cellar. When we reached the bottom step, a flashlight shone in our faces, and Summer had her arms around me in a bone-crushing hug.

"Oh, you're alive—you're both alive," Summer squealed into my ear.

"Just barely...way too close for comfort," Sam said as he herded us to the far corner of the cellar.

The memory of the first and last time I'd ventured into

the damp and scary place with Noah and my brother hit me, and tears began to flood my eyes. It had been the day I'd met Noah.

"What if Noah didn't make it to his house? He can't survive out there," I cried into the darkness.

"Why didn't he come here with you?" Sam asked as we huddled together against the rock wall.

"Maisy couldn't carry us both in the wind. He let me take her so that I'd get home in time. He made a run to his house to be with his sisters...they're alone."

Summer sighed and said, "He was brave to sacrifice himself for his pregnant love."

"Dammit, don't go putting the guy in the ground—he probably made it," Sam barked.

"I don't know, Sam. It was horrible—did you see it tearing up the road? The electric poles were gone, the trees... everything." Remembering the scene, I gulped for air and began crying.

Although the thick rock walls of the cellar underground muffled the sound of the destruction above, the house shook above us, and the shattering of glass could still be heard.

Suddenly, a booming wave vibrated through the cellar and century-old dust from the tresses above sprinkled our heads.

"What's happening?" Justin whispered frantically as he looped his arm through mine and leaned in close.

Sucking back the sob, I said, "I think the storm is passing over the house right now."

For all my worry about Noah, I knew he'd be proud of me. I'd made it to the cellar, with Sam's help, and was still alive. More than anything, he wanted me and the baby to survive.

I grasped Justin with one arm and Summer with the other, and the trembling of my body joined theirs. Hope whined, pressing her body tightly against my legs, and her fur tickled my nose, but I didn't dare move a muscle.

When the basement began to shake, Sam reached his arms around us all.

At least we were together....

34

Noah

My head was pressed against something sharp, and most of my body was covered in water. I was horribly uncomfortable, but I was afraid to open my eyes. Was I even alive?

Listening carefully, I strained to hear the storm, but only the whistle of a soft wind was on the air.

One at a time, I opened my eyes, blinking away the dust that still stung them.

The sky was brighter, and even from inside the culvert I could see fast-moving clouds drifting away to the east.

With a groan, I began to crawl through the water that was now filled with chunks of pavement and gravel. Poking my head out, I was relieved to see shards of sunshine peeking through the clouds here and there.

The tornado had passed by or maybe broken up. It didn't matter now. The ordeal was done, and although there'd be a lot of cleaning up to do, I was breathing easier.

My shoulder was bleeding, and pain coursed through it as I pushed myself up and away from the culvert. I counted myself lucky that it seemed to be the only injury I had.

The mooing down in the ditch immediately drew my attention, and I saw several of our cows walking sluggishly along the roadway. The fences must be down—one more thing to fix, I thought.

I began to turn, but something held me for an instant, keeping me in an invisible grasp. Tears began to rise in my eyes, and I let them fall. I could see the swath of destruction that tore up the crops and the trees straight up the road above the culvert I'd sought shelter in.

The tornado's path had been wide, and without much thought, I knew where it had gone.

Sucking in a breath, I found the courage to take the step around, only to collapse on the ground at the sight.

Our house was gone, and in its place was a heap of broken boards and crumpled tin.

My sisters…

Moving my legs, I rose and ran up the remains of our driveway. The fences on both sides of me had disappeared, the grass beneath them ripped away, too. The maple trees that Father had planted were snapped at the ground, and the larger oak near the house was split in two.

In a daze I noticed that the utility barn was leveled, but the stable was still standing. I ignored the whinnying horses and continued to cross the yard.

When I reached the wreckage, I knew it was hopeless. No one could have survived a force so strong that it splintered an entire house.

But still I began calling their names: Sarah, Rachel, Naomi, over and over again.

Grabbing boards, I threw them aside, trying desperately to clear a way to the basement. The gentle breeze at my back and the ever-brightening sky made me feel as if I were in a dream—one that I hoped to wake from at any moment.

A faint sound reached my ears, and I paused to listen. Yes, it was the coo of a voice.

35

Rose

The dead silence was almost scarier than the roar of storm. I kept my eyes closed and continued to grip Justin and Summer tightly. We were still holding our breaths, and no one moved a muscle.

For the first time since I'd entered the cellar, I felt the cool dampness that made my skin crawl. Yet even for the icky feeling, I decided that it was my favorite room in the house. Heck, it might be the only room left in the house.

"Are we alive?" Summer whispered.

Her voice broke through the paralyzing silence, and for the first time in many minutes, we began to shift our weights and look around.

"Obviously," Sam said smugly as he stood up. "Let's see if we still have a house."

"Do you think it's a good idea to go up there so soon?" I asked, feeling a cramp shimmy up the side of my leg as I rose.

"It's been several minutes since I heard a thing. I think the brunt of the storm has passed over."

"Dang, I hope the TV didn't blow away," Justin said as he followed closely behind Sam to the stairs.

"You've got a shallow mind. That was a tornado—who knows if everyone else in the neighborhood made it to their basements or not?" Summer said with strong disapproval in her voice.

She was right. The thought of Noah not reaching his house or the possibility that Suzanna and Miranda or anyone else had been caught outside when the twister struck terrified me.

Slowly we climbed the stairs. Sam took the lead with Justin, me and Summer following on each other's heels. When Sam pushed the door aside, light seeped into the darkness, and I held my breath.

The kitchen was still there. The outdated powder-blue walls still stood, and the faucet in the sink still dripped. The door was partially off its hinges, and the window above the sink was shattered, but otherwise, this part of the house had come through the ordeal unscathed.

"Look at the barn!" Justin said as he sprinted past us and out the door.

We quickly followed him, and my jaw dropped. Part of the barn was lying in the yard. Scraps of tin and boards covered the grass, and it was obvious that many of those pieces had struck the house where chips in the bricks could be readily seen.

"Good golly," Summer exclaimed.

The sun shone down through the clouds, and the air was warm—so different from twenty minutes ago. I marveled at the drastic weather change as I looked between the barn wreckage and the fallen trees beside the house.

"It must have just missed us," Sam said, and then added

enthusiastically as he pulled his cell phone from his pocket, "Hey, there are the horses."

I followed his pointing finger to the middle of the field between our place and the Millers'.

Sure enough, Lady was grazing beside Maisy as if nothing had happened. I began to fill with hope that Noah was all right, probably just stepping out of the Millers' basement with his sisters.

My gaze shifted...something was wrong.

I reached out and gripped Sam's arm. "I don't see the Millers' roof," I said slowly.

They all turned their heads where I was looking.

"What does that mean?" Justin whispered.

Sam didn't answer, but he started running through the yard, twisting and dodging the debris in his path.

I raced after him. "I'm coming, too."

Struggling to breathe normally, I tried to stay calm.

It can't be... Noah can't be dead. No, no, no...

A large portion of a tree was in the bed of Sam's truck, and a jagged crack spread across the windshield, but thankfully, the engine wasn't damaged.

I climbed in close to Sam, as Summer and Justin pushed against me.

No one said a word as Sam drove down the winding driveway, leaving it several times to go around large branches and chunks of wood in the path.

I hadn't breathed in a minute and was feeling faint when Summer picked up my hand and held it tightly. Meeting my gaze, she smiled reassuringly and whispered, "He's all right, Rose. Don't you worry—I can feel that he's alive."

36

Noah

With renewed energy, I began flinging the remnants of the house aside.

I didn't turn to look when I heard the clip-clops on the road. The driveway was far too broken for a buggy to cross over. I didn't have long to wonder who it was when shouts rang out.

Elijah Schwartz's voice cut through the air louder than the rest.

"Lord, have mercy, was anyone in the house?"

Finally, I turned to see how many men had arrived. I needed more hands to move the debris.

Paul and Micah stood beside their father with looks of shock, although Micah's expression carried a stronger emotion that I recognized for the same devastation I was feeling. Mervin and Matthew Weaver flanked them, and Raybon Yoder was jogging up from the road.

Matthew didn't hesitate and was beside me in an instant, dragging the pieces of the house at the place where I worked.

"The girls…my sisters were here. I tried to get home to

them, but I only made it to the culvert in the road when the tornado hit. I crawled inside and was protected."

I couldn't stand the look of sympathy that passed over Elijah's slender face, and I added, "They're alive. I think I heard a voice."

Silently, the Schwartzes got to work, and soon enough Raybon had arrived.

When I heard the soft voice again, I yelled out, "Stop and listen!"

Faintly at first, the voice grew until I knew it was Rachel.

"I'm here…be careful, the ceiling is caving in," she called out.

Relief flooded me, and I met Elijah's gaze. He nodded his head and smiled, and at that moment I felt the bond of the community.

Taking charge, Elijah began directing the other men to pick up the boards more gently while Mervin surveyed the area and pointed out the ones to take first.

"It's a miracle they're alive, Noah, but a blessed one. We'll have them free soon enough, no worries," Mervin said with conviction.

My throat was tight, and I swallowed, unable to speak. The last two men I thought would be aiding me were Elijah and Mervin, and yet, here they were, putting their hearts into it.

When I saw the delicate hand reach through the hole that we'd made, I jumped forward and grasped it. A minute later the opening was large enough to pull Rachel through, and with Elijah's help, I did just that.

Her cap was still on, but it was covered in dust like the rest of her. Otherwise, she appeared undamaged.

I hugged her and said, "Thank God, you're alive. You girls had me worried for a time."

Her body stiffened against me, and I held my breath.

"They're not with me… Haven't you found them? Sarah didn't make it to the basement. She was looking for Naomi. You know how she likes to hide…." Rachel burst into tears, and I held her sobbing body as I looked over her head at Elijah and Mervin.

Mervin took his hat off and wiped his brow with the side of his hand, while Elijah looked around at that wreckage.

"Where is she— Where's Sarah?" Micah's voice cracked, and I avoided his demanding gaze.

"Son, you must calm yourself. You'll be no good to anyone if you become emotional. We need to be ever more careful…there's always hope."

Paul patted his brother's back and then followed Mervin as they began to walk gingerly across the pile of sticks that had been my home.

I guided Rachel to a spot where the ground was clear. She didn't protest when I left her, instead continuing to cry as she grasped her knees to her chin and rocked back and forth.

My heart felt hollow and weak as my eyes wandered over the broken boards, shards of glass and sharp pieces of metal. Matthew was already clutching a bleeding hand, and Raybon had called out in pain several times.

There was no way they could be alive if they weren't in the basement—it was impossible.

Shifting my eyes again toward the Camerons' property, I took a breath and felt my nerves quiet. Being higher up, I could see the toppled trees in the yard and the roof and side of the barn missing…but the great old brick house was still standing.

I told myself again that Rose must be all right. Losing Sarah and Naomi would be very difficult, but as long as Rose survived, I'd survive.

In the distance hooves could be heard on the pavement, and I knew that more help would arrive in minutes. Father and Jacob were at the worksite, but Mr. Denton would have them on their way home soon enough.

Thankfully, Mother and the little boys were at the Hershbergers'.

At that moment I spotted Maisy with saddle still on. She was grazing in the field between our farm and the Camerons', alongside Rose's gray mare.

Matthew's voice rang out.

"I heard something…over here. It sounded like a child crying."

We all ran to the spot and stopped moving, with ears tilted to where Matthew was pointing.

The sniffling sound couldn't be denied, and I was the first to begin picking through the rubble where the noise had come from.

"Careful, Noah, don't rush now," Elijah warned.

I stopped to listen again and moved a few feet over.

"She's under the tin," I said.

Matthew and Micah grasped the edges of the large piece of roofing, and together we lifted it away.

I kneeled beside Sarah's body and touched her.

Her lavender dress was unsoiled and shining brightly in the sunshine. Her cap was still pinned neatly to her bun, and her eyes were closed as if she were in a deep sleep. Cradled in her arms was little Naomi. Sarah had shielded my youngest sister from the storm.

When Naomi saw me, she said my name and held out her tiny arms.

Carefully, I disengaged Sarah's hands from the child and lifted her into my lap. Her dress matched Sarah's, and for a moment I felt as if I were looking into Sarah's face, only she was a small child and I was running beside her in the pasture trying to catch the pony. I remembered her laughing as she begged me to run faster.

"You're as fast as old Smoky, Noah. Please catch him for me."

Tears dripped down my cheeks at the memory.

"No, it can't be. Father, please tell me she's all right," Micah cried out, but his voice sounded hazy and distant to my ears, even though he stood only a few steps away.

Elijah bent his head to Sarah's chest and then looked up at me.

When he slowly shook his head, I gripped Naomi tighter and began to cry.

37

Rose

When we reached the road and were about to turn out, Dad pulled up, blocking us. He jumped from his SUV and ran to the truck with Tina right behind him.

"Thank God, you kids are all right."

"The old brick house stood up to the storm, but I'm afraid the Millers weren't so lucky," Sam said.

"Oh, no," Father said as he pivoted and called over his shoulder, "Follow me."

The SUV and truck made it over the crumbled pavement but not the full-grown trees that littered the Millers' driveway. We parked in the road and sprinted up the hill toward the place where Noah's picture-perfect farm house had once stood. Only a giant pile of sticks remained.

Many of the Amish people were already there, gathered in small groups. Their faces wet with tears. I recognized Mr. Weaver, who stood beside the tall, slender man I'd guessed to be Constance's father at the auction. Matthew sat on the ground with his head in his hands, and another young man I didn't recognize stared off into space. A few more feet up the hill was Rachel—she stood like a statue, every few seconds sucking in a wet breath and blowing out again.

Suddenly, the fear became too much, and I stopped.

Noah was on the edge of the wreckage with little Naomi in his arms. His head was bent to hers, and his body rocked in silent sobs. Lying beside him was someone in a lavender dress....

Summer gazed at me with eyes full of tears before she turned and pressed herself against Sam's chest. He put his arms around her and looked over her head, his mouth gaping in disbelief. Justin hung back with Tina, who'd placed her hand on his arm to stop him from coming closer while Dad approached the scene slowly, bending down when he reached Noah.

Frozen in shock, I watched as Dad murmured quiet words to Noah and then to his little sister. His experienced hand gently picked up Sarah's wrist. My heart beat faster when he placed it carefully on the ground.

My vision began to haze over with wetness when Dad held out his arms to Naomi, and after encouragement from Noah she let him lift her. Tina passed by me and whispered to Dad and then pulled out her cell phone and made a call.

With steps that felt like walking in deep snow, I went to Noah and placed my hand softly on his shoulder. Without looking up, his hand closed over mine, and I knelt beside him. His gaze met mine, and brown eyes reflected the same grief I felt.

For a second his eyes roamed over my face, as if he were seeing me for the first time, and then he grasped me and pressed his head against my breast. I held on to him for dear life, wishing I could take away his pain and make everything all right.

But I couldn't. No one could.

38

Noah

I stared out the window at the pouring rain, thinking God was weeping along with the rest of us. The four coffins were in a line at the back of the Hersherbergers' shop, and I'd been working hard for the past couple of hours not to look at them. Seeing the pine boxes made the pain worse. I could still barely believe that Sarah was lying dead in one of them.

Marcus Bontrager, his eleven year-old son, Kevin, and Mary Katherine Hershberger filled the remaining coffins. Marcus and his son had been shutting the door to their welding shop when the tornado struck, bringing the wall down on them. A tree falling on Mary Katherine's buggy as she made her way home from visiting Emilene and her twin baby cousins had taken her life.

Amazingly, even though there was a mile-long swath of destruction through the heart of the Meadowview community, only four lives had been taken in the storm. Still, all the Amish were mourning. Every family was affected in one way or another, and they were all making their way in and out of the metal building to pay their last respects.

For a second I watched Martha embrace Ruth, who had

tears in her eyes. Sarah had told me that the two women had been at odds about Rose coming back to the community. Now, after this tragedy, they'd put their differences aside in mutual sadness. It was one of the things that I loved about being Amish—in the end, the community was one family.

Glancing at Elijah Schwartz, I pondered his reaction to the deaths, especially my sister's. He sat quietly and alone in the far corner of the building, twisting a few strands of his black beard between his fingertips. He'd already offered his condolences to Father and Mother, which they readily accepted. I wasn't sure if his contriteness was from genuine sympathy for my family or a reaction to his own son's distress.

I'd been told that Micah hadn't spoken since the discovery of Sarah's lifeless body, although I'd seen Rachel approach him right after the church service. She'd whispered a few words to him, not mindful of the inappropriateness of their contact, before she'd left him to sit with the Miller family beside Sarah's casket.

I'd walked toward Micah after he'd visited my sister's coffin, but after a second of our eyes meeting, he'd sprinted away into the rain. I had no idea where he was now, but my heart went out to him. I don't know what I'd do if death took Rose away from me.

Ever present in my mind was the pregnancy, although it felt bittersweet now. Just as the knowledge and excitement of new life in the family had taken hold of my parents and me, one was taken away. It wasn't fair.

"I'm so sorry, Noah. Is there anything we can do?"

The soft voice at my side startled me, and I turned, focusing my damp eyes. Suzanna's own eyes were red-rimmed and as wet as my own. Miranda stood slightly behind her, holding a kerchief to her nose and sniffling into it. Timmy and Matthew were there also, but they were trying to hold their emotions in. Matthew's bloodshot gaze was the only indication that he'd been crying, and Timmy's quick intake of breath and the shifting between his feet told me he was extremely upset also.

I had to clear my throat to speak. "There's nothing any of you can do."

Suzanna nodded her head in silence and moved to stand beside me. The others followed suit, although no one spoke a word. I knew it was their way of supporting me the only way they could.

The steady stream of people passing by blurred in my mind the same as the rain dripping down the windows obscured the world outside. Everyone stopped to shake my hand or hug me, depending on their gender, and whisper words of encouragement.

Ruth's squeeze was extrahard and her words affected me more than most of the others when she said, "'Let the little children come to me and not hinder them, for such belongs the kingdom of heaven.' Jesus told us this in Matthew, Noah. We must always trust in the Lord."

"Thank you, Ruth." Her words reminded me that Sarah was in a better place than any of us here, taking some of the sting from my heart.

"Be strong, child, be strong for your family," she added before she shuffled away into the dark-clad crowd.

Suzanna's hand pressed into my arm, and when I glanced down at her, she pointed toward the doorway.

My heart skipped for an instant and then calmed. Seeing Rose entering the building along with her father, Tina, Summer and her brothers immediately lifted my spirit a fraction. She was alive, and our child grew inside of her. There was light in the darkness.

I watched her walk with Summer, between Sam and Justin, as they followed David and Tina to the caskets. She wore a knee-length black skirt and a short black jacket that matched the skirt perfectly, following the curves of her body in the modern style. She still wasn't showing, which was expected, but my gaze strayed to her stomach several times with fascination, anyway.

They moved past the three first caskets at a slow walk and then stopped beside Sarah's. Rose began to shake, and David placed his arm around her. She pressed into his body, putting her face against his chest.

I wanted desperately to go to her, but I remained rooted in place. My warring insides left me nearly breathless. I couldn't approach her in such a public place. It wouldn't be fitting for me to go to her and put my arms around her. I wasn't allowed to comfort my girl…or let her warm spirit take care of me. Even now, at my sister's funeral, there were rules that couldn't be broken.

When Rose's head lifted, and she peeked around her father's arm catching sight of me, I saw the devastation in her gaze and something inside of me snapped.

To hell with the rules—I was finished with them all.

39

Rose

My heartbeat slowed when I saw Noah striding toward me. Suzanna, Miranda, Timmy and Matthew followed close behind, and, judging from their equally distressed expressions, they were as surprised as me.

As we stepped away from Sarah, the tears were still wet in my eyes, and my body quivered, but now it wasn't as much from sadness as fear. Noah was about to do something very stupid, and I couldn't help shooting Sam a pleading look before Noah arrived.

Sam's eyes widened, and he followed the direction of my gaze.

I heard him mutter, "Oh, great," before all hell broke loose.

Noah stopped a few inches from me, and the distress was clear on his face. In a fluid motion, his arms shot out, and he pulled me into a hug. The feel of his arms around me was glorious, but the thudding of my heart at the sight of so many Amish heads turning our way wasn't.

Noah mumbled into my ear, "I love you, Rose. With all my heart I love you."

"What are you doing—? Everyone is watching us," I spoke into his black shirt.

"I don't care anymore. I will do what I want from now on."

There was a strange note to his voice that raised the hair on my arms, and I leaned back to look up at him. He smiled at me with confidence just before the bishop appeared beside us.

"What's the meaning of this, Noah?"

"Rose is my girl, and I won't hide it any longer."

"This is not the place or the time for such declarations. Release her, this instant, before you upset your parents further," the bishop said in a low, threatening voice.

Noah seemed to become taller against me as he gazed at the man who'd always inspired such fear in me. He didn't loosen his hold on me, either.

"This is what Sarah would have wanted. She'd be happy for us."

"That may or may not be correct, but what is definite is that your behavior is unacceptable. I understand that you are mourning the loss of your sister, but Rose can't take that pain away from you...only the Lord can. As spoken in Psalm 34:18, 'The Lord is near to the brokenhearted and saves the crushed in spirit.' You are treading dangerously here."

It seemed everyone in the building stopped breathing. Not even the children stirred, nor did the babies whimper in their mothers' arms. The Amish community was entranced with the scene.

I feared what Noah was doing. Suzanna's and Miranda's eyes were wide with shock, and their boyfriends looked the same. Here, at this moment, Noah was making a stand against the entire premise of the Amish culture. A part of me gave a silent "hurray" that he was standing up to the bishop, but a bigger part was cringing that he'd picked his sister's funeral to do such a thing.

Dad must have felt the same way and came to the rescue when he placed his hand on Noah's shoulder and whispered into his ear, "Why don't you come over to our place for a while...before you say something you're going to regret later."

By this time Amos and Rebecca were standing close by, and my heart went out to Sarah's mother when she looked at me with a stricken face.

Noah nodded his head to Dad before turning to his parents and saying, "I love you both, and I'm weeping for Sarah as you are, but I can't go on like this. I should have been with Rose a long time ago. After almost losing her in the storm that killed my sister and nearly took my own life, I realize where I should be."

"What are you saying, son?" Amos's voice was quiet, yet it held a force that reached out and gripped my soul.

Noah took a breath and looked between the bishop and his dad.

When his eyes settled back on Amos, he said, "I'm going English."

The words that I'd yearned to hear for so long hit me like a physical blow...and that's when the world began spinning.

The last thing I remembered was the feel of Noah's arms tightening around me as the room went dark.

40

Sam

"Is it just me, or is this a bit sudden?" I asked the group gathered in the kitchen.

Dad shot me the "shut up" look, and I turned away. As I gazed out the opening that used to have a glass pane, I realized the darkness was nearly complete. Strangely, with the heavy rain falling all day, it had felt like nighttime hours ago.

Tina sat beside Dad at the table, and I briefly wondered why she was privy to such an important family discussion. After all, she wasn't my stepmother yet.

Before she spoke, she took a quick sip of her glass of cola and then cleared her voice. "Are you sure this is what you want to do, Noah? I'm not trying to change your mind, but I feel that you might be making a hasty decision because of your sister's death."

Dad nodded in agreement, while Noah shook his head vehemently.

"I've been thinking about this for a long time." When he saw the doubtful looks on their faces, he said in a rush, "No, seriously, I have. There've been problems in the community these past weeks that have made me question whether the Amish life is for me."

"Did Rose have anything to do with these problems?" Dad asked.

"Yes, in a way. When I broke off the engagement to Constance, it angered her family, especially her father. They weren't making it easy on us—that's for sure. But there were other things that have been bothering me lately, stuff that never really did before."

"Like what?" I said, still not believing what I was hearing.

Noah shrugged and leaned back into the chair. It was obvious the discussion was bothering him, but, what the hell, it was important.

"You wouldn't understand, Sam. Being English, you've never had kids gawk and point at you when you entered a store or had men whisper behind your back, only to have them put in a ridiculous offer on a work job, automatically thinking that you're ignorant—or even worse, getting nearly killed in a buggy wreck."

"Actually, I do understand. That's why I didn't get your insistence to stay Amish when Rose kept bugging you to convert."

Noah's eyes widened. He blurted out, "She never bugged me about it. Rose was content with the idea of living our ways." When I smirked and threw my head back, he went on to say, "She had no idea I'd decided to leave the Amish until today. After what happened, I feel really bad that I hadn't told her in private beforehand."

Tina nudged Dad with her elbow and said, "Don't you think Rose should come down for this conversation?"

"No, she needs to rest. I believe her fainting was a result of shock at Noah's proclamation and the stress on her body from the storm—not to mention the death of a friend. It's best if she keeps sleeping for now. There are dangers associated with teenage pregnancy, and she needs to care for herself."

"You still haven't answered me, David. Will you allow Rose to be my wife if I go English?"

I held my breath watching Dad. A month ago, I'd have bet money on what the answer would be, but not now. I'd seen how the neighbor girl's death had affected everyone, including my dad. If nothing else, Dad was a realist. Rose was pregnant, and short of killing Noah, there was no way to keep them apart. We'd tried just about everything already.

When Dad lifted his head and looked at Noah, I immediately noticed the change in his demeanor, and my heart raced before he said the words.

41
Rose

I pulled the covers over my head as the morning sun blasted into the room. My belly wasn't as queasy as usual, and I rolled over, enjoying the feeling. The relief didn't last long, though. Soon my mind wandered, and images of Sarah's dead body rose before me.

She'd looked like she was asleep lying there at the edge of the wreckage. Her dress hadn't even been ripped, and her eyes had been closed. You'd think that the house breaking apart in the twister would have caused my friend to have grotesque injuries, but no, she'd been much the same as on church day. The thought sobered me even more, and I wondered if Sarah had had a guardian angel with her during the storm, someone who'd made sure that she didn't suffer and felt no fear when the house collapsed. But then, if that were true, why wouldn't sweet Sarah have been saved?

The tears began dropping from my eyes once again, and I didn't bother to wipe them away. Instead, I pressed my face deeper into the pillow to absorb the wetness. It was so unfair that Noah's sister was taken away from us. She had been only sixteen, and she'd had her whole life ahead of her. Courting the handsome young Micah and eventually marrying him. She would have had eight or nine kids like her mom, and she would have been content with her life.

I remembered how kind she'd been to me the first day we'd met. I'd been clueless to Amish protocol, but she'd taken me under her wing, teaching me how to behave as an Amish girl. Early on, I'd secretly scoffed at Sarah's niceness, believing that no one could always be as friendly as she'd appeared to be. But I'd learned over time that Sarah had been genuine—and that made her death sting even more. Life wasn't fair at all.

And then there was Noah's speech in front of the entire Amish community at the funeral the day before. Was he really serious or had grief caused his mind to go funny? From the moment I'd first laid eyes on him, I'd wished that he'd leave his world and join mine. Even when I'd been living life as an Amish girl, I'd secretly hoped that Noah would decide to go English. In my mind it had been the solution to all my problems—a way for me to be with Noah and not give up my freedom and the lifestyle I'd grown up in. It's what I'd wanted all along, but now that he was agreeing to it, it didn't feel as good as it should've.

As I stared up at the old yellowing paper on the ceiling, I tried to figure out my strange emotions. Maybe I was worried that Noah couldn't hack it on the outside, or possibly I feared that someday he'd resent leaving his whole life behind to be with me.

After some more minutes of tossing and turning, I finally accepted the main reason I wasn't jumping up and down for joy at the news. I'd actually grown attached to the Amish community, and parts of their way of life appealed to me greatly. Now that I was pregnant, I wasn't as interested in having a career. I knew that when the baby arrived, I wouldn't want to leave it at a day care center while I went to school or worked a full-time job. I'd want to be home taking care of it myself. As an Amish woman, I would be expected to do so, but as an English one, I'd probably end up juggling a job and a family, the same as Mom.

So many thoughts were swirling in my head that I barely heard the soft rap on the door. Glancing up, I winced, not really wanting to talk to anyone at the moment. Couldn't Dad and the boys just leave me alone for a while?

Sighing, I said with serious agitation, "I'm still sleeping."

After a pause, the door opened slowly, and Noah's head peeked in.

"I'm sorry to bother you, sweetheart, but your father said it was all right for us to talk, and I didn't want to waste the opportunity."

He was grinning at me, and the sight of him chased all my worries away. Warmth spread through my body as I held out my arms.

Noah was careful to push the door almost closed, but not quite, before he crossed the room. His arms circled around me, and I pressed myself against him. We stayed like that for what seemed like several minutes, completely silent, except for our breathing and the creak of the bed when we shifted our weight. Finally, Noah released me and stretched out alongside me. He was careful to stay on top of the covers, but when he was settled, he pulled me back against his chest, and I placed my head in the crook of his arm.

I was right where I needed to be.

"How are you feeling?" Noah asked as his fingers smoothed down my hair.

"I'm much better this morning. I think I was overwhelmed yesterday."

"I know Sarah's death affected you, but I think you hit the ground because of what I said to Abram and Father." His fingers moved to my chin, and he tilted it up so that I was looking at him. His eyes were deep, dark pools, and I stared into them, mesmerized.

"Hmm?" Noah prodded.

I nodded and said, "Yeah, I was shocked. What made you change your mind? You were so dead against leaving the Amish— I don't understand."

He held me even closer and said, "I was stubborn. I see that now, and I'm sorry for it. I'm so sorry that I wasn't more open to your needs and desires. It was wrong of me to expect you to change your life, especially if I wasn't willing to do the same for you."

I sat up and interrupted, "I knew you loved me and only wanted what you thought was best. It made sense...but why now have you made this decision? Is it because of Sarah?"

He took a deep breath, and I wished I hadn't mentioned his dead sister. I could only imagine the pain he was going through, and here I was reminding him again.

"After losing Sarah, I realized that the most important thing in the world to me is you. If you had died in the storm, I would've wished death on myself. I can't imagine life without you. We've had our troubles. That's for sure, but in the end, we've always made our way back to each other. We're meant to be together—it's God's will, I can feel it inside of me.

"I've been selfish and controlling, Rose, and I'm going to change. Life is too short to keep making dumb mistakes.

I'm ready to marry you and start our family. It doesn't matter which world we live in as long as we're together. I know that now."

Fresh tears fell, but this time from happiness.

I leaned in and pressed my lips against his, and soon enough his were opening to mine. The feel of his tongue in my mouth caused a tingling to spread in my belly, and I reveled in the sensation, feeling more alive than I had in weeks.

When he broke away, I felt disappointed for an instant until I saw his eyes.

"I love you, Rose. With all my heart, I love you," Noah whispered.

I smiled and cupped his face in my hands.

"You know I love you, too, but what if our families insist on us staying apart?"

Noah's smile stilled my heart, but it was his words that nearly made me faint all over again.

"My folks have accepted my decision. They understand that our child is my priority." He shrugged and went on to say, "Sure, they aren't happy about me leaving the Amish, but they have accepted it."

"That's great and all, but it's not your parents I'm as concerned with. My dad will never approve—we'll still have to wait."

He reached out and took my hands between his and said, "Your father gave me his blessing last night. Will you be my wife?"

"Are you serious?" I whispered, realizing that Noah's decision to leave the Amish was probably the reason that Dad had finally relented.

He nodded.

The bubbles of happiness were too much to contain, and I flung my arms around his neck. "Yes, Noah, I'll marry you."

The hugging quickly turned to kissing, and as Noah's arms wrapped around me, I was filled with contentment.

Finally, everything was going to be okay.

42

Noah

"Won't you reconsider—for Rose's sake?"

"You know we can't go, Noah. It's not even fair for you to ask," Jacob said.

The little boys' laughter came from the sunny backyard beyond my brother's kitchen window, and I glanced outside to see them jumping on the trampoline. Peter, Daniel and Isaac's resilience after Sarah's death and the destruction of our home was truly amazing. Of course, they were still very sad, but already their lives were getting back to normal.

Katie leaned against the counter with a faraway look on her face. She was further along than Rose, and the swell of her growing stomach had recently become noticeable. When she glanced my way, her eyes were moist.

"Please tell Rose that I wish I could be there for her special day. After losing Sarah, it breaks my heart to miss it."

"You can be there—we can keep it secret," I urged.

Jacob's voice rose in anger, and I regretted what I'd said.

"No, we are not going down that road. It's your choice to go English, not ours. We will not jeopardize our relations in the community." He shook his head in frustration and added, "You knew it would be like this, so why even ask?"

"I guess I thought that after everything that's happened, you'd be more open to it."

"I'm sorry, Noah. You'll always be my brother, but our relationship is no longer the same."

I was about to speak when I heard the sharp wail of one of the boys. Jacob and I looked at each other with wide eyes, before we hurried through the doorway. Even as my feet thudded down the porch steps, I could see Daniel lying on the ground. He had his leg clutched up to his chest, and he was crying.

I reached my little brother a second before Jacob and knelt beside him.

"What happened?" I demanded as I pulled his upper body against me.

Peter, who was a year older than Daniel, spoke up. "I accidentally bumped into him. I didn't mean it— Really, I didn't."

I glanced up to see Peter's face tight with worry, and I knew he was speaking the truth.

"I heard a crack when he fell—maybe he broke his foot," Isaac added. He was only six, but he'd always had a thoughtful manner that made me cringe at his words.

"Oh, my, I'll call Mr. Denton. Your father should be with him," Katie said. She whirled and ran awkwardly toward the shed as she pressed a hand against her stomach to keep it from bouncing.

"Shh, Daniel, quiet down. You'll be all right, I promise," I told Daniel as he rocked against me.

Jacob asked with a grim expression on his face, "Where does it hurt?"

Daniel sucked in a deep breath and tried to be brave.

He held in the pain for a moment and pointed at his ankle. "Right there—it feels all loose inside."

Jacob carefully stretched Daniel's leg out and touched his ankle. When Daniel cried out, Jacob stopped and shook his head. "Guess it's best to leave it alone for now."

I nodded and whispered words of encouragement to Daniel while my three other brothers stood close by and watched. It hadn't been more than five minutes when Mr. Denton's blue pickup truck came rambling up the driveway at a speed that was unusual for the old man. He drove the work truck right through the yard and parked beside us.

Father jumped out and was on the ground with us immediately.

"What have you gone and done to yourself now, Daniel? I would have thought the trip you made last year to the hospital for that broken arm would have been enough for you."

Father spoke firmly, but I heard slight amusement in his voice. He was probably just relieved that the injury was fixable—unlike poor Sarah.

Peter had only heard the harshness of Father's voice and blurted out, "It was my fault, not Daniel's. I was doing flips, and I didn't look to see if he was close by. I hit him and made him fall."

Father sighed and looked up at Peter's distraught face. "That'll be lesson to you, young Peter. There will be only one person jumping on that contraption at a time from here on out. Do you understand?"

"Yes, Father." Peter nodded his head vigorously.

"Let's get you to the hospital, then," Father said. He took Daniel from my arms and rose fluidly with him.

After he'd placed Daniel into the truck, I went to climb in beside Jacob, but Father's hand stopped me.

"Not you, Noah."

"Why not? I can help keep Daniel calm while you talk to the doctors."

"Jacob will go with us. You are no longer a part of this family, and we all must get used to the idea." When he saw that I was about to argue, he held up his hand and said in a quiet voice, "Please, I've had enough difficulty this past week—don't add to it."

I stepped back as if he'd punched me. A quick look of sadness flashed over Father's face before he turned his back and got into the truck. Jacob slipped by, and his hand on my shoulder felt solid and warm for an instant, but he glanced away, not meeting my gaze.

After the truck had driven off, I stood on the driveway staring in the direction it had gone. Vaguely, I heard Katie instruct Peter and Isaac to head to the house for lunch before she walked up to me and placed her hand softly on my arm.

When I looked at her, her eyes were full of tears, and I sniffed, sucking in all the emotions I was feeling. I wouldn't let any of them see me cry.

"I wish only the best for you and Rose, and so does Jacob. You must believe that. We're not shunning you because we don't love you—we have no choice in the matter. If we wish to remain Amish, we must follow the rules of our Ordnung...you know that."

I nodded my head. "Yes, I do."

I turned away from my sister-in-law and went to the hitching rail where Lady was tied. The mare was pawing the gravel nervously, and when she saw me approaching, she paused and whinnied.

Her high-strung personality was more suited to Rose than me, but now that I was on my own and only had the untrained Paint yearling, Rebel, to my name, I didn't have much choice in the matter.

The sun shone down on my head, and I lifted my face to its warmth as I rode down the driveway. For all the grief of losing Sarah and my family, a small smile lifted on my mouth when a thought occurred to me.

In my new life, I wouldn't be restricted to using a horse for transportation. I'd be able to drive a car to get around in. The thought sent a spasm of excitement and fear through me at the same time.

But those feelings were quickly replaced with great heaviness some time later when I passed by the property where my house used to stand.

Sarah was dead, and my family was all but lost to me.

Taking a deep breath, I looked over my shoulder one last time to say goodbye to the only world I'd ever known.

I knew I was doing the right thing, but I still felt numb.

Straightening in the saddle, I focused on Rose's house and my future.

As long as Rose and our baby were with me, I'd be all right. I had to be.

43

Rose

I peeked around the corner at the interior of the church. Bouquets of wildflowers adorned the end of each pew, matching a larger display at the front of the room. The faces that looked out from the pews were smiling, the animated sound of their voices filling the air.

Amanda and Britney, my childhood friends from Cincinnati, were seated close to the front, and I smiled when Amanda spotted me and giggled. She whispered to her boyfriend, Heath, and then pointed at me. The two girls had been with me in the small room adjoining the chapel for most of the morning, and Amanda had even taken charge of rolling my hair up into an elaborate bun, while Britney had tucked the small purple flowers into my hair and curled some stray locks with the iron around my face.

I'd always assumed that the two girls would be in my wedding party, but it hadn't worked out that way. With none of Noah's family coming to the ceremony, he didn't have anyone to represent him. As it was, the only person we could think of to be his best man was Sam. Noah had only reluctantly agreed on the choice after much grumbling. Of course, Summer was my best friend, and it had worked out perfectly to have her be my maid of honor, beside Sam.

Summer's body was pressed against me in the doorway, and I glanced at her again to admire how pretty she looked in the dark green dress. The color complemented her eyes, and with her strawberry-blond curls framing her face, she looked like a model in a teen magazine. Sure, she'd complained about the dress and all the hair spray, but I'd caught her twirling in front of the mirror in the bathroom afterward.

Gazing back into the chapel, I searched the faces again, hoping to see white caps and long beards. I'd made sure that the entire Miller family and all our other friends from the community had received the golden embossed invitations, but sighing, I realized that there wasn't much hope that any of the Amish would show for the big day.

Noah had warned me not to bother, but I'd gone ahead and sent them out, anyway. Even though I knew about shunning, I still had a difficult time believing that Noah's beloved family would turn their backs on one of the most important days of his life—and all because he had chosen to live his life different than them.

It definitely put a dark cloud over the otherwise beautiful June afternoon, and I couldn't help but feel sorry for Noah and greatly perturbed with the community at the same time. Trying to push the negative thoughts aside, I raised my hand when Justin caught sight of me. He was sitting beside Tina and Uncle Jason, and I smiled at them both for a second before I continued searching the crowd.

There were many faces I didn't recognize, and I assumed they were Dad's friends, but I also spotted Mr. Denton near the back and a couple of men and their wives who I guessed were the English people that Noah had trained horses for in the past. He'd asked me to send them invitations, and I was glad that they'd actually shown up on such short notice.

There was a light beam shining through the stained-glass window to the exact spot where Noah and I would say our vows, and I swallowed down the tight knot in my throat at the sight. The awful morning sickness had left me a couple of weeks ago, and this was the first time I'd had a queasy feeling in a while.

Softly, I pressed my hand to my belly, which had begun to poke out in just the past week. A flash of worry shot through me when I heard Dad's words from a few days earlier replay in my mind. *Don't take this pregnancy for granted, Rosie— You're very young to be having a child, and sometimes teenagers have complications.* I'd figured that because Dad was a doctor and a dad at the same time, he was just being paranoid, but I'd searched the subject myself and was surprised to see that it was true. Women in their teens were more likely to have complications and premature birth than those over twenty. Since doing the research, whenever I felt an odd twinge in my belly, I found myself holding my breath and saying a silent prayer.

I would just die if I lost Noah's baby.

Trying to chase the ill thoughts away, I stroked the bump as I gazed at the painting on the wall across the way.

For some reason, seeing Mary cradling the baby Jesus in her arms made me think of Mom, and I had to take a deep breath to keep the emotions from spilling out. Even though she wasn't here in physical form, I still felt her presence, almost as if she stood beside me with her hand on my shoulder. She wouldn't have been happy about my teenage pregnancy, but in the end, she would have accepted it and my marriage to Noah.

When I closed my eyes, I could see her...and she was smiling.

Summer nudged me with her elbow and whispered, "Yep, looks like we're about ready."

"I'm so nervous," I said.

"Course you are—isn't every day you throw away all your freedom for a guy."

My eyes and mouth must have widened if Summer's amused chuckle was any indication.

"Just kidding—I'm really happy for you. It all worked out the way you wanted it to."

"I hope so," I said quietly and then met Summer's confused stare.

"It's a little late in the game to be saying such a thing, don't you think?"

"I'm just sad that none of Noah's family came—or any of our Amish friends. That's why we had the wedding here in Meadowview, just in case someone changed their mind about it. It feels like a bad omen or something."

"Don't go getting all gloomy on me now, girl. You're about to get married, and you're supposed to have a big fat smile on your face." She raised her chin and motioned toward the back of the chapel where the double doors were open. "Besides, maybe you jumped the gun a bit."

My eyes followed her gaze, and I caught my breath.

Coming through the doorway was Suzanna and Miranda, along with their boyfriends, Timothy and Matthew. I knew what trouble they'd be in if they were caught at our wedding, and my heart burst in happiness that they'd risked so much to be here with us on this special day.

I sniffed, and just as a tear began to fall, Summer pulled me away from the doorway and began dabbing the corner of my eye with the tissue.

"Good grief, you even cry when something good happens. Now, dry it up. That's an order," Summer demanded in a firm voice.

I laughed at her uptight face and hugged her.

"I'm so lucky to have a friend like you."

"Yes, you are, and don't forget it." She said the words in a joking way, but I could tell she was touched.

"Who knows, maybe it won't be so long that you'll be more than just a best friend," I said, grinning.

"Whoa, don't even go there. I'm not in a hurry to rush into anything with your hardheaded brother. He drives me crazy most of the time— We'd probably kill each other."

"Some things are just inevitable," I said.

Before Summer could argue, Aunt Debbie walked in. She looked very different than she had earlier when she'd entered the church in jogging pants and a sweatshirt. Her dark blond hair down on her shoulders and the sky-blue dress she wore hugged her figure attractively. She smiled deeply when she saw me and crossed the room.

Gathering up my hand, she led me to the mirror.

"Look at what a beautiful young woman you've become," she said.

I gazed at my reflection and was startled for an instant.

A mature face stared back at me that I hardly recognized. Yeah, Rose was still there, but I'd lost the childlike quality that I'd had when I'd first met Noah the year before.

The dress I'd chosen was satin, with a cluster of little white pearls on the bodice and continuing up the straps that went over my shoulders. The train wasn't long, but still flared out behind me for a couple of feet. It had been one of the more expensive dresses I'd looked at, but I was lucky that both Tina and Aunt Debbie had gone to bat for me with Dad. When he'd relented about paying the outrageous price, I was thrilled, and seeing how pretty it looked on me now, I knew I'd made the right choice.

Not everyone was aware of the pregnancy, and it was still early enough that no one would guess, thank God. I didn't want to be an obviously pregnant woman walking down the aisle.

That wouldn't be cool at all.

Aunt Debbie took my hand, and I turned to hug her. She even smelled like Mom, and having her close made the pain of Mom's absence more bearable. She'd also been very supportive of the pregnancy and even pulled some favors to get Noah a job at the market she worked at. Sure, he'd be stocking shelves on second shift, but the benefits were good, and we'd have health insurance. The only part that worried me was moving to the suburbs of Cincinnati. Would Noah be able to survive such a change?

When Aunt Debbie pulled back, she frowned and said, "What's wrong, Rose— Are you feeling okay?"

Aunt Debbie could read me like an open book, so it wasn't surprising that she picked up on my anxiety.

"I was just thinking about the move." I paused and searched her eyes for understanding. "I don't think Noah will be happy in the English world."

Aunt Debbie's face softened, and she nodded. I didn't

turn to look Summer's way, already knowing full well what she thought about the plan.

"Sometimes we have to take a more difficult path for a while until we can finally reach the easier one. We've already gone over this, Rose. This move doesn't have to be permanent, just until you guys get some money saved up. Noah can't start his own contracting business until he buys the tools, equipment and a vehicle. He's going to be out of his element, for sure, but there aren't many options at this point. At least in the city, I'll be there to help you with the baby, and your father and Tina will be moving back as soon as they get the house in Meadowview sold to be closer to you and the baby. Trust me, it will all work out." She forced a smile and made her voice cheery when she said, "Now, come on, you have a wedding to attend."

I finally looked Summer's way, and she grinned back at me, making me feel instantly better.

Pushing all worried thoughts aside, I picked up the skirt and said, "I'm ready," letting Aunt Debbie and Summer guide me through the door to where Dad and Sam were waiting.

When I saw their eyes light up at seeing me in the wedding gown, I relaxed even more.

The most important people in my life were here supporting me, and that's all that mattered.

Noah and I'd survive. As long as we had each other, we'd be all right.

44

Noah

I felt better seeing Timothy and Matthew sitting in the pews with their girlfriends. I hadn't expected them to come, but secretly, I'd prayed that they would. Out of the entire community, including my family, they were the only people I imagined would take the risk for me and Rose.

As I stood calmly at the front of the church, I watched my friends fidget in their seats, casting glances this way and that to take everything in about the ceremony. Of course, this was their first time at an English wedding, the same as me, and it was very different from what we were used to.

The flowers decorating the church and the brightness of everyone's clothes made the entire chapel light and happy-feeling. I had to admit that I agreed with Rose that a wedding ceremony should be a merry event and not as somber and quiet as an Amish one.

I was more relaxed and confident than I imagined I would be. The jitters that I'd felt earlier had all but left me, and now, knowing that within the hour I'd be officially married to my beloved Rose, I felt more sure of myself than I ever had. Sure, the fact that I'd left the Amish to be with her still weighed on my mind, but with the pregnancy, I knew I was doing the right thing.

Besides, after losing Sarah, I understood how short life could be and the importance of being with the person I loved. When my sister had died, all worries about leaving my world had disappeared. As long as I had Rose, I could survive anything.

When the organ's music suddenly sounded, I came to attention and searched down the aisle to the open doorway. Sam and Summer walked between the pews, side by side. His back was straight and his mouth was turned up in an amused smirk. The look was expected from him and didn't bother me much. I'd grown accustomed to his obnoxious ways and had come to terms with the fact that as his brother-in-law, I'd have to work hard to get along with him.

Summer looked pretty in the hunter-green dress she wore, and I had to admit that the two of them made an attractive couple. I guessed that they'd be exchanging their own vows in the not-too-distant future.

After Sam and Summer separated, each taking a place to the sides of where I stood, my heart stopped when Rose stepped over the threshold on her father's arm.

She was beautiful.

Her long brown hair was pulled up, but stray curls framed her face. The dress she wore was unlike anything I'd seen before. It sparkled of its own light with each step she took. It dawned on me what she would have given up if we'd stayed in the Amish world. She would have been wearing a plain smock and apron on her wedding day, instead of the glorious dress she had on now. And a girl like Rose was made to wear such a dress.

I felt a twinge of pain that I'd expected her to give up everything she'd ever known to be with me. How foolish I'd been. Rose would have tried, I know, but she'd never have survived the Plain ways. Over time, she'd have been drained of all her vibrancy.

As her father guided her to me, her eyes were wide and staring, and I smiled at her, taking her hands between my own.

When David stepped back, I caught the look on his face that stated clearly that he expected me to take good care of his daughter. I wasn't offended and nodded my head softly in reassurance. The look that passed between us was meaningful—feeling like a new beginning after so much strife.

Rose lifted her chin and smiled mischievously. I began to breathe normally again. Very soon we'd be officially joined before God, and all our troubles would be gone. The thought of moving forward with our lives made my heart light.

As the English pastor began to speak, I hardly heard him, being more focused on Rose's blue eyes and the trust and happiness I saw there. More than anything, I wanted to be a good husband to her and father to our baby.

When the man began speaking the Amish vows, I perked up, very grateful that they were included in the ceremony. Saying the words that I'd grown accustomed to made the joining firmer in my mind and put me at ease that the vows we were saying truly meant something.

"Do you acknowledge and confess it is as Christian order, that there should be one husband and one wife, and are you able to have the confidence that you have begun this undertaking according to the biblical doctrine you have been taught?"

"Yes," we both answered together.

"Do you also have the confidence that the Lord has ordained this, Rose and Noah?"

"Yes."

"Do you solemnly promise your wife that if she should be afflicted with bodily weakness, sickness or some such similar circumstances that you will care for her as is fitting for a Christian husband?"

"Yes."

"Do you solemnly promise the same to your husband that, if he should be afflicted with bodily weakness, sickness or some other similar circumstances, you will care for him as is fitting for a Christian wife?"

"Yes."

"And do you both also solemnly promise each other that you will love and be patient with one another and not separate from each other until God shall separate you through death?"

Together we said, "Yes."

Sam stepped forward and held out the rings to us. I took the smaller one and placed it on Rose's slim finger and then waited while she did the same to me with the larger gold band. The feel of the cold metal on my finger was completely foreign, and I glanced down at the ring in awe. My people didn't adorn themselves with jewelry of any kind, even wedding rings, and a part of me that had lain dormant since my announcement that I was going English suddenly flared to life in protest. Such a statement wasn't needed in the Amish world. Husbands and wives didn't have to make a show of their joining for it to be real, but this was a part of an Englisher's ceremony that I must accept and get used to, even though it made no sense to me in the least.

"The God of Abraham, the God of Isaac and the God of Jacob be with you and bless this union abundantly, through Jesus Christ our Lord, and what God has joined together, let no man put asunder. Go forth as husband and wife, live in peace, fear God and keep his commandments. Amen."

The chill of nervousness rushed through me, and I glanced out at the faces of so many staring people. Apprehension swelled in my gut as I bent down to kiss my bride in front of an audience. Such a display of affection in the open was completely forbidden in my upbringing—I'd never even seen my parents kiss. And even though I'd walked away from that way of life, it still felt wrong for me to do such a thing.

Rose understood, and as she tilted her head upward, I saw the sparkle of amusement in her eyes. The look made me bold, and when my mouth closed on hers, I suddenly forgot that we were being spied on by a hundred people.

The kiss was brief and not nearly as satisfying as our usual kisses, but it sealed the deal in the English world.

The pastor smiled at us and then lifted his hands to the congregation, saying, "I'm pleased to present Mr. and Mrs. Noah Miller."

Everyone stood and clapped.

We walked down the aisle between smiling faces and shouts of congratulations. The only thing that felt solid at that moment was Rose's arm hooked through mine, the warmth of her body pressed against me telling me that I wasn't dreaming—*she really was finally my wife.*

I was in a hurry to leave the building and reach sunshine and fresh air beyond the doorway when Suzanna suddenly appeared and placed a hand on Rose's arm, stopping us.

Her eyes were moist when she said, "I wish you both the very best. It was a beautiful joining."

As Rose hugged Suzanna and then Miranda in turn, I shook hands with Timothy and Matthew.

My friends didn't have to say a word—I saw it in their eyes.

This was goodbye. They'd shown me the respect of attending the ceremony, but our friendships would never be the same again.

We left them behind, and I knew that Rose didn't realize that her relationship with the girls was over—our English wedding had sealed the coffin, so to say.

I wasn't going to mention it to her, though. I wanted this to be a perfect day— She deserved it.

In time she'd discover the harsh reality.

The Amish world was just a memory now.

45

Rose

I looked down shyly at the light blue nightgown I wore. There wasn't a lot to it, only some flimsy material and a small bow in between my breasts. Suddenly, a million butterflies exploded in me at the thought of walking out in front of Noah wearing such a thing.

We hadn't had sex since that night at my aunt Debbie's house, which seemed like a million years ago. Although parts of our time together were still vivid in my memory, some things were blurred. I certainly didn't feel like I was experienced in the art of lovemaking. The whole business was still awkward, and being pregnant didn't help matters, either.

As I glanced out the window into the Gatlinburg wilderness, I wondered if it would be as nice as it had been the first time. I guessed it would be, especially since we were finally married and could do it without guilt or worry of being caught. And here we were in a cozy cabin at the top of a mountain in Tennessee—it was definitely a romantic location.

Still, as I clutched the doorknob in my hand, I hesitated.

What if Noah found the negligee offensive? He might think I was a floozy or something.

After glancing down one last time, I made up my mind and reached for the suitcase.

Noah was lounging on the bed with one arm behind his head and the other holding a tourist booklet when I entered the room. It was still strange to see him wearing blue jeans and a T-shirt, and I passed my eyes over the normal street clothes a second time, not totally sure that they suited him.

Hearing the door open, he said without looking up, "Do you feel up to taking a hike to Mount LeConte tomorrow morning?"

I stopped and stared for a few seconds, before he finally gazed up at me.

He immediately grinned and looked down, before raising his face once again with a more neutral face.

After clearing his throat, he said, "I was hoping you'd come out dressed in that pretty blue nightgown."

All uneasiness left me, and I leaped on the bed, grabbing one of the many piled pillows and throwing it at him.

He laughed as he ducked and rolled sideways. An instant later he had me tight in his arms, and I gave up the feigned fight.

"Seriously, sweetheart, why on earth are you wearing sweatpants and a T-shirt?"

His eyes were warm and still laughing, and I leaned back and chuckled myself.

"Were you poking through my things, Noah Miller—how else would you even know about it?"

He shrugged innocently and smiled. "Where did you get it, anyway?"

"It was a gift from Summer, if you can believe it. I thought she'd lost her mind when I opened the box."

"Don't you like it?" he said softly as his fingers began twirling circles on my arm.

His touch made my tummy do a flip, and I found it hard to concentrate, but I took a deep breath and managed to say, "Sure I like it, but I wasn't sure if you would."

He stopped moving his fingers and leaned back. "We're married now. You can wear anything you'd like around me... or nothing at all."

I blushed and turned away, but he caught my chin and pulled it back to face him.

"After everything we've been through, you aren't going to suddenly act shy around me—are you?"

"No, I guess not. It's just that it feels kind of unreal, don't you think? We've dreamed about this day for so long, and it's hard to believe that it's finally arrived."

He nodded his head and pulled me against his chest. The soft stroking of his hand on my head made me relax, and I savored the feeling, wishing that it would never end.

"I know what you mean, but you're my wife now—no one can keep us apart."

The look in his eyes was so intense that my heart skipped a beat. We really were married, and he was right; nothing in the world could change the fact. It was time to begin enjoying it.

I reached over and pushed the booklet off the bed and said, "I'm not interested in hiking plans."

Noah's smile deepened, and he teased, "What are you interested in, Mrs. Miller?"

When my mouth touched his, he got his answer.

At first his touches were extra gentle, as if we were afraid of harming the baby, but after a couple of minutes, desire took hold of both of us. In a sudden frenzy, our clothes were off, and his body was pressing me into the mattress.

I smiled against the side of his face when I realized that it didn't matter whether I wore the pretty nightie—it would have been off just as fast as the sweats were.

I hadn't realized how heavy my heart had been with sorrow until this moment, when it all disappeared. Noah's arms around me and his warm breath on my neck erased the heartbreak of the previous year and deadened the ongoing pain of losing Mom and the new pain of Sarah's death.

I was finally happy again.

46

Noah

I stared at the small white house in utter disgust. The neighbors to the right and left were only an arm's length away, and there was no yard to speak of, only some packed dirt between the porch and the busy roadway and a few yards of grass in the back.

"It's not as bad as it looks, and besides, it's all we can afford at the moment."

I glanced at Rose. Her hair was pulled up in a ponytail, and she'd chosen to wear a large shirt that hid her growing belly. To most people, she would have appeared calm enough, but I knew better. The tightness of her lips and the rise of her eyebrows dared me to complain about the living arrangements that she and her aunt had picked out.

Turning to watch the cars streaming along the street, I admitted there wasn't much I could say about it. After the honeymoon trip to the Smokies, I'd stayed in Meadowview for a couple of weeks in order to do some handyman jobs around the farm of an Englishman I'd come to know through Father's business, while Rose had gone to the city. I had been thrilled to have the opportunity to make some extra money before the move to the city, especially since the job had required me to be on the roof of a barn with the sun on my back, instead of stocking shelves in a warehouse-type store.

The absence from Rose had been the most difficult part, but I'd held on to my connection with Meadowview until the last possible moment. I didn't want to move to this ugly, crowded place, but I had no choice. It was the best for my wife and unborn child, and I'd have a way to earn a living.

Looking back at Rose, I forced a smile and took her hand when she reached out to me. Letting her pull me up the stairs and through the door, I did my best to be upbeat about the ridiculously tiny rooms. Each time I glanced out a window, I saw only the outside walls of other houses, and the air coming through them was corrupt with the smells of exhaust and pavement. Still, I murmured words of encouragement and nodded my head when Rose would point out something that she thought was special—like the dishwasher or the flat-screened TV that one of her grandmothers had gifted us for the wedding.

For an Englisher, the place was probably pretty nice, but for a fellow that was used to a large, sprawling home and hundreds of acres of crops, fields and trees beyond its windows, this place was quite a disappointment.

The tour ended in the bedroom, and she sat on the edge of the bed, wearing a frown once again. I hated seeing her lovely face marred with unhappiness, and as I sat beside her, I put my arm around her.

"The place is very nice."

"Don't lie—you hate it," she pouted.

I blew out a breath, clearing my thoughts. Of course, she'd see through my act. Rose knew me better than anyone.

"All right, to be honest, it's definitely not what I'm used to, but for all that, it's not too bad, either. And like your aunt keeps saying, it's only temporary."

"I know it sucks. All the nicer places I looked at were too expensive, and Dad and Aunt Debbie agreed that we should get a cheap place that's close to your work so that we can save money quicker."

"They're right. We need money to start up my own construction business and put a down payment on a small farm. We have to be patient."

She looked up at me with doubt. "Can you really survive living like this, Noah?"

Without hesitation, I said, "I'll have to."

She nodded, and then her mouth lifted into a grin.

"You promised that today you'd come out with me and practice driving."

I couldn't help rolling my eyes and dropping back onto the mattress.

"I only barely passed the permit test. I don't think it's a good idea."

"But you did pass, and that's all that matters. Now you have to get out there and start driving!"

I thought hard for a few seconds and smirked up at her. "You're only seventeen. I can only go out with a driver who's eighteen."

Quickly she answered, "I already thought about that. Sam should be waiting on the curb by now."

I shot off the bed and threw my hands in the air. "No way am I practicing driving with your brother."

"You're being unreasonable. Sam came all the way to the city, taking a day off from his job to help you learn to drive." Her eyes widened as she looked up at me, saying in a louder voice, "Do you really want me to send him away?"

I stared out the window at the peeling white paint on the neighbor's house. This place was a gold mine of work possibilities. If I had some of my own tools, I could earn income on the side. And, if I could drive my own pickup truck, I'd be one step closer to moving back to the country.

My stomach tightened when I said, "No, you're right. It's nice of him to take his time to help me out. I'll go."

"Great, I'm going to stay here and attempt to make pork chops the way Ruth taught me. Sam said something about guy-bonding time."

Then I knew that I was really up a creek. Time alone with Sam was never a good thing.

47

Sam

"You need to speed up or we're going to get rear-ended."

"I'm going as fast as I'm comfortable with. Why did you direct me on to this busy road, anyway?"

I rolled my eyes and thudded my head back against the seat. The past half hour riding around with Noah had been a real pain in the ass. The guy didn't know the first thing about driving—he didn't even understand basic directions. We'd already been beeped at several times and had run over a couple of curbs.

Taking a deep breath, I tried to be patient and said, "When you're learning to drive, you need to throw yourself into it and not be afraid of the highway. Rose wants to coddle you on this, but it won't do you any good if you stay on the half-dead secondary roads all the time. You won't learn a thing."

"I don't feel like I'm learning much at the moment, except maybe how to avoid having a wreck," Noah said as he gripped the steering wheel and leaned forward.

"Hey, man, that's what it's all about at first— Not getting killed," I said, chuckling, but absently I did check that my seat belt was tight again. "Besides, those damn buggies you drive are a hell of a lot more dangerous than a car or a pickup truck, like this one."

Noah shook his head and said, "The only dangers for us in the buggies are the motorized vehicles and their ignorant drivers."

I snorted. "Well, you're one of those ignorant drivers now, so suck it up. You better learn how to drive safely and pretty damn quick, too."

"Why are you so interested in my driving skills, Sam?"

"Because my little niece or nephew and my sister will be at your mercy, that's why."

His face sobered, losing the arrogance that had developed during the argument. Sure I felt a little bad for the guy—after all, he'd been thrown into a world of craziness compared to the slow-paced country existence he'd grown up in.

"Hey, take the next exit, and slow it down," I shouted, deciding at the last minute to go on an excursion.

Noah mumbled something under his breath about going too fast and then too slow, before he barely made the turn on to the ramp.

This part of Cincinnati was a shade on the dark side, and I scanned the beat-up-looking houses for a clue to where we were.

"There's this burger joint down this way that I went to with the football team last year after a game. I think it's somewhere on this road."

"You don't even know where we are?" Noah's voice hit a higher pitch, and I had to smile at him.

"Sure I do, somewhere on the east side of town." After noticing small groups of men huddled on the street corners, I added, "Just in case, you should lock the doors."

"You've got to be kidding me. I'm supposed to be learning how to drive, not how to survive the city."

"Now is a good time to do both." I said the words jokingly, but it had just occurred to me that we'd taken the wrong exit. I was scrambling in my mind, trying to decide which way would be the fastest to get our asses back on the interstate.

Noah's alarmed voice turned my head suddenly. "Something's wrong with the truck. It's slowing down by itself."

"What are you talking about?"

I leaned over and looked at the gauges. My heart landed in my stomach when I saw that we were out of gas.

"Dammit, didn't you notice the little yellow gas tank blinking?"

"I was too busy trying to stay in between the lines and not hit the other cars. You should have known that you were low on gas," he growled back at me.

He was partly right. I'd been so busy directing him every inch of the way that I'd forgotten that I needed to fuel up. Most people would have noticed the gauge warning, but not Mr. Suspenders.

Even though my new brother-in-law was wearing a pair of regular jeans and a solid blue T-shirt, I still couldn't help calling him the nickname I'd given him a while ago in my mind. There was something foreign about him—his mannerisms and speech were all wrong. Sure, we could dress him up like one of us, but deep down he was still one hundred percent Amish.

Noah was smart enough to turn the wheel so that we ended up stalled close to the curb, and then he turned and demanded, "What do we do now?"

I pulled my cell phone from my pocket and said, "I'll call

Rose. She can drive out here with a container of gas, just enough to get us to a gas station."

"No way—I don't want Rose coming to this run-down part of the city by herself. What if she gets lost like you did?"

"I'm not lost, just a little off track. But, yeah, I see your point." I thought for a few more seconds and said, "I'll try Heath. He's probably home."

Heath didn't answer and neither did Uncle Jason. I even tried Hunter, but he was working and said that I'd have to wait until his shift was over. From the dull sound of his voice, I knew that he was still bummed out that he'd lost Rose forever. After hanging up, I regretted even calling him, but I was surprised that he was willing to drive all the way to the city to help Rose's new husband out. It proved what a stellar guy he was.

The sun had dropped low enough in the sky that a string of street lamps came on. I could hear the hum of the one closest to the truck through the small opening at the top of the window. The evening was warm, and I was beginning to sweat. Wiping my brow, I reached over and turned the ignition enough to allow me to drop the window a few more inches.

"Do you think that's wise?" Noah asked in his usual uptight voice.

I shot back, "It's better than dying of heat stroke."

Before Noah could reply, the tap on the window had us both turning.

"Are you guys in some kind of trouble?"

The voice belonged to a middle-aged man on the pavement. He smiled, showing a missing front tooth, but the clothes he wore over his husky body looked in good condition. I could even smell the tangy scent of the same laundry detergent that Aunt Debbie used.

I glanced at Noah and absorbed his wide eyes and shrug. He had no clue how to handle this. It was all me on this one. Unless it came to a fight— At least I was confident that Noah could hold his own in a rough situation, unless a gun was pulled. I tried to squash the thought and smiled up at the man.

"Yeah, man, we're out of gas. Is there a station nearby?"

The man nodded and said, "Sure is." He pointed up the road and said, "A few blocks that way, you turn right and head another couple of blocks to a small ma and pop joint."

I turned to Noah, and asked, "Are you ready for a stroll in the city?"

He rolled his eyes but gripped the door handle, anyway. Once we were out and had the truck locked, the man walked up beside us and said, "Here, wait a minute. If you want, you can borrow my gasoline jug." Without giving us a chance to respond, he sprinted away to the closest driveway and added, "I'll only be a sec."

"Can we trust this guy?" Noah said in a whisper.

"No telling, but at least I have insurance on the truck."

I wasn't going to get all worked up over nothing. We'd probably be back on the highway within twenty minutes.

The sudden shout beside the house that our Good Samaritan ran to jolted both of us, and I motioned Noah to follow me.

When I turned the corner, I was amazed to see the tall man in a scuffle with three other men. The other guys were grabbing for the red jug, and I heard one of the men say, "What you helping that fool for? That big ol' truck has some valuable parts in it."

My stomach did a flip at the words, but I didn't let the

queasy feeling get to me. Stretching my legs into a run, I closed the distance to the fighting men quickly. Noah was at my side, and for an instant I wondered what he was thinking before I jumped into the melee.

I got a hold of the man who'd spoken and pushed him away with both hands. Noah had the guy to the right in his grasp, and before I began to tackle the third guy, I saw him punch the man soundly in the face.

The fighting seemed to go on for minutes, but in actuality, it probably only lasted thirty seconds before Noah, me and our gasoline jug guy had the other three men running up the alley.

With a huffing noise, the man said, "Why, thank you, young men. Those boys you helped run off are nothing but trouble."

Noah shook his head and then spit a wad of blood from his mouth. Blood trickled down his nose, and I cringed thinking about what Rose would say when she saw the condition I brought her husband home in.

"No, sir, we should be thanking you for your willingness to stand up to those men for us," Noah said.

"Sir. Why, I don't believe I've been called that before." The big man laughed and went on to say, "This isn't a good neighborhood to have car problems. I was hoping to get you out of here before anyone was the wiser."

This time I didn't hesitate when I hit the numbers on the phone.

Startled, the man said, "What are you doing?"

"I'm not taking any more chances—I'm calling the cops."

"Wish you wouldn't do that—will only make matters worse for me when you're gone. But if you must, I'll be on my way."

He handed me the jug and added, "Just leave it on the stoop at this house when you're done with it."

When the man had disappeared into the darkened house, Noah and I returned to the truck. We waited a few minutes for the two officers to show up and then told them our story before they drove us to the gas station themselves. Once we had gas in the tank and the jug on the stoop, the shorter officer with the mustache asked us again if we wanted to be checked out at the hospital or file a complaint, but we both shook our heads no.

Noah climbed into the passenger seat, and I didn't argue with him. Following the officer's directions, I headed out of the seedy neighborhood and breathed out a sigh of relief when I saw the bright lights of the highway come into view.

After several minutes, Noah finally broke the silence. "That was awful. How can anyone live in such a place?"

When I glanced over, Noah was staring at me. His face was milk-white and there was dried blood below his nose and on his cheek.

I reached into the console and pulled out some tissues. "Here, wipe your face and get yourself together, bro."

Noah took the tissue and said, "Your English world is horrible."

"That was completely random." I glanced back to reassure him, but he was facing the window. In a more determined tone, I said, "Really, that sort of thing never happens in the real world. We were just incredibly unlucky tonight. You need to buck up and stop referring to your new life as my world—because it's yours now."

"I've made a mistake bringing my family here." Noah sounded completely depressed.

"No, you haven't. Just be careful when you're driving to not get off at the wrong exit," I teased him, but he didn't smile at me in return.

"What have I done, Sam?"

I stared out at the passing cars, not able to find an answer for him.

Maybe he'd been right a long time ago when he'd insisted on raising his family in the Amish community.

But it was too late for that now.

"You have no choice—you have to make it work."

Noah nodded and said, "I will, but it won't be easy."

"Nothing ever is, bro."

48

Rose

Staring out the window at the drizzle falling around the street lamp, I felt the twinge of loneliness. Thank goodness, Noah would be home soon. When he left for work each afternoon, I'd cry for a few minutes until I finally pulled myself together. My shift at the animal clinic was in the morning, giving me very little time to spend with Noah before he left for work. Summer was too far away to hang out with, and Amanda and Britney had all but abandoned me when I'd begun looking like a pregnant girl. Sure, I understood where they were coming from. I didn't even enjoy spending time with me lately. I was uncomfortable and cranky most days, and my emotions were like thin ice.

Besides hormones, lack of sleep was probably to blame for my moodiness. Nightmares about Sarah's death had plagued me for weeks now. Images of a black, churning tornado descending on to the Millers' farmhouse like a hungry monster rose up whenever I closed my eyes to sleep.

In the dreams, Sarah was always standing in the window, looking out. She was clearly visible, wearing a lavender dress and a white cap, and her body had an unnatural glow around it, making her shine brightly against the darkness of the raging storm around her. Strangely, instead of a look of terror on her face, she smiled back at me.

I didn't know what to make of her happy face, being more obsessed with the really unsettling part of the dream—the baby in her arms. Who was it, and why was it even there? The first time the nightmare had struck, I thought it was just a way I was grieving over losing my friend. After all, Noah and I had been married soon after she'd died, and we hadn't had the proper amount of time to digest the fact that she was really gone forever. But after the same dream persisted each night, I began thinking more and more about the baby she held, and anxiety grew within me. Maybe it was her unborn niece or nephew she cradled in her arms, and if so, what kind of ominous sign was it?

I might not have taken the dreams so seriously if I hadn't been plagued by nightmares during Mom's illness. Even before her body had distorted and the shine had disappeared from her eyes, I'd seen her clearly in her diseased and dying state while I'd slept.

Maybe it was just an overactive imagination, but I was becoming increasingly more worried with each passing day that something bad was going to happen to my baby. What if Dad was right, and I was one of those unfortunate teenagers whose pregnancy ended tragically?

Glancing at my phone again, I sighed. Noah was the one person who could soothe my troubled mind and make me forget the dreams. Only when he returned from work and put his arms around me was I calm and safe again.

The last few minutes always took the longest to go by. There was nothing else to do except wait. I'd already vacuumed and tidied the small house to perfection. Heck, I was sure that even an Amish woman wouldn't be able to find a speck of dust or grease in this home.

I knew that Ruth would be proud of me.

The soft rap at the door caused my heart to skip and I forgot about everything else. Noah would have just walked in, so I knew it wasn't him. If Amanda had reconsidered about the visit, she'd definitely have texted me, and besides, she wouldn't come over at nearly eleven o'clock at night.

The knocks on the door sounded again, a bit louder, and I reluctantly got up and made my way to the door. Noah had given me direct orders to never answer the door unless I was expecting someone. He'd been worried about my safety ever since he'd had some strange experience out driving with Sam that he wouldn't tell me about. I'd agreed wholeheartedly with him on the matter. Our neighbors to either side were not exactly upstanding types of citizens.

I was convinced that the young couple to the right was dealing something illegal, if the constant stream of late-night, short visits were any indication. The old man who lived to the left frowned constantly, and when he did occasionally say something, his voice sounded more like a growl than a person talking.

Taking no chances, I looked out the small glass window in the middle of the door. Seeing no one, I became confused, until the knocking started up again.

Getting on my tiptoes, I craned my neck until I glimpsed blond hair. Immediately, I opened the door.

The little girl belonged to the couple next door, and I'd heard her called Lucy. I'd seen her many times playing between the houses with her brother. I guessed she was about five, and at the moment she was barefoot and wearing only a T-shirt and pajama pants. It was a usual late October evening in Ohio and must have been pushing thirty degrees outside.

When she looked up at me with saucer-sized eyes, I wasted no time reaching down and guiding her into the warmth. I kept the door open a crack, though, still wondering what the heck what was going on.

Bending down to the child's level, I asked, "Lucy, what are you doing here?"

She sniffed and said, "Mommy and Daddy are fighting."

My heart sank. I wasn't surprised in the least. Her parents went at it several times a week. They weren't shy about screaming, slamming doors and peeling away in anger from the curb with their dented Saturn, either.

For a second I was at a complete loss about what I should do, but then I moved closer to the doorway and strained to listen. Sure enough, I could hear angry words and the occasional explosion of something hitting the wall.

"Is your daddy hurting your mommy?" I said, turning to the child and thinking about some of the crime shows I'd watched in the past.

"They're hurting each other, and my little brother is crying 'cause he can't sleep. Neither can I— I want them to stop."

When the voices rose again, I picked up my phone and dialed 911. I had a very uneasy feeling about getting the cops involved, but what else could I do? Taking the child back to the crazy people wasn't an option for me personally. The man was taller than Noah, with tattoos of swords, barbed wire and strange symbols on his arms and neck. His head was shaved, and his eyes were always bloodshot.

His wife wasn't much gentler to look at either, with her dyed jet-black hair, anorexic skinny body and a cigarette always hanging from her lips.

It was impossible to believe that people like that could have spawned a sweet child like the one looking up at me.

I whispered, "Don't worry, Lucy. I'll take care of everything. Why don't you go over to the refrigerator—I think there's a piece of peanut-butter pie with your name on it."

She grinned and headed that way, reminding me of the resiliency of children.

After I got off the phone, my heart began pounding harder. The dispatcher had told me to keep Lucy at my house until the officer arrived, but I worried that her parents would suddenly realize they were missing a kid and come looking for her. I could only imagine the hostility they'd direct at me if they thought I was poking my nose into their business.

I was so distracted when Lucy spoke that it took me a second to realize it.

"When's your baby going to be born?"

"It's due in a couple of months—in December."

Lucy forked another piece of the pie into her mouth and then, between chewing, said, "Is it a girl?"

The child's eager face told me that she hoped it was, and I couldn't help smiling at her enthusiasm.

"Actually, I decided that I wanted to be surprised when the baby is born. I told the doctor not to tell me when she did the ultrasound."

"Really? I'd want to know. How else are you going to buy baby clothes and stuff?"

Her little voice had taken on a more adult twang to it, and I wondered about how many babies she'd been around to be so interested in mine. Her question was legitimate, though, and I took a few seconds to think before I answered.

"Well, you see, I spent some time with a group of people who normally don't want to know the sex of their babies until after they're born. It makes it more exciting, you see. You can always have the basics in neutral colors for the birth and shop for the rest later."

She rolled her eyes and said, "Maybe, but I'd want to know if it was me."

I laughed. "Hopefully, you won't have to worry about it for twenty years or so."

It was probably only a few minutes, but the time I spent making small talk with the child at the kitchen table seemed to last an hour before the flashing lights shone in through the front windows.

Taking Lucy's hand, I quickly went to the front door and opened it. I felt instant relief when I saw the officer was already walking up the steps.

It didn't take long to explain to him what was going on, and he thanked me for taking the child in and contacting authorities. His name was Drew Prescott, and with his round face and rosy cheeks, he didn't appear that much older than me.

"I've been to that residence on a number of occasions for both domestic violence and narcotics." He leveled a hard stare at me, suddenly looking older, when he added, "You should step lightly when dealing with them, Mrs. Miller. They aren't the kind of people to mess around with."

His words sent a shiver up my neck. I asked, "Will you take Lucy back to them?"

The little girl was standing between the two of us and

looking up expectantly at Officer Prescott. If I had to guess, I'd say she didn't want to go back.

"I'm calling social services this time. Don't worry about Lucy. She'll be fine."

He patted her head and then took up her hand.

Lucy glanced back at me as she walked down the steps and said, "Thanks, Mrs. Rose—I'll bring your hoodie back tomorrow and we can hang out again."

Her face was so bright with hope that I didn't have the heart to tell her that I probably wouldn't be seeing her again for a long while.

"You just keep it. I have another one that fits me better, anyway."

She smiled and nodded vigorously before turning away with Officer Prescott.

The bus stopped across the street, and Noah wasted no time getting off and hurrying across the road. As he passed them on the walkway, he greeted the officer at the same time he looked anxiously at me.

"What's going on?" Noah said when he reached me on the porch.

I took his hand and pulled him into the house, closing the door behind me with my body as I leaned against it. Finally, I exhaled.

"The little neighbor girl came over here while her parents were fighting."

"Why didn't you just tell her to go back?"

The look on Noah's face immediately put me on the defensive.

"I couldn't make her go back to them. She was afraid. You know, they do this all the time. It's not healthy for a child. Besides, they're into other stuff, too, that's not good for Lucy to be around."

Noah shook his head and moved forward to pull me into a hug.

On the top of my head, he muttered, "I know you wanted to help the little girl, but you should have thought about the consequences."

"What are you saying?"

He sighed and said, "Our neighbors aren't going to be happy with us for this. They'll probably be downright angry. Now we'll have enemies living a stone's throw away."

My own anger swelled inside of me, and I blurted out, "I tried to help Lucy, and I wouldn't do a thing different. Sometimes, you have to take a risk in life and do the right thing."

"Not everyone would agree what the right thing to do in a situation like this is. But I won't argue with you about it anymore. I just hope the authorities use discretion when mentioning your involvement. The last thing we need is a neighbor with a serious grudge. Trust me, I know how that can go."

I relaxed against him and said, "I'm sorry, I just couldn't stand the thought of her going back to those insane people."

He brushed my hair down with his fingers and whispered, "We've got to get out of here, Rose. I'm afraid to leave you here when I go to work. The job is bad enough, but worrying about my pregnant wife for hours is even worse."

I shrugged and muttered, "Not much we can do about it now."

Noah leaned back, and his face instantly brightened. "Actually, there is."

I raised my brow questioningly, and he continued, "My

department manager gave me the weekend off. I was thinking that it's the perfect time to head to Meadowview for a visit."

I suddenly felt lighter and exclaimed, "Are you serious—can we go back? I didn't think they'd see us so soon. You said they were still upset about your decision."

He nodded his head. "I talked to Mother this morning while you were working. They still believe I've made a huge mistake, but they love us, anyway. She's anxious to see you—says she'd made a quilt for our baby. It's the perfect time, really. Jacob and Katie had their little boy last week, and I'd like to see my nephew."

"Oh, it would be wonderful. Will there be enough time to visit our friends? I miss Summer and Suzanna so much."

"Of course—we'll make the time. It will do us good to get away from this place of pavement and problems and smell the fresh air again." Noah paused and stared down at me for a second before saying, "Does this make you happy?"

I nodded as the tears developed in my eyes.

"I know you've been depressed lately. The testing time of our lives is still with us, but it won't last forever. I promise you that."

As he hugged me tightly and my swollen belly rubbed between us, I almost believed him.

But I couldn't help glancing around his arm out the window at the flashing lights. Another car had arrived, and I could just make out Lucy's parents talking to Officer Prescott and another, older man in the light rain.

The scene caused my heart to begin pounding faster again.

Yes, it was a very good thing to get out of town.

I just wished that we never had to return.

49

Noah

As we walked through the mowed field between our families' properties, I glanced down at Rose. Amazingly, her belly seemed to have popped out more overnight. Even with the wool jacket she wore partially concealing the middle part of her body, it was apparent that she was pregnant.

I hid a smile at her waddling stride and slowed even more to accommodate her inability to move any faster. She was such a good sport to be hiking the distance to the farm. Without me having to explain my feelings, she'd understood.

It would be difficult to reunite with my family after so many months, but arriving in a truck would have been even worse. The last thing I wanted to do was rub my decision to go English in my parents' faces. The meeting would be awkward enough without a grand show of how different I was now.

I'd even chosen to wear extremely plain jeans, a button-up blue shirt similar to the ones Mother used to sew for me and my old pair of suspenders. It wouldn't have felt right to appear in front of Father wearing a shirt with a strange picture on it. Rose, for her part, had dressed in a subdued manner, too, squeezing into a pair of maternity pants that looked like jeans, with a white sweater that just made it over the baby bump.

We were lucky. With just a few days left to go until the end of October, the weather was still fairly mild, making the hike through the sunny field enjoyable and not much of a chore, even for my very pregnant wife.

I smiled at the thought and once again looked at Rose. This time, she caught my glance and said, "Why are you staring at me?"

Squeezing her hand more tightly, I replied, "I was just thinking about how beautiful you are and how lucky I am to have you for my wife."

She rolled her eyes and snorted, "Oh, yeah, I'm a real hottie right now."

I pulled her to a stop. "Don't mock me. You are beautiful. The pregnancy has heightened your beauty."

"I feel like a bloated tick. Didn't you see how Sam laughed at me when I got out of the truck?"

I rolled my eyes. I'm sure my face had turned red with the heat of anger when I said, "Your brother is an idiot. I know you're not very comfortable at this point, but you're still a sight for sore eyes—I just wish you were always as happy as you seem today."

"I think it's just the hormones making me so emotional." She took a deep breath and glanced away. "I have to admit, being home has made a world of difference. I feel like I've woken from a bad dream."

For a second, I scrunched my eyebrows together and

watched Rose as she avoided my gaze. She still wouldn't open up to me about the nightmares that had her tossing and turning each night. Sometimes she'd wake drenched in sweat and crying out Sarah's name or saying the word *baby* in the middle of the night.

I understood. I had my own ill dreams to deal with, but I'd been becoming increasingly more concerned as dark lines had developed beneath Rose's eyes and her skin had turned paler. The lack of adequate sleep was taking a toll on her— I only prayed that this trip would take away her fears and give her peace.

Having her own family visit us on a regular basis hadn't helped Rose. She needed something else, and now I was pretty sure what it was. Not so different from me, she felt city life draining her life away. Deep down, Rose loved the country and the slower pace as much as I did.

When she finally looked at me again, her wide smile nearly took my breath away. I would do anything to make her face light up like that every day—anything.

"I feel the same way. Smelling the acres of grass and the scent of cows on the wind calms my soul. Other than you and the baby, the one thing that keeps me going is the hope that we'll have our own farm one day."

She gripped my hand more tightly and promised, "We will."

Picking up our pace, we started walking again. Several times Rose pointed at the display of autumn colors in the distance. Unfortunately, all the trees that used to line the roadway were gone, splintered from the same storm that had taken my little sister to heaven. Most of the devastation had been cleared away, but here and there were reminders of the horrible storm in the form of bulldozed piles full of broken trees and pieces of the house and barn.

In the city, it was easier to block thoughts of Sarah from entering my mind, but here, so close to home, I couldn't stop them from flooding in. I pictured sweet Sarah racing against me on her fat pony and her laughing face when she kicked hay down on to my head while she hid in the barn loft. I could still smell the wonderful aroma of her special oatmeal raisin cookies when she pulled them from the oven, and I remembered her soft hands when she'd placed bandages on to my cuts and scratches. She was the best sister anyone could've asked for. I only wish that I'd realized it before God had taken her away—and told her how much I loved her.

Carefully, I turned away and quickly sniffed in the emotions that I hoped Rose wouldn't notice. I had to collect myself. The last thing I wanted to do was show her how my sister's death still affected me. I had to be strong for her—for the both of us.

Closing my eyes for a few seconds, I swallowed down the lump in my throat.

Goodbye, my dear Sarah. I love you.

The breeze picked up, and for a strange second, I swore I smelled cookies baking. Shaking my head, I gazed up at the puffy clouds that dotted the blue sky, and the hairs on my arms went up and my heart began to race. Sarah was with us—I could feel her presence all around me.

I couldn't help smiling. Sarah had heard me—she wanted

me to know that she was all right and that she knew my feelings for her. She was saying her own goodbye.

Rose tugged me to a stop and said, "What's caused that silly look on your face?"

Someday, I'd tell her about it, but not now.

Pulling her into a tight hug, I murmured into her hair, "Have I ever told you how much I love you?"

Rose pulled back and raised her chin, squinting into the sunshine. "Several times a day, actually. If you want to avoid the subject, that's fine with me. I have ways to get it out of you."

She giggled and pinched my side playfully.

I sighed, knowing full well that she'd have me talking about it by tonight. Rose could be very persuasive when she wanted to be.

My smile broadened at the thought of her tactics, and I pulled her up under my arm. There was no need for any more conversation and we both knew it. The promise of what was to come when we were alone later in the night was enough as we walked in silence, holding each other tightly.

When the entire farm came into view, Rose gasped and clutched my arm. All remnants of the old house were gone and replaced with the frame of a new one. The shine from the silver tin roof glared at us, and the white paper on the walls showed that the building was almost dried in. There were no trees in the yard, and the shed hadn't been rebuilt yet, but other than those things, the place had an air of rebirth about it, almost as if the land itself was happy to be fixed up again.

"They've done so much work since we left," Rose breathed out in awe.

I understood her amazement, but I wasn't shocked. I knew that the entire Amish community had come together to put the house up for my family. With so many master builders working together and the threat of winter approaching, the work would have gone quickly. Even at this distance, I could see a couple of buggies parked in the driveway and could hear the sound of pounding hammers.

"I wish Father would have allowed me to help rebuild the place. It feels strange to see all that's been done and not to have lifted a finger for any of it."

"Let it go, Noah. Just be happy that they're seeing us at all. Maybe you can help with the shed when they start on it."

Her suggestion was reasonable to an Englisher's mind, but I couldn't help the snort that erupted from my lips.

"No, they will never accept my help again."

Quietly, we closed the distance to the farm. Once again, I'd added to Rose's growing anxiety, and I hated myself for it, but I didn't say anything more to try to soften my words. This was the part of leaving the Amish that I'd always feared.

When we got close enough to the house to see Father and Jacob hanging a window on the second story and Matthew finishing the last board on the stoop leading up to the back door, I stopped and whistled in admiration.

All eyes turned my way, and I couldn't help feeling my heart jump when the looks were accompanied by large smiles, even from Father. Matthew wasted no time in throwing down his tools and running toward me.

The force of his body against mine as he grabbed me into a hug took me by surprise. Even though Matthew was known for his freely shown friendliness, I would have reckoned he'd have been more reserved in front of Father.

"Good golly, I can't believe it's you, Noah. What, it's been four or five months now?"

I pulled back but kept my arms braced against my friend. "I'd say nearly five months since the wedding. It's hard to believe that so much time has passed that we haven't seen each other."

Matthew finally released me and peered over at Rose shyly.

"Boy, will Miranda be thrilled to see you, Rose." Matthew stopped and looked at me with wide eyes, and said in a pleading voice, "You'll be here long enough to see everyone, won't you?"

"That's the plan."

"I'll go call Timmy. Maybe he can bring the girls over here. Would you like that, Rose?"

"Very much," she said with a brilliant smile.

Matthew nodded and turned away. With a faster stride than my large friend was known for, Matthew began crossing the yard to the barn. He looked back over his shoulder and shouted, "The phone is in the stable for the time being."

I nodded at the information and then turned to watch Father and Jacob approach at a slower pace. Noticing that Jacob's beard had filled in more, I reached up and touched my clean-shaven chin without thought. The spread of nervousness in my stomach caused a cool sweat to erupt on my skin, and I took a breath as I made a mental note that Father's own beard appeared to have grayed considerably since last I'd seen him. The stress of losing a daughter, a house… and a son…had aged Amos Miller, and I suddenly felt the weight of guilt on my shoulders.

When they reached us, Father went first to Rose and took her hands up between his own. "It's so very good to see you. You're absolutely glowing."

"Thanks, Mr. Miller. You look pretty good yourself."

Father smiled warmly and then turned to me. He was more serious when he faced me, but there was no anger in his eyes. I breathed a little easier when he shook my hand heartily before stepping aside and allowing Jacob to follow suit.

"What brings you to our neck of the woods?" Father asked.

"Didn't Mother tell you that we were coming?" I said, wondering if she'd misunderstood me.

"Yes, she did. I'm simply wondering why you're visiting us."

The blood began to drain from my face when I realized that Father wasn't going to roll out the welcome mat.

Quietly I said, "We wanted to visit our family and friends. Isn't that reason enough?"

Father and I stared at each other for several long seconds before he broke eye contact first and said to Jacob, "Why don't you take Rose down to your place, son, to see Katie and the baby."

Jacob motioned for Rose to follow him to the nearest buggy. Rose looked at me for confirmation, and when I nodded, she joined Jacob. Father then turned to Matthew and ordered him to drive to James and Ruth's place to inform Mother and the other children that we'd arrived. I'd heard that the family was staying at the Hershbergers' while the house was built and was suddenly happy that most of the people I wanted to see were in one place.

"Sure thing—Timmy is picking up the girls. Maybe he can meet us at the Hershbergers'?"

Father shrugged, but I said, "That would be fine if you could arrange it, Matthew."

"I'll do the best I can," Matthew said before he sprinted to his own buggy.

As I followed Father to the barn, I glanced over my shoulder at Jacob's buggy which had just turned on to the roadway. Apprehension coursed through me when I saw the buggy speeding down the pavement. It was a strange feeling and one I'd never had before, even after my own near-fatal wreck. It suddenly dawned on me that if I'd stayed Amish, I'd have worried about my wife and children every time they got into a buggy. I knew firsthand how dangerous the mixing of buggies and motorized vehicles were, and a small part of me was glad that I didn't have to deal with it anymore.

The sun was still bright in the sky when I entered the dimmer interior of the barn, and I breathed in the scent of hay and leather as I took my usual place on one of the hay bales left in the aisle for just such occasions.

Father didn't sit down, though. Instead, he chose to slowly pace while he rubbed his beard with his hand thoughtfully. I sat patiently waiting for him to initiate the conversation. Nervousness still poked at me, but I was calming down.

After all, I was a grown married man with my own child on the way. I was no longer a green boy who Father could intimidate.

When the silence was finally broken by Father's voice, I was surprised by what he asked.

"How is that little Paint rascal doing?"

An image of the young black-and-white horse sprang to mind, and I chuckled, letting go of any apprehension that still clung to me.

"He's biting and kicking a whole new group of horses at the stable where Rose boards her horse in Cincinnati."

Father stopped and leaned back against the stall. He said, "That horse will always be difficult, because it's in his nature to be so."

Knowing that there was hidden meaning to Father's discussion of my horse, I asked with reluctance, "What's your point?"

Father sighed and then smiled sadly. "You're not much different than that colt of yours. Even as a small child, you were rambunctious, always questioning everything, forever gazing down the road." He took a deeper breath and continued. "I always prayed for you, son, more so than any of your siblings, because I *knew* that you were at the most risk of being tempted away. You couldn't help buying that obnoxious horse the same as you couldn't stop yourself from falling in love with an English girl. It was inevitable, because of your difficult nature."

I straightened up on the bale and said, "I didn't come here to argue with you, Father."

"No, of course not—we are beyond that now. You've

chosen your path, for ill or good. I won't be changing your mind."

"Then why bring up how disappointed you are in me?"

Father shook his head and said, "I'm not disappointed in you, just disappointed in how your life has turned out. I'll always believe that you've made a huge mistake by leaving the Amish, and breaking your oath to the church, but I'm not really surprised that you did it and I'll always love you."

Quietly I said, "I told you the reasons for my decision. I have no regrets, but I'm sorry that my actions have hurt you and Mother."

Father's brows lifted, and he asked, "Really, no regrets at all? That's amazing. Even I have some regrets, although I live every day for my God, my church and my family, knowing that some things can't be undone…or shouldn't be."

The strangeness in Father's voice bothered me. He wasn't behaving at all as I expected, and I wondered why. It would have been easier to deal with him if he'd been raging mad at me or completely friendly. This going back and forth with his emotions was making the conversation uncomfortable, to say the least.

"I want nothing more than to have some semblance of a relationship with you, Mother and my siblings. What do you want?"

The barn was quiet for a minute, the only sounds the birds chirping beyond the doorway and the occasional snort of a horse in the stall at my back. I was about to stand and leave the barn when Father decided to answer me.

"I want you to have a relationship with our Lord…and

to be happy." When he turned to look at me, his eyes were wet, and I rose, standing before him. "After losing your dear sister, I don't want to lose you, too."

I took the few steps to reach him and flung my arms around his strong body. Father grasped me in a bear hug that nearly took my breath away, but I wouldn't have dared to complain. The squeezing pain felt good.

"You should come back to Meadowview, son. You should raise your family close by. It's the right thing to do."

I pulled back, gaping.

"But I'm shunned from the community. How could I make a life here as an English man?"

"Pray for an answer. Ask for guidance, and I'm sure you'll receive it. But I feel it in my heart that you and Rose aren't happy in the city. Just like that colt will always be difficult, you'll always be drawn to the land. You must return to the basics. Whether you're Amish or English, you must live a simple life to be closer to God and truly happy."

His words resonated deep inside of me, and I knew he was right.

"How can I do it without your help?"

Father's eyes brightened, and he said, "Never fear, Noah. I will always help you if you ask it of me and it's within my power to do so."

"I don't understand," I whispered.

"Pray about it and I'm sure you'll get your answers."

He patted me on the back and then left me alone in the barn. Searching out the doorway, I gazed at the open fields for several minutes before I finally bowed my head and prayed.

I only hoped that God was merciful to me and showed me the way quickly.

For Rose's sake, I'd made the best of my circumstances, learning to drive a car, working at a job I hated and living in the city; but I didn't know how much longer I could survive what my life had become.

50
Rose

The heat coming off of Ruth's wood stove was glorious, and as I leaned back in the rocking chair, I sipped the cup of tea in my hands.

Feeling at peace for the first time in so very long, I reveled in the feeling, unable to drop the smile that had erupted on my lips the minute I'd entered the house and had been embraced first by Ruth and then by Noah's mom.

The two women had talked my ears off for a half hour, and the conversation had only just calmed to a normal pitch in the past few minutes. Rachel sat close beside me, and for the first time ever, I felt the beginnings of a kinship with Noah's younger sister. She'd been genuinely happy to see me and even touched my belly several times tentatively with a whimsical smile on her face.

She was now staring into her cup, and I wondered what she was thinking when Rebecca asked, "Do you have any names picked out?"

"We've talked about quite a few, but haven't decided for sure yet."

"It's such an exciting time, the birth of a first child. Enjoy these last weeks of time alone with your husband, Rose. Soon enough everything will change."

Rachel woke from her trance and said, "You make it sound awful, Ruth. Why go scaring Rose that way?"

Ruth snorted and said, "I'm doing no such thing—simply giving young Rose a wise bit of advice."

Rebecca nodded and supported the other woman. "Yes, she's right, my dear. There is so very little time when we are alone with our husbands in the world—very soon the babies begin arriving, and life changes, but in a wonderful way. We want Rose to enjoy this time with Noah and to understand that it's special."

"I don't know why all the girls are in such a rush to get married. I'd be happy living on my own without the worry of a husband or children," Rachel said.

Rebecca's eyes widened, and she scolded her daughter, "Hush now, Rachel. Don't be talking like that."

Ruth had a tight smile when she said, "Don't mind her, she'll be changing her mind soon enough."

"No, I won't." Rachel rose abruptly, nearly knocking her chair down with the motion.

I looked at Katie with wide eyes, and she only shrugged as Rachel left the room in a hurry.

Rebecca sighed and said, "I don't know what's got into that girl. She's always been temperamental, but lately she's been impossible."

Ruth reached over and patted Rebecca's hand and reassured her, "Maybe losing Sarah has been harder on her than you think. Don't forget, she survived the house collapsing when her sister did not. That's a difficult burden to bear, I'd say."

Rebecca nodded and sniffed, rubbing the wetness from her eyes.

The warmth of the wood-burning stove in the kitchen kept the numbness from setting in. Even though there was grief in the room, there was also friendship and love. As long as these women had each other, they could survive anything.

I suddenly realized with a sharp pain that I was only a visitor now, and I was filled with envy of what I'd lost when I'd help convince Noah to go English.

A loud knock was immediately followed by the door bursting open and Suzanna and Miranda rushing in from the cold, dark evening.

Almost breathless, Suzanna said, "I hope you don't mind us stopping by, Ruth. We desperately wanted to see Rose."

Ruth stood and said, "Of course not, girls. You're welcome to stay as long as you like. I have some mending to do in the other room." My ex-foster mom took the few steps to me, and I rose and let her embrace me tightly. She murmured against my ear, "It's been wonderful seeing you, my dear. I do hope you'll visit again soon."

When she stepped back, she eyed me with a wise and knowing stare before she left the room.

Rebecca followed suit but was completely silent during her hug. I could tell she wanted to speak, but the words must have caught in her throat. When she left the room, tears were falling down her cheeks.

Katie touched my belly softly with her hand and said, "May the grace of God be with you when you deliver, Rose... and please bring the sweet angel by for a visit. I hope that he or she will know their cousin, Stephen. They will be close in age, and I'm sure they'll enjoy playing with each other."

"Do you think that's possible?" I asked hopefully.

Noah had been so vague about whether we'd be able to return anytime soon, I really didn't know what would be allowed.

Katie's nod was hesitant. She said, "Only time will tell for sure, but I'd welcome seeing you again." As if the emotion of the situation was too much, she quickly went to the bassinet that Ruth had set up in the corner of the kitchen for just such visits, and reached in to gather up her baby boy.

"I'd best be heading home myself. Peter, Daniel, Isaac and Naomi are staying with me tonight, and I reckon they've worn Jacob out. It was good to see you, Rose."

Katie's smile lit up her face, and then she was through the door. The blast of cold air entered the kitchen just long enough to leave a harsh impression of her departure before the door closed.

I didn't have long to miss her, when Suzanna crossed the room and embraced me. Unlike everyone else, she didn't worry too much about the great bulge of my belly and pressed right into it. I laughed at her exuberance and then received a calmer squeeze from Miranda before we were all seated in front of the stove.

Although I'd enjoyed my time with the other women and even felt a strange bonding toward Noah's sister, these two were among my closest friends in the world. And, unlike with Amanda and Britney, the fact that I was pregnant made no difference to them. It was a way of life in their world—I was just experiencing it a little before them.

"What have you two been up to...getting into any trouble?" I teased.

Suzanna rolled her eyes and barked, "Ever since you left the community, getting into trouble isn't as much fun anymore."

I knew she was joking, but I put on an offended face for a few seconds before I began giggling.

"You're rotten, you know that, Rose. You had me going for a minute." Her tone changed, and her voice slowed when she added, "Actually, I have some news for you. We both do."

The following silence from the outspoken girl was strange, and my curiosity made me burst out, "Well, out with it."

"I'm getting married in March and Miranda a month later."

I let the words sink in and then reached out to grasp each of their hands. "It's about time."

Suzanna's face went from an excited grin to a sudden frown. She said, "Don't go telling anyone...only our families know. We'll make the announcements in early February."

I leaned back, quickly counting the months in my mind. "That's almost four months before you even let the word out. Honestly, I don't know how you'll be able to keep it secret for so long."

"Time will go by fast—there's so much to do to prepare," Miranda said in her quiet, birdlike voice.

I looked between the two of them and said sullenly, "I wish I could be there."

"I know. So do I, but it would never be allowed for you and Noah to attend." After a few seconds of uncomfortable silence, she added, "We'll get together right after the wedding. Once Timmy and I move in to the farmhouse we're going to rent, you can come by anytime."

"I don't know, Suzanna. I don't want to get you into trouble."

Suzanna's face firmed with a determined look. "Don't go acting like that. Sure, you're not Amish and things won't be the same as before, but you'll always be my friend, and Noah and Timmy have been best buddies since they were two. It'll be all right—we'll have more freedom once we're all married."

Miranda sighed and said, "That's what we hope, anyway."

Suzanna turned to her and said sharply, "What's that supposed to mean?"

"Everyone talks about having more freedom when they marry, but it doesn't seem to work out that way. You know it deep down to be true."

Suzanna leaned back in her chair and folded her arms across her chest. Her silence was her way of agreeing.

"How can that be so? Once you are out from under your parents' thumbs, you can do what you want." I directed the question at Miranda.

Miranda shook her head softly and replied, "We change from the authority of our parents to that of the church, which is even more diligent about watching us and keeping us in line. Our parents don't have much more freedom than we do now."

"Then, why do it—? Why stay Amish?"

Miranda said, "Because that is who we are. We trade our freedom for the support of community. Some would think us crazy, but others might be jealous of our blessings at the same time."

"Yes, I have been, at times," I murmured, thinking about Lucy and the neighbors I'd traded Meadowview for when Noah and I had moved to the city.

Wanting to wipe the melancholy feeling from the room, Suzanna exclaimed, "Oh, I have more news for you." She paused and said with a grin, "Guess what? Constance is also engaged— They've been trying to keep it secret, but I've heard that it will be a week before mine."

The news shocked me, and I asked, "To whom?"

"John, the oldest Yoder son— Do you remember him?"

Searching my memories, I tried to pinpoint him but couldn't. There were so many Yoder boys, and they were all blond. Their faces glazed together in my mind, but having Noah's ex-fiancée hitched was a good thing in my book.

"I wish them all the best." I tried to sound sincere, but the girls knew better. They burst into laughter, and I joined them.

After we all sobered, a thought popped into my head, and I asked, "Do either of you know what's going on with Rachel? She's in quite the mood."

Suzanna nodded and leaned in to whisper, "She hasn't been right since the tornado. When she's not snapping at someone, she refuses to speak at all." Lowering her voice to the point I had to strain to hear her, she added, "And, to top it off, I have it on good authority that she's been flirting with two boys."

Suzanna's words directly conflicted with what Rachel had said to us earlier about not wanting a husband or children. My shock must have shown, because Suzanna said,

"I definitely think it's true, and you won't believe who the boys are."

What she said next made me almost fall out of my chair.

"It's Micah Schwartz...and your little brother, Justin."

51

Sam

When Rose came through the family room doorway with Noah two steps behind her, I wasn't expecting her to bypass me completely and head straight to the TV. She yanked out the Xbox cords. The fuzz of static lasted for a second, before she turned off the power to the television and faced Justin, her hands on her hips.

"What are you doing—are you insane?" Justin yelled, jumping out of the recliner.

I glanced at Noah, who met my gaze for a second, but he only frowned and remained on the couch.

Rose stood up straighter. Her stomach bulged, but she was still formidable when she blasted back at Justin, "You're the insane one. What are you thinking, getting involved with Rachel Miller?"

The words split my head like an ax. No way... But looking back again at Noah, I knew with sickening surety that Rose was indeed serious. Damn.

Justin sat back down in defiance and shrugged. He said in a milder tone, "You could hardly call it getting involved."

Justin's nonchalant attitude seemed to placate her a bit. She said in a more civil voice, "How do you even know her?"

"I've only talked to her a few times when I went next door to help clean up the mess from the storm. Dad ordered me to."

Piping up in Justin's defense, I said, "Yeah, Dad did tell us to go over there and help out whenever we could. We've spent a lot of cleaning up, and I even helped with the framing of the new house. I don't see why you're making such a big deal of this."

"Oh, it might sound all nice and innocent, Sam, but Justin isn't really being honest with us. There's more to this than he's saying."

Before I had the chance to follow up, Justin's voice rose again. "There's nothing going on, so just leave it alone, will you? That girl's totally bent, anyway." He looked up at her and smirked, and I knew he'd either lost his mind or he was desperate to cover his ass.

Rose's eyes widened at his challenge, and she said, "You shouldn't be messing with her, Justin!"

I jumped up and put my arm in front of her just in time. Even though Noah was married to my sister, he still had no clue to her volatility. He was several seconds too late.

Rose gripped my arm and threatened, "If you don't move, Sam, you're going to be a casualty when I kill him."

"You're not going to kill anyone...at least not in your condition. Really, do you want your baby experiencing this kind of violence while it's still in the womb?"

Rose leveled a hard stare at me and said, "Don't patronize me." She pointed at Justin, who was still sitting leisurely in his gamer chair. "Justin shouldn't be getting involved with Rachel Miller on any level. She's nothing but trouble—the entire situation is nothing but trouble. I know. Justin, you don't want to end up with the problems Noah and I have had. Tell him, Noah. Tell him to stay away from your sister!"

Justin was unfazed and looked up at his brother-in-law with an "I dare you to" look, and I suddenly had a lot more respect for my little brother. Staring at him for the first time in forever, I saw that his face and body had matured into a good-looking fifteen-year-old when I hadn't been paying attention. He had the same brown hair and bright blue eyes that Rose had and could pass as her twin, but whereas her face was extremely pretty by anyone's standards, his was beautiful in a masculine way.

It suddenly dawned on me that he had the capacity to be more of a headache than Rose ever had. Justin was a bad boy in a zoned-out gamer's disguise...and the little shit was smarter than us all.

Noah put his hands gently on Rose's arms and tugged her away from me and Justin. In a calming voice, he said to her, "Rose, sweetheart, if your brother says nothing is going on, then I believe him. You know how the Amish girls gossip—Suzanna probably misunderstood."

Rose screeched, "Oh, I'd take Suzanna's word as the gospel compared to Justin's— He's lying!"

Justin stood again, and the four of us were facing off in the center of the family room when Dad walked in.

"What's going on in here?"

The silence that followed Dad's question was palpable. For once, I didn't dare to say a word. I would leave it to Rose to decide how to proceed. After all, she was probably right to be worried about our little brother and whatever mess he was getting himself into.

Noah just stared at the ground and Justin looked straight into Rose's gaze, unflinching.

In a sudden release of energy, Rose let out a breath and said, "We were just arguing about the television. Noah and I wanted to watch a movie, and Justin wouldn't get off the Xbox."

Dad frowned at Justin and said, "Justin, don't be rude. Your sister doesn't come to visit often. The TV is hers tonight."

Justin smiled and said, "Fine," before he left the room.

I had a few seconds of feeling relaxed before my gaze met Rose's.

She was backing off for now, but the look she gave me said it all.

Rose might be completely wrong about Justin and this Rachel chick, but either way, she wouldn't let the matter drop until she got her answers.

52

Rose

The man's finger came alarmingly close to my nose, but I held my ground, although my insides felt like mush. Darkness had settled in a few minutes earlier, and the street lamps illuminated my neighbor's angry face. His wife stood a few feet behind him puffing on a cigarette. She hadn't spoken, but she didn't need to. Her glare conveyed her hatred easily enough.

"You made a big mistake, girlie, and you're going to fucking pay for it."

Noah wouldn't be home for several hours. I tried to close the door, but the man's hand shot out and kept it in place. As panic swirled inside of me, I said with effort, "Please, go away. I don't want any trouble with you."

"If you'd minded your own damned business, I wouldn't be here on your porch. You brought this on yourself." He smirked and said with a mock sweet voice, "And you being about to pop out a baby. How unfortunate."

Behind his shoulder, the green dually truck pulled to the curb and parked beneath the lamp post. I breathed a sigh of relief. When my neighbor had hurled obscenities at me earlier in the day when I'd returned from shopping, I'd called

Sam, crying. He'd been getting ready to pick Summer up for a date, and I wasn't sure if he'd actually come to the city on such short notice to stay with me until Noah got home. But here he was, and just in the nick of time.

Sam shouted out, "Rose, are you all right?"

The man let go of the door and turned. He grabbed his wife's arm and dragged her along with him off the porch as Sam and Summer reached it. Just as I thought—the man was a complete coward.

He growled over his shoulder as he was crossing into his own yard, "She'll be fine if she learns to keep her trap shut."

Sam rushed the man and grabbed his shoulder, spinning him around.

"Don't you threaten my sister, you loser," Sam said.

"Sam, stop!" I yelled, terrified. The man was bigger than Sam and probably nearing thirty. Even if he weren't a violent drug dealer, he'd have been a lot to handle for anyone.

"Fuck you," the man said as he shoved with both his hands on Sam's chest.

Sam swung, hitting him soundly on the side of the face. The crunch was loud, and a spurt of bright red blood flew through the air. Summer got a hold of Sam's midsection and held on, and the wife grasped her husband, whose nose was now bleeding profusely. I ran outside.

"Sam, are you okay?" I asked, clutching his arm.

"I'm all right," he said. "He didn't get me."

"Who are these people?" screeched Summer.

"Dwayne, stop it. We don't need this kind of trouble on top of everything else," the woman pleaded with her husband as she wrestled with him in the yard. He was a lot bigger than her, but she was one of those scrapper types of women who had more strength than she looked like she had. Slowly, she pulled Dwayne to their house.

Right before they went inside, Dwaye turned back and, in a strangely calm voice, said, “You’re all going to regret this.” And then he disappeared into his house.

Sam turned to me and said, “You need to move.”

Maybe it was relief that we’d survived the encounter with my crazy neighbor, but I was overcome with sudden mirth, and I started laughing. The laughter continued to build until I was making hysterical sounds. When Sam and Summer looked at me, frowning, all the emotions I’d been holding at bay for the past several hours hit me.

I began to sob, and Sam pulled me under his arm and guided me into the house.

“Please, don’t leave, Sam. Stay the night with us.” I choked the words out and looked up at him.

“Of course we’re staying. It’ll be like a slumber party—don’t you worry about a thing.”

I had my pajamas on and a cup of hot chocolate perched on my belly. Summer was brushing my hair, and Sam and Noah sat in the chairs at the table playing chess. Fear still had a slight hold of me, but Summer’s soft downward strokes with the brush were distracting me in a nice way.

When my baby’s foot jabbed my insides, I quickly grasped Summer’s hand and brought it to the swell. I turned to watch her face light up in astonishment.

“Holy cow, that little booger is strong. How do you put up with being kicked like that all the time?”

I smiled. It didn’t bother me in the least that Summer

called my baby a booger. I knew she meant it in the nicest way.

Noah must have thought differently, though. He said, "Summer, please don't call my child a booger."

"Well, maybe if you'd tell us what you're having and its name, I'd know what to call it," Summer replied.

"It's going to be a surprise for all of us," I said cheerfully.

"I can't believe you haven't cheated and found out what the sex is yet. How can you be so patient?" Summer demanded.

More quietly, I said, "I want to be surprised, but I have a feeling what it is."

Summer's green eyes brightened instantly. "Really—what?"

I rolled my eyes at her intensity and said, "I'm not saying a word. Besides, it's just a feeling and probably doesn't mean a thing. We'll all know in six weeks, anyway."

"It's hard to believe that I'll be an uncle before Christmas. The months have gone by so fast," Sam said.

"You aren't kidding," Noah said, and then his voice became softer and he changed the subject. "Sam, I don't know how I can thank you enough for driving all this way to be here for Rose when she needed you. If you hadn't shown up, who knows what that awful man might have done?"

Sam shook his head and said, "First off, you can stop thanking me. Rose is my sister, and even though she's given me a hard time ever since she was big enough to start running around, I'll always be there for her and you and the baby."

Noah looked at me with a tight face and said, "I just wish

you'd called me, Rose. I could have gotten here within minutes."

"You need your job. You've already missed too much work as it is, staying home with me so I wouldn't be alone. I couldn't jeopardize you being fired."

"The job means nothing if something happens to you."

The worried look on his face sobered me. He was right. I should have called him.

Before I had a chance to respond, Summer tugged me off the couch and said, "It's late for a pregnant woman to be up. Let's hit the hay."

Sam said, "Ah, babe, are you sleeping with my sister instead of me?"

Noah didn't catch the teasing ring to Sam's voice and said firmly, "It wouldn't be appropriate any other way."

Sam rolled his eyes, and Summer said, "Don't you worry, Noah. I'll make sure Sam behaves himself."

I couldn't help grinning when Sam clutched at his heart in mock distress.

Summer wagged her finger at him as she pulled me into the bedroom.

When Summer closed the door and then climbed onto the bed beside me I knew something was up.

"What?" I asked with extreme reluctance.

"Oh, don't go getting your panties in a wad. It's nothing about you...or even me. I was just wondering what's going on with Justin. Sam only told me a little bit, said something about you laying down the law to him about Noah's little sister."

I leaned back against the headboard and rubbed my belly absently. At the moment, the pressure was almost unbearable. I felt like I was about to explode. Breathing in deeply, I waited until the sensation passed, and then I said, "My friends told me he was flirting with Rachel. I just don't want them to get in trouble. Honestly, maybe I overreacted. Justin has always been difficult to read. He seems zombielike most of the time, and then out of the blue he'll surprise me with how very aware he is. Maybe he can handle it."

Summer said, "But Sam said he wasn't even sure if Justin had ever talked to Rachel."

"I don't know. One of the Amish must have noticed something or Suzanna wouldn't even have heard about it."

I stopped and pictured Rachel's wide-spaced brown eyes and her dark hair. She was definitely a pretty girl, but her gloomy temperament had always lessened her beauty in my eyes.

"Justin wouldn't go for a bitchy girl like her. He was just being nice. One of Noah's little brothers probably misunderstood and began spreading gossip, is my guess."

I sighed. "I hope so."

Summer frowned and said, "It really isn't any of your business, anyway."

Anger coiled in my gut but passed quickly. She was right.

"Yeah, I know. I just don't want to see Justin make the same mistakes I did."

"Aren't you happy with the way it all turned out?"

I looked at the concern on my dear friend's face, and I had to be honest. I'd kept my true feelings hidden for so long that I wasn't sure how to begin. After returning from Meadowview, I'd had fewer nightmares, but a deep melancholy had spread inside of me.

"Yeah, I'm happy and all, but there's something missing. It's like I'm still waiting, and I don't even know what I'm waiting for."

"My mama once said, life isn't much fun most of the time, and for once I agree with her." She bumped softly into my shoulder and patted my leg. "You've got a lot going on, Rose— About to have a baby, and all the crap with Noah being shunned by his family is enough to bring any girl down. Heck, you have psychopaths for neighbors. It's no wonder you're depressed."

"Gee, thanks," I muttered.

"All I'm saying is it can't get much worse."

I turned to her and exclaimed, "Oh, please don't say that. I've learned from personal experience that it can *always* get worse."

Summer shrugged and then rested her head on my shoulder. For a long time we sat their together in silence until she began breathing deeply, and I knew she'd fallen asleep.

Sleep wouldn't come for me for a long time, though.

53

Noah

I didn't care that I'd let Sam have the couch, but as I lay awake on the hard, carpeted floor, I quietly complained about his loud snoring.

Throwing a pillow at him hadn't worked, and I'd given up getting any sleep an hour ago. Still, I had to work the following morning, one of the rare day shifts, and I kept my eyes closed, desperately trying to drift away.

My mind was distracted, though. Too many worries were floating around in my head. As if it wasn't bad enough to have my first child about to born, now I had to worry about a crazy, drugged-out neighbor.

After going over every possible scenario for several more minutes, I decided that I'd contact the police first thing in the morning—and after I got home from work, we'd begin the search for another place to live. It would be difficult to move with Rose being less than two months from delivery, but we couldn't stay here any longer.

I felt a rush of relief for having made the decision, and the incessant ramblings of my mind began to ebb. When the heaviness of sleep pushed in, I welcomed it, relieved that our lives would be changing real soon.

★ ★ ★

The smoke parted, and I saw Rose. She was standing beneath a tree, and she was holding our baby. Hope nuzzled her legs, and her horse, Lady, grazed beside her. She smiled and held the child out to me.

I took a step forward, but the air clouded again, and I couldn't see anything.

Frantically, I clawed at the haze, trying to reach Rose and the baby, but I couldn't get through the thick smoke that surrounded me.

My throat was on fire, and my eyes burned.

With sudden clarity, I realized that it was real. My dream was real.

Pushing off the floor, I saw the red flames leaping through the air in the kitchen. I could hear the crackle and hiss of fire burning and feel its heat. My mind froze in fear, but my body acted on instinct.

Grabbing Sam's shoulder, I jerked him off the couch, shouting, "Fire, there's a fire."

Sam sputtered and cursed, but I quickly turned away, racing to the bedroom.

I opened the door, and the smoke that was flooding the rest of the house exploded into the room that had been untouched until that moment.

"Summer, Rose, come on, wake up," Sam shouted from behind me, but he was by my side when I reached the bed.

Rose coughed, "What's going on?"

I put my arm around her and gently pulled her away from the bed.

Summer was instantly awake and shrieking, "Oh, my God, is it a real fire?"

Sam didn't answer her. Instead, he pulled her off the bed and then extended his arm to help me with Rose.

The four of us left the temporary shelter of the first-floor bedroom and entered the family room, but the fire had spread there, and the flames were licking the ceiling. I was shocked that in the minute we'd left the room to get the girls, the inferno had grown rapidly. The way to the front door was blocked, and the kitchen was already engulfed.

Sam looked at me over Rose's head with terror, shouting, "We can't make it to the door."

The thick smoke made it impossible to breath, and I coughed out, "The window—we'll break the window in the bedroom. It's only a first-floor drop."

Rose and Summer hugged each other while I pulled the blinds up, and Sam brought his foot up and kicked at the window. The glass shattered, and I used my foot to help Sam knock the remaining shards away.

The window was reasonably safe when Sam helped Summer through. The blaring of sirens filled the cold, early morning air, accompanied by the flashing of lights. Silently, I prayed that the firemen would work quickly and save some of the house, but as fast as the blaze was spreading, I knew it was hopeless. The house and all of our belongings were as good as gone.

Rose began to put her leg over the sill but then hesitated and glanced at me with wide eyes. "I can't do it. The drop is too high."

Normally, Rose would have jumped the same way Summer had, but in her condition, she was awkward and had difficulty tying her own shoelaces.

"Sam, you go first and help catch her."

Sam went through the window in a fluid motion and yelled, "All right, come on, Rose, I'm here for you."

I helped her put her legs through the window and grasped her beneath her arms. The smoke rushed past us out the opening, and blazing heat touched my back. I didn't dare turn around, though. Even when I heard the crash of the ceiling caving in behind me, I focused on gently holding Rose out the window as Sam reached up to help her down.

By the time Rose's feet touched the ground, several firefighters had come around the corner of the house. I'd barely cleared the window when a portion of the house exploded. The rush of hot air and debris whipped out, hitting my back as I fell onto the grass. As I went down, I could see firemen shielding Rose, Summer and Sam out of the corner of my eye.

There were several seconds of complete silence, like a vacuum in my ears, until suddenly the world had sound again. The sirens and shouting mixed together as I was pulled away from the rental house by strong hands. Other firemen were dragging hoses through the yard, and I watched as they aimed the water streams at the neighboring houses. There was only one hose on our rental house, because there wasn't anything left of it. They needed to keep the fire from spreading through the neighborhood.

The scene blurred, and my eyes saw only Rose as she huddled beside Summer and Sam near the ambulance. Pulling away from the fireman who was helping me walk, I sprinted over to Rose quickly.

When I had her in my arms, I finally breathed again. Pressing my face to the top of her head, I said, "It's going to be all right. We're all alive and that's what matters."

She pulled back suddenly and gripped her stomach. The way she looked down between her feet made my heart race once again.

She glanced up in terror and cried, "I think my water broke."

"Are you sure?" I asked, stepping back in disbelief.

The closest paramedic must have heard Rose's shout. She jumped from the back of the vehicle and rushed over to us. I stepped aside and let the woman do her job, but I continued to hold Rose's hand, not willing to release her until it was absolutely necessary.

Panic began to spread through me as Rose was guided into the ambulance. She still had six weeks to go…it was too early for her to have the baby.

"Are you the father?" the lady paramedic asked, and I nodded, stepping up into the vehicle.

Right before the door shut, Sam reached in and grabbed my arm.

"I'll call Dad. It'll take him some time to arrive from Meadowview, but I'm sure he'll hurry."

"It's too early, Sam. She can't have the baby."

Sam's face looked grave when he said, "Bro, I don't think she has a choice. You've got to be strong for Rose. Whatever happens, be there for her."

Then the paramedic asked Sam to back away, and she shut the door.

I moved forward and knelt beside Rose and pushed damp hair on her forehead aside. I forced a smile and said, "Are you excited to meet our baby?"

"It's too soon." Her voice trembled, and she sucked in a

breath and said, "It hurts really bad— I thought the pain would build slowly."

The paramedic began taking Rose's blood pressure and said, "Because of the trauma of the fire, you've gone into sudden labor, young lady. Basically, you skipped the beginning of the process entirely."

As Rose asked the woman questions and the ambulance moved through the still-darkened morning streets, I couldn't help but wonder about the fire and how it started. I had the bad feeling that it wasn't a random thing at all. I remembered what Dwayne had said to us.

I knew that when I left the Amish community, I was taking my family into a more difficult world, but I'd never imagined it would be so dangerous.

54

Rose

Thank God for the epidural. Instead of the painful cramps that twisted from my back across to my groin, I now had the wonderful feeling of nothingness. Well, there was some pressure along my lower back when the monitor would begin to rise in higher, more spastic lines, letting me know that I was indeed having a contraction, but other than that, I felt pretty good.

Dad had arrived on the scene an hour ago, and I had to give the man credit for getting the hospital staff in high gear. His personal call to the anesthesiologist brought the man quicker than the request of my *real* doctor.

They were trying to be discreet, but occasionally, either my dad's or Doctor Puzzo's voice would rise, and I'd catch the gist of what they were saying. Dad wanted to waste no time and prep for a C-section while my doctor believed that I could have the baby naturally. I liked my doctor and was rooting for her, but in the end, I was betting that Dad would get his way. Although, I was impressed that she'd stood up to Dad as well as she had so far.

Noah walked through the doorway with the pitcher of

chipped ice when Doctor Puzzo approached the bed. Dad was one step behind her.

I eyed Dad for only an instant before I focused on Doctor Puzzo's face. She was younger than Dad and kept her blond hair pulled up in a ponytail. When she smiled, I relaxed, thinking that maybe she'd won the argument, after all.

Noah sat on the edge of the bed and took my hand into his, but he didn't say a word. Smudges of soot still stained his face and the scent of smoke clung to his clothes. I wrinkled my nose at the smell and looked back at the doctor.

"Rose and Noah, as we've already discussed, it's not the ideal time for you to have the baby, but now that your water has broken and you're already dilated at nine, there's no stopping the arrival. The baby will be almost six weeks premature, so it's borderline how developed its lungs will be. If we're lucky, it might not need a ventilator at all or only for a short time, but we'll be prepared for the worst."

Noah must have read my mind when he asked, "How long will the baby need to stay in the hospital?"

"I can't tell you that for certain at this time. We'll need to wait and see how the delivery goes and its size." She paused and glanced at Dad and then back at me again. "Are you ready to have this baby naturally, Rose?"

I nodded my head and said, "Yes."

"All right, then, I'll get the nurses ready."

When she left, I looked up at Dad as he took my hand. He began to explain everything that would be happening to me and the baby, but I ignored him and asked, "Where's Sam and Summer?"

Dad looked bothered for a second that I'd interrupted

him, but then his expression changed and he said, "As far as I know, they're still in the waiting room."

"Can they come in for the birth?"

Dad sighed and ran his hand through his hair before answering. "Really, Rose, with the birth being early and having just escaped a burning building, I think it might be wise to keep the room as quiet and stress-free as possible."

I glanced at Noah, and he nodded in support. Turning back to Dad, I took a quick breath and said, "I'd really like for them to be here."

Dad sighed loudly, but said, "All right, then. I'll go tell them."

After Dad left the room, Noah and I were completely alone for a minute. I savored the time and especially the kiss he placed on my forehead.

"How are you feeling?" Noah asked as he rubbed my shoulder with his hand.

"I don't feel the pain anymore...and I have all kinds of energy—almost like I'm about to pop."

Noah chuckled and said, "Well, you kind of are."

I swatted at his arm playfully, but the serious look on his face stilled my hand.

"Are you ready for this, Rose?"

His soft voice and concerned face reminded me of why I'd fallen in love with him. A few strands of his dark hair fell down, partially covering his left eye, and I reached up, brushing the locks back. He was so handsome, and my heart did a little jump at the thought that he belonged to me.

We'd been through so much, but here we were—finally married and about to have our first child. I'd certainly not planned on being a teen mother, but I was sure at that instant of staring into Noah's dark eyes that I wouldn't change a thing.

I sniffed and whispered, "Yeah, I'm ready."

"I love you, Rose."

"I love you, too."

His mouth touched mine softly, and I sighed between his lips.

"Isn't that what got you into this mess in the first place?"

Sam's annoying voice cutting the air broke off our kiss, and I suddenly regretted inviting him in. What was I thinking?

Summer came to my aid, smacking her boyfriend on the back as she passed by him.

"Thank you so much. I wanted to be here for you, but I was afraid to ask."

My eyes became moist, and Summer was quick, grabbing a tissue for me. She said, "No crying allowed. That goes for weddings and childbirth as far as I'm concerned."

Her businesslike manner made me laugh, and even Noah smiled at her.

I was scared to death of what was about to happen, but I had Noah, my best friend, Dad and even Sam with me. I'd be all right.

Doctor Puzzo came back into the room, accompanied by three nurses, one pushing a baby incubator. The flurry of activity and bright lights of the room added to the surreal feeling I was experiencing. The only thing that made any of it real were the voices.

"It's time to have a baby, Rosie."

I looked up into Dad's anxious face and nodded.

I was ready.

* * *

"Come on, Rose, you can do it—just one more push." Noah voice was close to my ear, but I still barely heard him.

I was exhausted, and I was over hearing people tell me, just one more push. It would probably take a dozen more pushes to get the baby out.

Summer understood and said, "It needs to be a big push, a really big one."

"I can see the head, Rose, and there's a lot of black hair," Doctor Puzzo said with excitement.

With renewed energy, I leaned forward. "You can see the head? Really, you're not lying to me?"

"You're almost done. I promise you," Doctor Puzzo reassured me.

"Come on, Rose. Don't wimp out on us now." Sam's words caused the intended reaction in me.

I shot him a look that would have torn most guys to shreds and gripped Noah's hand more tightly. Gathering all the strength I had left, I bore down and pushed with all my might.

I cried out only once, right at the end, and then opened my eyes to see Dad wrapping his grandchild in the blanket. It was already making loud squawking noises, and I didn't take my eyes off of it as Dad came forward.

That had come out of me?

"It's a girl, Rosie. You have a daughter. She's breathing just fine on her own, too."

Summer cooed excitedly, and Sam let out a loud breath as if he'd been holding it in the entire time.

When Dad set the baby on my chest, I hesitated, looking

at Noah. He took my hands and guided them to the baby, and together, we touched her.

"She's so tiny," I said in both awe and fear.

"But, she's perfect...and she's all ours." Noah leaned forward and kissed my nose and then hers.

"We need to to examine her thoroughly. All things considered, she's doing fabulously, but she's still pre-term," Doctor Puzzo said.

"Have you decided on a name yet?" the blond-haired, older nurse asked.

The baby's face was red from squalling, and her thick, black hair was standing up in soft spikes. Her face was round, and her eyes were widely spaced. Just as Noah had said, she really was perfect.

I glanced up at him, searching his face for confirmation of the name that we'd discussed calling the baby if it was a girl, and he nodded. Our daughter's name would be in honor of two very special women, who'd meant the world to us and had left us too soon.

"Her name is Sarah Ann Miller," I said proudly.

55

Noah

When I came around the corner, I stopped abruptly and stepped behind the wall. I was careful to keep most of my face hidden when I looked back down the hallway. Father was holding David's hand and arm in a friendly way, and Mother stood to the side.

My heart sped up at the thought that they'd made the trip to the city hospital to see their new grandchild. I hadn't been expecting it, but I sure was pleased, just the same. I couldn't hear the words exchanged between the men, even though I turned my head and strained to listen. The interaction only lasted another minute before David left my parents alone in the hallway.

When they began walking in my direction, I took a deep breath and went to greet them.

Mother's hug was extra tight and lasted longer than was usual for even her.

"Congratulations, son, I hear you have a fine daughter of your own," Father said.

I couldn't help smiling proudly. "Did David tell you her name?" I asked, hoping that he hadn't.

Father shook his head, and Mother looked up expectantly.

"We named her Sarah Ann—after our Sarah, of course, and Rose's mother."

Father nodded and Mother exclaimed, "Oh, Noah, how wonderful to honor your sister." She paused, taking a few seconds to get her emotions in check before saying, "And how is Rose doing? Was the labor very difficult?"

"She was incredibly strong through it all. Even before she had the epidural, she didn't cry or complain about the pain." I stopped and looked closely at them. "Did David tell you about the fire?"

"Yes, we know," Father said. "We are just thankful that you were all spared and made it safely out of that house. Since we weren't speaking, I'd asked David a while ago to call us and let us know when Rose had the baby. He told us when he called. Mr. Denton drove us by the place before coming here." He shook his head. "It's a complete loss. Everything burned."

"I know." I hadn't had much time to think about the devastation since Rose's labor had begun so soon after. Father's words were sobering.

"It's a Godsend that none of your neighbors' homes went up also as close as they're all packed in," Father said.

Bitterness took hold of me, and I spoke harshly. "It would have been poetic justice if the one neighbor's home had caught fire."

Father placed his hand on my shoulder and said, "David told us that arson is suspected. You mustn't let anger take hold of your spirit, Noah. It will only bring more trouble into your life."

"Our neighbor threatened Rose that very same day. I have no doubt that he did it in revenge for Rose calling the police on him during a fight he was having with his wife. His small child came over to our house seeking help from Rose, and she did what she thought was best."

"Poor Rose, to have to deal with such a thing." Mother sighed.

Father stroked his beard and said, "The English world hasn't been kind to you, has it?"

What he said was true, but still, I bristled at his words.

"If you remember, the Amish one wasn't all that friendly before I left, either. At least now, I'm free to raise my family as I see fit, and not be governed by people who might not have my best interests at heart."

A couple of nurses walked by and glanced away quickly when I noticed them staring at my parents. Amish people were not normally seen in the city. I understood their curiosity, but their rudeness still bothered me.

Father said, "This isn't the time or the place for this discussion. We came to see the baby and give you and Rose our best wishes."

I was relieved that he didn't want to argue, but it still angered me that he'd brought the matter up in the first place. I'd made a lot of mistakes in the past year, but I was working hard to be a good provider for my family. It wasn't my fault that the woman I fell in love with was an outsider.

Pointing down the hallway, I said, "She's in room three-twenty-six. I'll be there in a minute."

Father looked questioningly at me and said, "You obviously need help. Will you not ask for it?"

"I have to figure this out on my own, Father. You can't help me this time."

Father's smile hinted that he had a secret, but the look

passed briefly before he tilted his hat to me and turned away with Mother.

I watched them disappear into the room where Rose and little Sarah Ann were before I pulled the cell phone out of my pocket and dialed the Realtor.

When I had been Amish, I wouldn't have hesitated at asking Father for help, but it wasn't an option anymore.

I had to straighten things out on my own, and I'd have to do it in a hurry. Rose and the baby would be released from the hospital in a week, and although her aunt Debbie had offered for us to stay with her and Jason indefinitely, we needed a place of our own.

And, time was running out.

56

Rose

The snow falling was picture-perfect beyond the window. The trees looked like they were covered with white icing, and the field was blanketed and sparkling. Sarah Ann's murmur brought my gaze down to her, and I smiled. Her little mouth was moving in sucking motions, and I figured that she was dreaming about eating. She was only a month old, but she'd already gained two pounds and was filled out like a proper baby now.

Her first week had been nerve-wracking. She'd been quite small, and even though all her organs were developed, she still got a respiratory infection and had to be put on a ventilator a few days after birth. Her sickness delayed our leaving the hospital by another week, but I was kind of relieved. It had taken me all of the two weeks to become comfortable with caring for my baby on my own.

I'd chosen to breast-feed, which had been the most challenging of all, but Sarah Ann was nursing easily now, and I was glad I'd stuck it out. Noah had been a saint, catering to my every need. He even surprised me with daily foot massages, but for all his helpfulness and exuberance, I knew it was all for show. He was brooding about something, and no matter how I pestered him, he wouldn't open up to me.

Losing the house in a fire had been rough on both of us. We'd lost all our furniture, clothes, the television and computer, but in the end we turned out to be truly blessed when family, friends and even some strangers came to our rescue. I'd been amazed at the outpouring of generosity. By the time we'd left the hospital, most of our things had been replaced.

The investigation proved that the fire had been purposely set with an accelerant at the back porch, and after a couple of weeks, the police had enough evidence gathered to arrest the neighbors for arson. I still didn't know what happened to little Lucy and her brother, but I hoped that they were in a better place with kind people.

Living with Aunt Debbie had been fine with me. She'd taken time off from work to help with the baby, and I felt more comfortable having people around me, especially after everything that had happened at the rental property. I still had some anxiety swirling in me about the whole thing, but it was getting better. I was lucky to have a steady stream of visitors, which kept me distracted.

I could thank the baby in my arms for all the company. No one could resist her, and mock fights broke out about who was going to hold her. Sam had surprised me the most. He'd turned out to be the one person, other than me or Noah, who could easily get Sarah Ann asleep. He'd walk around the entire house holding her against his shoulder, never stopping and talking constantly. It did the trick every time.

"Let me have her," Summer said, startling me.

I carefully lifted Sarah Ann to my friend and then slid over on the coach to make room.

"I still don't understand why Dad insisted we come out this weekend. It's supposed to keep snowing, and if we can't make it back to Cincinnati, Noah may lose his job."

Summer glanced at the open doorway of the family room and then lowered her voice. "I don't know any more than you do, but I think Sam is keeping a secret."

Her words made my heart beat faster, and I whispered back, "Sam doesn't keep secrets well. What do you think is going on?"

The loud knock at the door interrupted our conversation, and I looked questioningly at Summer, who shrugged and went back to cooing at Sarah Ann.

Before I got up, I turned and searched out the window behind the couch, and the car I saw there made me catch my breath.

Hunter.

As I leaped from the couch, I said, "You aren't going to believe who it is."

Summer's confused face turned to shock when she, too, saw Hunter's car parked at the end of the stone walkway.

"He better not be here to cause trouble," Summer warned.

Putting a finger to my mouth, I shushed her and asked, "Please, stay here with the baby—I'll take care of it."

Summer nodded, but her expression was suspicious.

I felt jittery when I reached the door. It had been nearly nine months since I'd seen Hunter. After his fight with Noah in the barnyard last spring, he'd completely disappeared from my life—no phone calls, text messages, nothing. Not only had he erased me, but Sam had also been a casualty of his jealousy. From what my brother had told me, he hadn't spent any time with Hunter since the day he'd come to ask me to the senior prom.

Even though my feelings for him had never been as deep as what I'd always felt for Noah, I still cared about him, and losing his friendship had stung. He'd said that he'd always be my friend, no matter what, but he broke his promise. Now, out of the blue, he arrived in the heavily falling snow.

Maybe I was freaking out for nothing. He could have stopped by to see Sam.

As I turned the knob, the realization that Hunter probably wasn't here for me deflated me a bit, and I opened the door slowly.

The melting snowflakes blended into Hunter's blond hair quickly, and after a second of eye contact, I focused on those flakes, feeling incredibly uncomfortable, all of a sudden.

Hunter's smile was lopsided when he said in a friendly voice, "Hey, Rose, it's good to see you."

I looked back at his hazel eyes, and they were sincere. He really was happy to see me.

"You probably weren't expecting to run into me, huh?" I said.

He shook the snow from his head and replied, "Actually, I came here specifically to see you and meet your baby girl."

I looked over my shoulder into the foyer to see if anyone was there. As far as I knew, Noah was still sleeping, having pulled a double shift the days before. When I saw the coast was clear, I stepped out into the brisk air and shut the door behind me. Luckily, I wore a thick sweater, but I still folded my arms across my belly, instantly feeling the cold.

"Noah's here, and I don't know if he'll want to see you."

Clearing his throat first, he said, "I'm sorry for fighting with Noah that day. It was ridiculous for me to do such a thing. It's just...well...it hurt a lot to finally realize that you really were going to be with Noah, instead of me."

Instinctively, I reached out and touched his arm, saying, "I'm sorry, Hunter. I never meant to hurt you."

His eyes met mine, and a small smile touched his lips. "I know that. All along, you kept telling me how crazy you were about Noah, and I wouldn't listen. I thought I could change your mind."

"In another life, you probably could have," I said softly.

"It's taken me all these months to deal with it, Rose. I would've come to see you sooner, but I wasn't ready until today."

Raising an eyebrow, I asked, "Why today?"

His smile deepened, and before he said the words, I already knew.

"I met a girl in college who's helping me get over you." He ran his hand through his hair nervously and went on to say, "I think you'd like her. She's a tomboy like you—she even rides horses."

A million emotions passed over me in that instant, but in the end, after searching Hunter's face, I was more than okay with the news.

"She's a very lucky girl."

"I don't know about that, but she's the one who encouraged me to come here and see you and the baby. She thought I needed some closure or something before we went to the next level."

"She's a smart girl. I hope you don't let her get away."

He shook his head and said, "This time I won't."

The look that passed between us was bittersweet. The connection was still there, but it was fast disappearing with every snowflake that drifted down.

Pulling a small wrapped package from the inside of his jacket, he handed it to me and said, "Well, I better get going. Please, take this for the baby."

After he handed it to me, he turned away, and I reached out and grabbed his arm.

"Where are you going? You should give this to Sarah Ann in person."

"I thought I should leave since Noah didn't want to see me."

Shaking my head, I tugged him toward the door.

"I was being stupid. You were a good friend to me when I needed one most." I tried to stop my quivering lip but failed. "Please, come in and see the baby. Noah will handle it."

Hunter nodded, and we quickly made our way into the warmth of the old house. When we walked into the family room, Summer's eyes widened in surprise, but she got herself together quickly and greeted him.

"Hi, there— It's been a while."

"Yes, it has," Hunter said as he walked across the room and knelt beside Summer, where Sarah Ann was lying happily on her legs.

He looked at her for several long seconds before he glanced back at me and exclaimed, "She's a beautiful baby."

"Why, of course she is," Summer informed him as if she thought he was an idiot for having to say it out loud.

I smiled and, remembering the package in my hands, I joined Summer on the couch and unwrapped it.

The bright pink rattle had a star in the middle with the words *Drama Queen* on it.

"I figured if she's anything like her mother, it's the one for her," Hunter said, grinning.

I laughed. "It's perfect. Thank you."

"We have an unexpected visitor?" Noah said from the doorway, turning all of our heads.

Hunter quickly rose and crossed the room with an extended hand.

"Congratulations on your baby. She's a real beauty," Hunter said.

Noah only hesitated for an instant before he grasped Hunter's hand, and I let out a breath of relief.

"Thanks, she's a keeper," Noah said, looking Hunter straight in the eye.

Hunter must have needed closure on all sides, when he went on to say, "It's taken some time for me to work things out, but I've moved on and am content with my life." He glanced back at me and then faced Noah again. "I really do wish the best for both of you."

Noah nodded his head slowly in acknowledgment and then reached out to squeeze Hunter's shoulder in a friendly way.

I could hardly believe what I was seeing.

"I better get going before the roads get any worse. You guys, take care. Maybe we'll see each other again sometime."

Before he had a chance to leave the room, I jumped up and raced over to him. I was careful not to give him the hug goodbye that I desperately wanted to. Noah could be taken out of the Amish world, but the Amish would never fully be taken out of him, and his wife hugging her former boyfriend in front of him would have ruined any progress the two young men had just made.

"Don't you want to hang around and talk to Sam before you go?"

Hunter quickly said, "Tell him I'll give him a call next week." He looked over my shoulder at Summer and added, "Maybe we can arrange a double date or something. I'd really like him to meet Hailey."

"Sounds like a plan to me," Summer answered with a smile.

"I'll walk you out," Noah said, turning away with Hunter.

When they were both out of earshot, Summer exclaimed, "That was plumb weird."

I nodded in agreement and sat down beside her again.

"I'm glad he came by, though. The way our friendship ended had been bothering me for a while now."

"And you're not at all jealous about this Hailey chick?"

"No, not at all." When Summer raised her eyebrows in doubt, I said, "Seriously, I'm surprised myself, but seeing Hunter's eyes light up when he spoke about her made me really happy. He's a great guy, and he deserves to be in love."

"With a girl who loves him back," Summer agreed, but then her voice became sharp when she pointed out the window and exclaimed, "You have more company."

I swiveled and gasped when I saw the buggy being pulled by the dark bay horse coming up the driveway. Getting on my knees, I leaned over the back of the couch to get a better look.

"It's Noah's parents— What on earth are they doing here?"

"I was hoping you could tell me that." Noah's voice

popped up behind me as he bent over and looked out the window himself.

"They might want to see the baby," I suggested, watching Amos help Rebecca out of the buggy after it had stopped beside the pathway.

"I wasn't expecting them."

"What's the big deal? They probably want to see Miss Precious here," Summer said.

I looked up at Noah and saw the worry on his face.

"Usually, my folks wait for us to come to them. Taking the horse and buggy out on a snowy day like this is unlike them," Noah told Summer.

Before Noah and I could get to the door, Dad was already there, welcoming the Millers in. Rebecca came straight to me with a hug before she sat down beside Summer. Summer quickly relinquished Sarah Ann without being asked, and soon enough, Rebecca had the baby resting in her arms.

Noah and I exchanged worried glances while Dad and Amos stood talking about the winter weather for a minute. Sam, whose hair was still damp from the shower, appeared and slipped by the men to settle comfortably into the recliner.

I was nibbling my pinky nail when Amos finally turned to Noah and spoke up. "Noah, your mother and I came here today with an idea. One that I hope you'll consider for the well-being of your young family."

Noah looked confused and said, "I don't understand."

Amos glanced at Dad, and I held my breath.

Dad said, "I've been trying to figure out what I'm going to do with this old house. You see, it's too big for me and Tina, especially with Sam in college and Justin following him out the door in a few years." He took a breath and looked between me and Noah before continuing. "The house market isn't very good right now to sell for any kind of profit and Meadowview has begun to grow on me."

I couldn't take the suspense any longer and blurted out, "What does this have to do with us, Dad?"

Dad smiled and glanced at Amos before speaking. "I've decided to stay here in the town. I'm going to move into Tina's house, which is closer to the hospital." He spread his arms and added, "That means this place will be empty and in desperate need of its own family."

My heart jumped, and I said, "Are you kidding me?"

Noah was more reserved with his emotions and asked, "What exactly do you have in mind, David? I can't afford to buy this house...were you thinking about renting it out?"

Dad shook his head. "That's where your parents come into this, Noah. They are willing to lend you the money for a down payment on your own mortgage. I'm going to let you and Rose have it for a fraction of what I bought it for. Consider it a kind of housewarming gift."

I held my breath, waiting for Noah's reaction and desperately trying to keep the excitement from bursting out of me.

Noah turned to Amos and said, "Is that true, Father? Why would you do such a thing when you're so upset that I left the Amish? The last thing I thought you'd ever want is for me to be close by, corrupting the younger kids."

Noah's resentment cut the air like a knife, and I sagged in the seat, suddenly afraid that a fight was about to break out.

"This has been a year of change for all of us. Yes, we'd rather you remained in our faith, but we aren't willing to turn our backs on you for the decision. You must get away from the city and all the bad things that go with it. You belong here. You always have."

Noah ran his hand through his hair and said, "I don't know what to say."

Usually, Rebecca let her husband do the talking, but this time she spoke up herself, and all heads turned her way. Since she was holding the sleeping Sarah Ann in her arms, her words carried even more meaning.

"Noah, nothing has changed as far as the shunning is concerned. In order to preserve our way of life and guide your younger siblings to join the church, we won't be able to be with you and your family the way it would have been if you'd stayed with us. But we can help you, and we want to do so. This precious little angel deserves to grow up away from the city, safely surrounded by her kin on both sides of the family. We want to be a part of her life."

The silence in the room was unbearable, but I didn't dare to speak. I understood what was going through Noah's head—he was afraid that being so close to the Amish, without being a part of their world, would be more difficult than staying away.

I knew what I wanted, though, and I looked into Noah's eyes, waiting.

"There is one catch."

Sam's voice broke the tension, and I said, "What?"

"Sorry, Dad, nothing personal, but when I come home from college, I'm staying here. Tina's kind of irritating, and I consider this place *home*." He looked straight at Noah and added, "If it's all right with you, bro."

The smile that erupted on Noah's face made me suddenly

relax. Dad and Amos were grinning also, and Summer rose and pulled me into a hug.

"You're never going to be able to get rid of me," she whispered into my ear.

"I never want to," I said.

The throat-clearing in the doorway got everyone's attention. Justin stood there in his pajama pants and Halo T-shirt.

Looking directly at me and ignoring the others, he said, "I'm staying, too."

"Now wait a minute..."

Dad began to protest, but Amos smacked him on the back and said, "That argument is better left for another day, friend." He then turned to Noah and asked, "Have you made your decision?"

Noah reached his hand out to me, and I took it, allowing him to pull me under his arm and against his side. He looked down and said, "I believe I know what you want to do...."

I nodded my head vigorously, and he laughed and said, "Then we're moving in. I still don't know what I'll do about work, but, by the grace of God, something will surely come up."

"Oh, I almost forgot about that." Amos laughed, and I could see the joy on both his and Rebecca's faces. He said, "I've got several jobs lined up once the weather breaks. I won't be able to get around to all of them, and even though Elijah's mood softened considerably toward our family after Sarah's death, I certainly won't be recommending him to my customers. It's my understanding your friend Matthew

Weaver isn't enjoying his time working for the man...he might be persuaded to join with you on the jobs."

"Thank you, Father, for everything... And you, too, David. Rose and I are blessed to have our families."

"And, it doesn't even matter that you're from different worlds. In the end, family is family," I said.

Noah nodded, and Amos said, "Amen," before he joined Rebecca on the couch. She handed him Sarah Ann, and he bent down to kiss her forehead. When he pulled back, her little fist was clamped around the end of his beard. Everyone laughed, Amos the loudest.

Noah joined his parents, and Summer sat down on Sam's lap. She whispered something into his ear, and he chuckled. Dad went to meet Tina who'd just arrived, and I wandered over to stand beside Justin.

Seeing all of the most important people in my life gathered together made a honey warm feeling spread inside of me.

Finally, after so long, I'd found where I belonged.

Glancing sideways at Justin, I said, "I'm going to be keeping an eye on you."

He laughed and turned away, taking the stairs two steps at a time.

Pausing in stride, he looked back and smirked. "I don't think you'll be able to keep up with me...but we'll see."

Now I knew how Sam felt.

At that moment, my gaze met Noah's, and with a brilliant smile, he motioned for me to join him on the couch. After I squeezed in beside him, his mouth brushed my ear, and he whispered, "I'll love you forever."

His lips against my skin caused the tingling sensation to erupt inside of me that only Noah could create.

I sighed against his face and murmured, "Forever."

After all the struggles we'd been through, we'd finally made it.

★★★★★

KAREN ANN HOPKINS

THE TEMPTATION NOVELS

He's Amish. She's not. Will love be enough?

Coming February 2014

"Belonging, The sequel to *Temptation* (2012), places the reader in an Amish community filled with danger, suspense, romance, and mystery. The writing is addictive and fast-paced, leaving readers breathlessly waiting for more."

—*Bethany Fort, Booklist Online*

Available where books are sold!

HTKAHFETR

THE GODDESS TEST NOVELS

Available wherever books are sold!

A modern saga inspired by the Persephone myth.

Kate Winters's life hasn't been easy. She's battling with the upcoming death of her mother, and only a mysterious stranger called Henry is giving her hope. But he must be crazy, right? Because there is no way the god of the Underworld—Hades himself—is going to choose Kate to take the seven tests that might make her an immortal...and his wife. And even if she passes the tests, is there any hope for happiness with a war brewing between the gods?

Also available:
THE GODDESS HUNT, a digital-only novella.

HTGSTR3